The
Daughters *of*
Simon Lamoreaux

A Novel by DAVID LONG

SCRIBNER

New York   London   Toronto   Sydney   Singapore

SCRIBNER
1230 Avenue of the Americas
New York, NY 10020

Designed by Brooke Koven
Set in Walbaum MT
Manufactured in the United States of America

1 3 5 7 9 10 8 6 4 2

Library of Congress Cataloging-in-Publication Data is available.

Long, David, date
The daughters of Simon Lamoreaux: a novel/by David Long.
p.   cm.
I. Title.
PS3562.O4924 D38 2000
813'.54—dc   00-022212

ISBN 0-684-85414-7

S.S.L.

Acknowledgments

Major thanks to my editor, Gillian Blake, agent, Sally Wofford-Girand, and right-hand man, Dennis Held, for their dedication to this project. And to my friends Hamilton Cain, Claire Davis, Bonnie Dowell, Rick and Heather Hodsdon, and Linda Longo for their encouragement and generous suggestions. To Phillip Aaberg for his counsel on the music business, my esteemed sisters-in-law, and the others who helped with information along the way. Thanks to my boys, Montana and Jack. To Jane Senter, *metta*. And to my long-ago friend, Peach Warren.

For Fanning and Ryugi's discussion in chapter 3, I'm indebted to Robert Adams, *Beauty in Photography: Essays in Defense of Traditional Values*.

Julia's quotation, chapter 7, is borrowed (slightly altered) from Saul Bellow, *Seize the Day*.

The
Daughters *of*
Simon Lamoreaux

In the dark the mind runs on like a devouring machine . . .
——Don DeLillo, *White Noise*

Hartford 1973

Psalmus
Hungaricus

FANNING WAS NO SINGER. His roommate, Sully, now *he* could sing. Possessed a lovely Irish tenor. His chin rose, his soft eyes struggled to stay open—a pure thin sound escaped, obliterating the routine foolishness that had occupied him moments before. Michael Sullivan, with his shock of black hair, his talent for mimicry, his passions. Often received the plum parts, often found his transgressions overlooked. *Ah-ve-Ma-ri-i-a.* Fanning might have gone sick with envy, if he was the sort to covet others' gifts. His own voice was adequate, nondescript, baritone. At least he could read music, he could be counted on to hit the note square.

A hazy Friday in May and they were in the state capital to rehearse with the choirs of six other schools, the last of the joint rehearsals before the following Saturday's full run-through and Sunday's massive choralfest. Fanning's girlfriend went to Moorcroft, and the Moorcroft bus was late. Ironic, because Moorcroft was a day school here within the city. He sat squinting at the double doors, chin on fists.

"Now, 'is old 'eart's a 'ammerin," Sully intoned. "'e can't 'ardly contain 'isself."

Fanning returned him a dark look. Sully lay his head back and gazed up at the ceiling. A pigeon had gotten inside and was momentarily at rest on one of the struts.

Words were spoken from a megaphone. The schools assigned the Te Deum filed from their seats, then onto risers. Fanning's family—mother Marjorie, father Walter—were nominally Presbyterian. The Te Deum's sobering Latin diverted Fanning briefly, its threat, its dire implication. *Lamb of God,* he translated. *Help me in my hour of need.* At last, just as Fanning was really beginning to wonder, the Moorcroft girls drifted in, skirts and blouses, a beret or two, bookbags swaying against their backs. Fanning's eyesight was less than needle-sharp at this distance, but there was Carly, hand on a railing, scanning for him. Unobtrusively, he made *Love you* in sign language, the way she'd taught him.

Three blocks from the Civic Center ran an alley, barely the width of a modern-day delivery van, and to one side was a recessed area furnished with a wooden bench—curved, thickly lacquered, the sort once common to train stations. He and Carly had lucked onto this spot the previous Friday, strolling toward Bushnell Park, had squandered the remainder of their lunch break kissing. Carly tasted of wintergreen, her skin was moist at the hairline. She unbuttoned the top three buttons of her shirt so that Fanning could insert his hand. She was a steady, handsome girl with chin-length hair the color of a Hershey bar, and short hard legs. Virtually every afternoon one of her blue envelopes appeared in his mail slot at Griffin, where he and Sully were seniors. Most nights, if he could, Fanning called from the phone booth built into the wall of the Common Room. Fanning's father had written again recently mentioning the excessive charges on his calling card.

After the Te Deum, known as The Tedium, came the Kodály, *Psalmus Hungaricus.* They'd have professional soloists on Sunday, a full orchestra—for now there was only the piano. Years later, Fanning happened onto Laszlo Eosze's biography of Kodály, paged through it one drizzly weekend, but that spring all he knew was how the name was said. *Koh-die.* He couldn't have put his finger to Hungary on an unmarked map. The music, though—it shook him, bore through his defenses. One section where the voices swelled and collapsed in waves, diminishing finally into silence, as if from exhaustion, or the peace that follows some monumental heroism. At night, in bed, he heard this passage over and over, despite himself. Three hundred voices.

The plan was for Fanning and Carly to exit the building separately. A little before noon, Fanning grabbed his sack lunch, darted outside, and arrived first at the bench. Someone had sat here, smoking, pitching the butts in the direction of a Chase & Sanborn can, thirty or forty of them, lipstick-marked. The day had turned muggy but this alcove was a pocket of shade, cool like the bottom of a well, having the faint smell of old mortar. On a ledge across the way, one flight up, red flower petals clumped out of two clay pots. Overhead, criss-crossing wires. Fanning loosened his tie and waited. He stood, stuffed his hands in his pockets, and peered around the corner. A truck backed into the alley, rocking on the lip of the cobble-stones, blew its brakes, pulled out. He glimpsed cars as they passed, glinting chrome. He went back and sat again, drew his feet up on the slats. He watched with a sick feeling as half the lunch break evaporated, then the other half.

Already he was jumping ahead to the next time they'd be together in the flesh, which was the run-through, and then after the concert when the four parents were scheduled to eat at a restaurant. Her folks were an odd pair: birdlike mother, gaunt towering father who was deeply, disturbingly religious. He gave Fanning the willies. Also there was a younger sister. Already the thought of this little ceremony was suffocating him. He and Carly would salvage a few minutes alone, but that was worse, almost, the frustration.

Back at rehearsal, Fanning caught the shoulder of the first Moorcroft girl he encountered, asked about Carly.

"Oh, she's here someplace," the girl said.

Fanning asked if she'd seen Carly *specifically*. The girl went vague. A big mob was in the ladies' room, maybe there?

But when it came time for the buses to load and leave, Carly still hadn't shown. Fanning waited unhappily in the lobby, watching faces as they passed. A man in a wheelchair was selling candy out of a kid's red wagon, attracting a crowd, but it soon thinned and the lobby was virtually empty again. Not sure what else to do, he started toward the doors himself, but was intercepted by one of the Moorcroft chaperones. A fraught, angular woman. Wasn't he Carly's friend, had he been with her today?

Fanning said he hadn't laid eyes on her since the Kodály, offered nothing more.

"What about the Buzzati girl, Sophia? You know which one she is?"

What Griffin boy didn't know Sophia?

Well, the two of them were unaccounted for. Not the kind of stunt you'd expect from Carly, this chaperone said. "Led astray, no doubt."

Fanning climbed aboard his own bus. He passed the hour back to school with his head against the glass. The late afternoon light was drifting with pollen, a green-gold Fanning associated with an old Pontiac of his mother's. After supper he walked the lane behind the infirmary, down into the woods as far as a weed-choked pond, trying to get a handle on his mood—the letdown, the acute sense of dislocation. Carly wasn't in Sophia's erratic orbit, nonetheless, he could picture the two of them going AWOL if Sophia had a need for Carly's talents, some urgent mess to remedy. And he could hear Carly explaining, accounting for herself. *Oh, M., I didn't have a choice. You know how she is. I promise I'll make it up to you—*

In their dorm room, Sully was restringing his Martin,

snipping the excess wire with nail clippers. Fanning considered calling the Lamoreaux house, but what if the father answered, and if it was Carly, he didn't want to sound shaken, or give the impression of being pissed. So, no phone call tonight—he'd make himself wait until morning. He read a few pages of *Death in Venice*, but couldn't hold his mind to it. He went down the hall and brushed his teeth, then undressed. Sully hadn't said a word. He could be good like that, Sully. Sometimes he chided Fanning for being a worrier, for hanging back, for being too goddamned deliberate, but always half-kidding, never with any venom. He was probably the closest friend Fanning had ever had.

Past midnight, Fanning was awakened by the dorm master, a sweet wreck of a man known as Captain Marvel. He'd taken a few quiet vodkas and clearly wanted no part of this. Fanning pulled his pants on, thrust his bare feet into a pair of loafers.

The headmaster and another man awaited Fanning in the Captain's overlit sitting room. Fanning was asked to take a chair.

"Miles," the headmaster said, "I'm told you're close to Carolyn Lamoreaux."

Fanning nodded, then the headmaster nodded. A small precise man, Mr. Beatty. He taught one section of calculus every year, but Fanning hadn't taken it, not being mathematical. In Fanning's time at Griffin, they'd had perhaps a half-dozen short conversations.

"You wouldn't know where Carolyn is?" he asked.

Fanning explained that Carly and Sophia Buzzati had skipped out together.

"Apparently not," Mr. Beatty said.

"An incorrect assumption on someone's part," the other man said. He was stocky, sweating at the neck. He had a suit on, where Mr. Beatty was in a windbreaker and chinos, his hair standing up funny.

"We didn't even talk today," Fanning admitted, and quickly regretted the childish, affronted tone of voice.

They lobbed a few more questions at him, trying to gauge his degree of intimacy with Carly, short of asking outright. Fanning answered obliquely, embarrassed.

"And why was it you didn't talk?" the second man asked.

Here was Fanning's opportunity to tell about the meeting place, or not. He thought: What point is there in holding out?

When he was done, and when he had clarified several small items, Fanning was told he could return to his room. Sully was out cold, forearm a dead weight across his eyes. Fanning sat at his desk a minute, then knelt at the open window and had a cigarette, which was forbidden, but screw that. If Carly was having second thoughts about him, they'd come out of the clear blue. He retrieved her most recent letter from the metal box in his drawer, held it so the yard light fell across the words. He knew what they said, but under the circumstances, he needed to see them again. *I want you, Miles. I do. Soon, okay?* He lay on the bunk, still in his clothes. He thought he'd never return to sleep, and yet, somehow, he did.

Seattle 1997

1

IT WAS AFTER ELEVEN when Fanning put the quietus to his day, retreating to the "Hospitality Suite" where he'd been hanging his hat these past weeks. He was dehydrated, hollow with hunger. There was half a container of Thai noodles in the minifridge, but he settled instead for a few handfuls of Raisin Nut Bran. This was the third and uppermost floor of 40 Tarbox Street, studios and offices of SunBreak Records, Miles Fanning, founder. An importer of futons and rattanware occupied the ground floor, the one below SunBreak housed a warren of solitary, glass-doored offices, some vacant. The Hospitality Suite was an old SunBreak joke: a storeroom at the end of the corridor, catchall, refuge for the indisposed. Corroded, soot-furred pipes across the ceiling, banks of steel shelving, caches of dysfunctional electronics and water-spotted cartons of very old product. A miserly, plywood-sided lavatory built into one corner. Fanning had ordered a second phone line for the computer, he'd sent downstairs for new bedding.

He poured a beaker of club soda and cranberry juice and knelt on the kneeling chair in front of his computer to check his e-mail, found spam headed "Svetlana Introduction & Marriage Agency, St. Petersburg, Russia." *Dear Friend: Soon you will be get letters from nice, family-oriented Russian ladies. Please come visit our Website.* Fanning guided it to the trash. There were replies to his query about some Monk sessions from '56, and a long dispatch from a copyright attorney in L.A. Fanning scanned them, nodding, filed the latter under *Headache, minor.*

Plus he found this:

Are you the Miles Fanning who went to Griffin?

Fanning could go weeks without Griffin crossing his mind—unless Sully phoned, which he did every few months, taking Fanning by surprise, though it was a joy talking to his friend, a relief. Less often, Fanning called him. Sully had lived abroad after college, and in the mid-eighties he married a French woman, a cellist, sinewy, placid Pascale. The longest fingers Fanning had ever seen on a woman. Sully was wildly enamored. *My-kul,* she called him, in teasing mock-American. Both taught now, and summers they operated a music camp in the Adirondacks. They were happy. Sully was virtually Fanning's only contact with the East Coast of his adolescence, nor had Fanning kept up his college friendships. No one else had migrated to the Northwest, and gradually, without meaning to, he'd lost touch. Not that he'd ever run with much of a pack. His life seemed to have started fresh in Seattle—what came before felt oddly remote, irretrievable.

His but not his.

Sully didn't have the number for the Hospitality Suite, Fanning realized. The thought of his wife, Kyra, fielding a call at the house, explaining their current living arrangement—it gave his stomach a sour little turn. But, as for Griffin School, Fanning wasn't up to reminiscing with an old alum tonight. Lacked the energy, the bonhomie. He logged off, drained the juice, stared down at the street, where nothing much was shaking. Stray foot traffic. It was only then, though he couldn't say why, that the e-mail address snagged his attention.

julamo@netrisys.net

He logged back on, typed *Yes* without deliberating, clicked on Send.

He sat a few moments, mildly disoriented.

He'd been cold all day and was cold now, cold in his fingers and feet. Bad peripheral circulation, Kyra kept telling him. He needed *exercise*, why didn't he move around more? "You'd sleep a whole lot better if you did, you know that, don't you?" Fanning liked to walk around his adopted city just fine, but his knees ached if he overdid it, and for another thing some people happened not to be athletes. "Try tai chi or something," Kyra said. Sorry, no, no tai chi. He broke from his trance and ran himself a shower and stayed in it, shoulders drooping, bony chin uplifted like a sea bird's, until, too soon, the hot water began to fail. He toweled off and threw on a robe and returned to the machine, where he found:

> I won't keep you in suspense. If I'm not mistaken, you were my sister's boyfriend at the time of her "disappearance." I'm going to be in your fair city on business next week and I wondered if we could meet. I've lived in the Bay Area for a number of years.
>
> Julia Lamoreaux

Fanning read the message a second and third time, picked at it for motive—why look him up now, after all this time? Curiosity, he supposed. Nothing but that, most likely.

Yes, all right, he typed. *Would dinner be good?*

He sat up, waiting. No reply from *julamo*.

*　　*　　*

Fanning slid into bed, tested his body's interest in relinquish-
ing the day. In recent years, he'd hit a run of nights, sometimes weeks on end, when he'd wake between three-thirty
and four, often *exactly* at four, four-oh-oh. He'd get up, traipse
to the bathroom and drain his bladder, and maybe nod off, or
maybe not, but the first ten minutes would tell the story.
There was no rousing Kyra for any charity sex, either—she
required vast quantities of sleep, untrespassed upon. Now
that he was bivouacked downtown, Fanning occasionally rose
and pedaled the stationary bike somebody had abandoned
here, the city lights vaguely hallucinatory without his glasses.
Early on, he'd jettisoned the idea of using these hours con-
structively. Sometimes he listened to music, but nothing he
had to render an intelligent opinion about. If he dictated
notes at that hour, his voice sounded wrong the next day, like
another man's, querulous, uncertain. A strew of travel books
lay about his chair: Patrick Leigh Fermor and *In Patagonia*
and *The Colossus of Maroussi* and one by Evan Connell. Also
paper-bound atlases and gazetteers. These required only a
quiet submission to the names, the ragged shorelines and
archipelagos. One night he broke out a new disc of Keith Jar-
rett's *Köln Concert*—he hadn't heard this in years, afraid he'd
find his reverence for it unsupportable, yet the piece seemed
brilliantly moody, elemental. Near dawn, Fanning might
creep back under the covers. He remembered Hemingway's
story where the waiter couldn't sleep until daylight, but Fanning seldom allowed himself a good fear of the abyss anymore, Fanning-less time unfurling without end. Sometimes
he encountered a grace period just before morning—if he
slept even a little then, his day might be salvageable.

But *Carly Lamoreaux*—

She was a room he had rarely visited as a grown man, and
never with his guard down. He owned no photo of her, the box
containing her letters had been lost in a move years ago. He

lay on the futon wondering if he could recall her voice, the timbre, the way she worded things. So much of their relationship had been conducted long-distance, Carly stretching the cord of the Lamoreaux's upstairs phone beneath her bedroom door, while Fanning contorted his long body inside the sweaty phone box at school. (The following year, 1973–74, Moorcroft and Griffin had both gone co-ed. Exquisite timing.) But the voice he heard tonight was indistinct, more like a grown woman's than a girl's, as if Carly had been allowed to age along with him. For all this, Fanning was unconscious in a matter of minutes and didn't stir until well after six. He was shaved and on the street before seven. A chilly morning in late October. Gray, windy. He took coffee and biscotti at a storefront place a few blocks up the way, resting his elbows on a narrow shelf along the plate glass, watching the early parade. Another long day in the offing, heavy on the business side: sales meeting, two conference calls, tête à tête with a banker. Fanning wiped his lips and stepped outside again, buried his hands in his pockets. A low blat from the Bremerton ferry. She'd be thirty-eight, thirty-nine, *julamo*. Fanning took the elevator, emerged on the third-floor landing, saw the office doors open, the lights burning. He stuck his head in. Gloria gave him a look. "Bad night?" she asked.

"No, not so bad," Fanning said.

Gloria disapproved of him living in the Hospitality Suite, found it unbecoming. *If she wants this, you tell her she can find herself another place. Shouldn't be you who has to camp out like a hobo.*

Fanning appreciated the loyalty, but he told her things were all right. Just a temporary situation. A little solitude never killed anyone, right?

"I hate to think of you having bad nights," she said. She'd been with Fanning from the start. Gloria de Santos with her bright lipstick and yard-wide hips, her emphysemic husband.

And what she didn't say, *You can afford to stay in a nice place, why you doing this to yourself, huh—? You're not crapping out on us?*

Fanning put a hand up, cut short further discussion of his condition by saying he was going next door, be back in a second.

On his machine:

No, I don't think dinner. Could you come by my hotel? The Queensbury. Meet you in the lobby. Let's say around eight.

Fanning slipped off his jacket and knelt to fashion his reply.

2

FANNING CIRCLED the block, humming a Billy Caughlan
tune, "Hard Knock Turn," that had been looping through his
head all afternoon. The rain had let up and the streets shone
like graphite. On the third pass, he found a spot on the down-
hill side of the hotel and squeezed in. It was a raw night,
squalling. "Will I recognize you?" he'd asked online. "I'll
have a flower in my hair," she answered, and though he didn't
take it literally, he kept picturing a woman with an orchid
anchored in a spill of hair. Dark, copious. The truth was he
couldn't call up any likeness of Julia at all, much less calculate
what time had wrought.

The Queensbury was an older hotel, off the beaten path,
nine or ten floors, revamped during the eighties. He stepped
inside and got his bearings. The place was deserted but for a
pair of gnomish Korean gentlemen waiting at the elevator.
He took a seat, checked his watch. Quarter past already. The
business section of the *P-I* lay on the chair adjacent. He left
it there. Murkily, he made out the Sonics game. Five or ten
minutes elapsed, his thoughts eddying. He didn't begrudge

her what he remembered about her sister—if that's what she wanted, and why else would she have bothered with him?—it was just that he remembered precious little.

Now a woman in a black raincoat swept out of the revolving door and came in crisp strides, swinging a satchel-like bag of pebbled leather. Tall, handsome, the hair a deep walnut, glossy, asymmetrical in cut. She made eye contact. Fanning rose, drying his palm on his trouser leg. "Julia," he said, offering the smile of an old ally.

A momentary discomposure around her mouth now. "*Richard?*" she asked.

Fanning shrank back a half-step, involuntarily. "No," he said, "I'm sorry."

She stood blinking, as if this might yet be a joke and turn out happily. She was prepared to be a good sport. "You're not Richard?" she said.

Another night, he might've joked with her—"No, no, just kidding, of course I'm Richard. How *are* you?" Now he simply apologized again. He watched her go to the desk, where a message was handed her. He watched her read it, take three or four steps, lower her satchel to the terrazzo, then read it a second time, head bowed. She glanced up sharply and caught him staring. He turned away, feeling, absurdly, as if he had a part in this news.

He kneaded his face and sat. He'd give Julia another five minutes.

He waited five, another five.

Then the doors of the elevator parted and she approached him, and he *did* recognize her—something in the fretted expression, and there were the same bangs she'd worn as a girl, almost obscuring her eyes. The hair was dyed now, eggplant, cordovan. She was very thin, wearing a rayon tunic, plain and loose-hanging.

She came artlessly, head shaking, gave her hand. "This is a fool's errand," she said.

Fanning greeted her, assured her it was no trouble, he was pleased to see her.

"You look de*lighted.*"

"No," he said, "I am." He asked if she'd like a drink.

Julia cast a glance at the shadowy entryway to the lounge, The Embers, said no, she didn't care to, here would be all right. So they sat in two tall-backed leatherette chairs, with the blue flame of a gas jet hissing in the fire grate, Julia slumping into what Fanning took to be a customary slouch. "I'm going to smoke," she announced, taking a flat box of some imported product from the tunic's one floppy pocket. He picked up a ghost of accent in her voice, working-class New England. He hadn't heard it in years.

"You're married?" she asked.

Fanning nodded.

She said, "Nice."

"To be honest," Fanning said, "we're not cohabiting at the moment."

"Her idea or yours?"

"Some of both, I guess."

"And how's it going to play out?"

"Can't answer that one," Fanning said, attempting a smile. "You?"

She shrugged.

Fanning didn't press. "Your business got taken care of?" he asked.

Smoke leaked from her nose in two desultory plumes. "I'm afraid I fibbed about that part," she said.

Fanning took this to mean he was her business.

Her skin was an off-white, yet pale, with no veneer of makeup—hours ago, there might've been a coating of lipstick. Her eyes were far apart, tipped . . . Fanning couldn't decide if she was pretty or not. But she was a champion smoker, went for it avidly, hungrily. Plain air must have seemed a thin broth.

She said, "You two were sleeping together?"

"Excuse me?"

"You and Carly."

"I'm sorry, I don't think I want to get into that," Fanning said.

Julia looked off.

Her pants were the same material as the tunic, taupe or mushroom. "Willfully austere," Fanning's wife would have remarked. The shoes were flats, suede worn to a gloss over the toes, which never stopped flexing, Fanning noticed.

"It was an awfully long time ago," he said at last. The words struck him as criminally insipid. He rearranged himself in the chair. "Look, Julia," he said, "I'll tell you as much as I recall. I'm afraid you'll have to take it or leave it." He hadn't meant this to sound so curt, but strangely it was the first thing he'd said that seemed to agree with her. "You sure you don't want a drink?" he asked.

"No, it's okay."

"You not drink?"

"I *drink,*" Julia said. "I'm not in a drinking frame of mind right at present."

"I was just offering," Fanning said.

"Noted."

Fanning said, "I drove down that summer to see your folks. I don't know if you were around."

"Be*lieve* me, I was around," Julia said. "I barely left the compound."

The Lamoreauxs had lived on the Old Post Road in Clarion, well outside Hartford, a good two-plus hours from his own town in Massachusetts. A white, post–Civil War house on a knob of stony ground. Black-shuttered, a wraparound porch with reefed-up floorboards, a row of elderly plum trees. Respectable, but not in exquisite repair. He had a memory of Mr. Lamoreaux bumping along spectrally on a mowing tractor.

"I meant, when we were having our actual . . . conversation," Fanning said.

She rolled her lip, retrieved a flake of tobacco with her thumb, studied it as if it might be a piece of tooth. "The boyfriend," she said. "Rimless glasses, madras shirt, good chinos with a crease. Iced tea with mint served in the blue tumblers. Store-bought sugar cookies."

"You can't *remember* that——"

"Well, I'm blessed."

Somehow Fanning didn't doubt it. Already he'd begun to suspect nothing got past her, nothing lapsed into a saving obscurity.

"A command performance on your part," she said. "That's how it seemed."

"My mother'd been at me for days," he said. "*You've got to go see those people.* She didn't call it my Christian duty, she didn't talk in those terms, but that's what she meant. I didn't know what to say beyond how sorry I was."

"You'd accepted the worst. You held out no hope?"

"But how else could you possibly make sense of it?" Fanning said. "Weeks had gone by."

"Very true. And yet, I mean, the abduction and slaying theory . . . three blocks from the Civic Center, what could happen? Great improbables with that scenario."

Fanning said he realized that.

"*C'mere sweet pea, hop into my vehicle.* Broad daylight."

"Well, not like that exactly."

"Then you tell me."

"Honestly, I have no idea."

"Take a *stab*," Julia said.

Twenty-four years ago, the city police had questioned Fan-

ning at length and then he'd led them along the precise route
he'd taken, past the delicatessen, the luggage store, the eye-
glass place, past Tony Rome's tavern on the corner, and across
the exposed cobblestones in the alley mouth. The party
veered into that strange recessed area, and there was a
woman's blouse knotted on the arm of the bench, a yellow
polyester with stains that appeared to have been made by a
bicycle chain. Fanning was asked if he recognized the shirt,
but he didn't. "And that other time, you didn't stop anywhere
on the way here?" Fanning said no, they'd been aiming for
the park, just had a short time. "And this shirt's nothing you
seen before." No, Fanning repeated. The alley, previously
cool, grottolike, now seemed hot and airless. Fanning couldn't
get his breath and thought he'd be sick in front of these
grown men. Again and again, he presented his story, then,
some weeks later, reprised it for a private investigator Mr.
Lamoreaux had hired. They all dunned him with the same
question Julia was asking now: What was his own explanation? He knew nothing, he insisted, he couldn't help—every
time they started pressuring him his thoughts seized up. For
all that, Fanning seldom relived these events. He wasn't fond
of the past, didn't court it, his *own* past. True, certain
moments had the clarity of engravings: his father in a brown-
checked shirt rowing them back across the lake after shearing
the cotter pin of the boat's propeller on a submerged stump.
His father's calm acceptance, the smile on his dry lips. A great
hummer, his father, Count Basie tunes. He dipped the oars in
the lake water and pulled, humming, the oarlocks giving little
yelps. Or the afternoon, in the pale lime Pontiac, en route to
Watson's Market in Fitchburg, where she bought her roasts,
his mother had undertaken to explain girls' periods, extracting from him the solemn pledge not to push any of his female
classmates into the water . . . or the time, performing some
similar errand, on the plaid bench seat of an earlier vehicle,
she had attempted to allay his fears about death. Yet most of

it was simply not there. Day stacked on day, erased or remembered in shreds or skewed into untruth.

Fanning sat forward now and looked at Julia and said, "I suppose she could've come out a different exit from the one we used the Friday before, she could've gotten turned around, gotten going in the wrong direction, then tried to improvise, or even hitch a ride."

"Because by then it was late."

"Yes."

"And she was hot to see you."

"Yes, I guess."

"So you two could make out."

Fanning found it mortifying to remember that the anticipation of skimming his hand across Carly's bare skin had once consumed him. That he'd been imagining touching her when whatever happened to Carly was happening, or starting to happen.

"And as luck would have it," Julia said, "she ran into just the wrong man. Or men."

"It's not out of the realm of—"

"You don't think she lit out for greener pastures?"

"But she wasn't like that. She was *happy.*"

He expected an immediate objection, but Julia only studied him, smoking, a phantom smile camped about the lips. Fanning found himself unnerved, yet couldn't stop watching her. At length, he asked, "Do you *know* something? You have something to tell me? Is that what this is about?"

A slight, bangs-clearing toss of Julia's head.

He said, "You haven't got . . . new information?"

"No new information. Not a whisper."

Fanning sighed.

He sat rubbing his corduroys. "You don't think she was happy?" he asked.

"Mitzi always said, *Carolyn's my sunbeam.*"

The mother. Fanning wouldn't have been able to dredge

up the name if he were before a firing squad, but now he recalled how freely Carly used it, *Mitzi says, Mitzi's in one of her famous moods . . .*

"And the chronically cheerful are immune from rash acts?" Julia said.

"I'm not saying that," Fanning said. "I just don't see her running off—without a word? The worst I could say is she was impatient for school to be out, but who wasn't? We had the summer in front of us . . . we were driving up to Wells Beach in June."

Fanning had only just remembered this, just as he said it. "And she had her job at the stables," he went on. "Which she loved, I know that for certain. If there was something else, I'd have seen it. But she wouldn't have done that to you, to your family. She wasn't *cruel.*"

"No, not cruel," Julia said. "Not our Carolyn."

Fanning stared. What to make of this tone of voice?

She said, "Why are you so sure she came out the wrong door?"

"I'm *not.* You asked me to speculate."

"But that is what you think."

"I don't think anything," he said, sorry to be so blunt, but there it was.

She eyed him through the scrim of smoke.

She said, "We surely didn't see much of you after that."

"I worked during the week," Fanning said. "I was on a framing crew out of Leominster that summer. And then, you know, in August I left for Ann Arbor, for college."

"You'd have come if we'd had a funeral."

Fanning frowned. Yes, of course, he said.

"Maybe they'd have let you carry the box."

Now here was a thought that had never once crossed his mind: Carly in a box, himself pressed into service. Six men sweating in dark suits. But then, it appeared, Carly never got a box.

Julia said, "Were you waiting for us to call you?"

Fanning shot his gaze around the near-deserted lobby, found nothing substantive for it to light on. "I don't know if I acted honorably or not," he said, unclear how he'd wound up on the defensive. "I can't answer that. I was barely eighteen myself, I didn't know your family all that well. Your father in particular, he scared the bejesus out of me if you want the honest—"

"No kidding."

"*Simon,*" Fanning said.

Julia nodded.

"Is he still—"

"No."

Fanning felt he should ask about the mother then.

"Nope," Julia said. "Her either."

"Recently?"

"This past summer," she said. "In Mitzi's case."

Fanning sat back.

After a moment, she said, "We just thought you might've been more curious. We thought you might've had the urge to check *in.*"

Was this what she was after? he asked. A pound of flesh? After so long?

She brightened. "Fanning," she said, "to be perfectly goddamn honest, I don't know what I want from you." She raked at her bangs, and was ambushed by a horrendous yawn, disclosing a mouthful of fillings. She refocused on him as if coming back from the void. She said, "I feel like I've been up a year."

Fanning had no trouble believing this. He recognized the glassy intensity. Four hours a night, max. Four hours on a good night.

"You take anything?" he asked.

She said, "One time they put me down with a horse needle and I slept the sleep of the righteous. I came to, it was the next day. I showered, put on coffee water. Almost eight and I had to be clear across town in three-quarters of an hour, but the sun was in the wrong window, and the traffic noise was screwy. I couldn't make my mind function for the longest time. I was all goosebumps, goggle-eyed. Then a streetlight came on, then another and another."

Fanning smiled without having meant to.

She said, "I do hate to miss a single moment of this extrava*ganza.*" She waved her free hand in a grand sloppy arc, rattling two thin bracelets.

"So your wife look anything like Carly?"

"Why?"

"Just nosy."

"Not really."

"No resemblance."

"She's extremely blond," Fanning said. "And bigger, closer to my height."

"Big strapping girl?"

"Really, there's no similarity. Everything about her's different."

"Nice legs?"

"Very decent."

Julia nodded. "Long in the shank," she said. "What's her name?"

Fanning balked a moment, then gave it.

"But she's another look-on-the-bright-side type, isn't she."

And here Fanning retreated from this badinage, as if from a hot burner, because Kyra *was* that way. She suffered brief frustrations, brief hard bouts of sadness, like anyone, but her system seemed to flush them. She lacked the capacity for gloom. He'd come to believe it was genetic. No canyons of indecision for Kyra. Even this experiment of theirs, this hiatus from physical proximity . . . she'd gone at it like a scout leader.

"And she knows the Carly-and-Miles story."

"Of course," Fanning lied.

It wasn't true at all. Kyra believed in full disclosure, complied herself, but in seven-plus years' worth of talk about old heartthrobs, Fanning had omitted Carly entirely. He'd given Kyra the women he'd dated at Michigan, the dancer, the future hematologist, he'd given Bridget Piersall from when he'd reviewed concerts for the paper, treading lightly, it was true, on the breakup with Bridget . . . they'd been edging toward matrimony, but she'd drawn back, accusing him of what, a certain coldness of spirit? Fanning had taken pains to demonstrate his buoyancy then, his good heart, but the horses were already out of the barn. After that, no serious involvements until Kyra. She was nine years his junior and seemed from another generation entirely. "But what about high school?" she prodded. Fanning said he'd been a slow bloomer.

Now he stood abruptly. "Would you mind if I went and got myself a glass of scotch and brought it back here? Could I get you a spritz water or something?"

Julia stared up at him. Her limbs had a lank, convoluted look. "Scotch is okay," she said.

"We could go *in*to the bar."

"I don't know," she said. "I'm here now."

Fanning nodded. He wasn't about to push. He asked, "You partial to any particular kind?"

She said, "The kind from Scotland."

Fanning idled before the wall-mounted TV, watched Vin Baker receive an alley-oop from Payton and pound it down, then watched the replay. What an elegant thing, he thought. *So sudden.* "Show it again," he whispered, but the game had proceeded on. He was tired himself, had a needling pain behind his eye sockets. How tempting it was to stand here and not move, but after a moment, he withdrew bills from his wallet and left them and carried the drinks back to the lobby. From the rear, Julia's chair appeared to be smoldering, about to burst into flame.

She accepted the glass without comment, rolled it against her cheek before bringing it to her lips. "Liar," she said.

"How's that?"

"You didn't tell your wife the first thing about any missing girlfriend."

"No?"

"Tell me I'm full of it."

Fanning held his own drink in his lap, two-handed.

"Carly wasn't pregnant?"

Fanning shook his head.

"You know this for fact."

"Yes."

"Because things hadn't progressed that far."

Fanning said, again, he wasn't comfortable discussing this. Weren't he and Carly entitled to a certain baseline of privacy?

"Mitzi found her pills," Julia said.

Fanning had no memory of pills. "She told you that?"

"I was a snoop, okay? She told Mitzi they belonged to a friend from school. It was an unopened package. *What friend?* Mitzi asked. Carly said she couldn't tell her, this girl's parents were tyrants, they ransacked her belongings, she and her mother didn't have the kind of close relationship *they* had . . . Mitzi would just have to trust her that she couldn't betray this friend. And Mitzi couldn't bring herself to believe Carly'd lie straight to her face, and so she believed her and said nothing to Simon. That was in April. I have to admit it was an impressive performance, very much out of character."

She produced a new box of smokes and gave it three smart taps against the waxy curve of her wrist. She said, "But, as I say, the pills were unopened, which could mean anything." She stared at Fanning. "You didn't know any of that, did you?"

What possible good is this doing anyone? he wondered. *It's over and gone.* He drew his glass to his lips and found it already drained to the ice.

"Don't you think it's bizarre no one ever took credit?" she said.

"Took credit?"

"Time goes by, somebody needs something. *I know about this missing girl*— A little click of information they've been holding onto like a 'Get Out of Jail Free' card. The ones who clam up are rarer. It takes talent to hold it in, your accomplishment."

She drank. She seemed to be sieving the scotch through her teeth like an astringent. "And it's not that easy to lose a body, takes an expertise. An amateur, you might expect a poor job. The garbage guys find it, the wild dogs dig it up, it floats out of the river and snags in the goddamn bulrushes. It doesn't turn up, now that's blind luck."

"*Julia*—" Fanning said, leaning in.

"Not that anyone uttered the word *luck* in the Lamoreaux house," she said. "Oh, shit no. Verboten. Luck was for people who didn't comprehend the Lord's mystery, the Lord's intricate handiwork."

Now she went silent, but her eyes were on him and there was no way for him to consult his watch, which, having knobby wrists, he stored in a jacket pocket.

"So why was it you didn't tell the wife?" she asked finally. "Feel a little tarnished by all this Lamoreaux business?"

"Julia," Fanning said quietly, "I'm not someone who says everything out loud. Can't we leave it at that?"

"If you want."

"I honestly do," Fanning said.

Julia nodded.

After a moment, she said, "You know what, I'm more the other way."

Fanning said he'd figured as much.

"Can't seem to shut up."

He should offer to buy another drink now. He should say, despite appearances, he often thought about her family, that it was too damn bad they had to know one another under such ugly circumstances. Instead, he stood. His knees cracked. He said, "I should be going. It's been a hellish week. I'm sorry if I haven't been as helpful—"

Now Julia stood. Fanning thought for an instant she'd spring onto her toes and give him a ritual kiss, one cheek then the other. He was mistaken. She held her bare forearms together at the waist, precluding even a handshake. "Good night, Fanning," she said.

Fanning could think of nothing useful to add, so he said his own good night. He walked the length of the lobby and outside where the sky was again spitting rain. He passed by the side windows of the lobby and saw that Julia had slumped back into the big chair. He was a few blocks up Boren, peering through the greasy sweep of the wipers, before it occurred to him that despite his relief at being quit of her, he might at least have said, "I hope you sleep."

3

"YOU REALIZE YOU can have me," Kyra said. There was no taunting to this, no blandishment. They were in the main studio, drinking sodas.

"I'll take that under advisement," Fanning said.

It was late, the night of 30 April 1990. Billy Caughlan and his bleeding ulcer were in the bathroom. Two hours earlier, Billy had been playing with excellent concentration, improvising fluidly, but now he was pissed: at the wimpy medication he was on, at his own lumpishness, at Kyra for giving pale comfort, at Fanning for having suggested they call it a night. Kyra was in black stretch pants, a white T with a scoop neck, Kyra with her braid like a hawser reaching the lower back, swaying as she moved.

Fanning and Caughlan had a business relationship, perhaps more, not quite a genuine friendship, but there was no possibility Fanning would interpose himself between Caughlan and his girlfriend. None. No matter that Fanning's attraction had been immediate, that he'd daydreamed of Kyra Cannaday with a precision he never afforded women he actually knew. Saw her strolling across white tiles in a taut black tank suit. Saw her on her back, gripping the spindles of a bed-stead.

"Don't study it too long," she said.

Fanning gave her the smile of an old comrade-in-arms, an old uncle.

She said, "He's done with me, he just doesn't know it yet."

She rubbed the sleeve of his jacket with her knuckles. "I'm too wholesome," she said. "He thought that's what he wanted but it wasn't."

Billy Caughlan reemerged from the can, hair beaded with water, eyes red-rimmed yet not so crimped. Whatever had transpired there, Fanning didn't want to know of it. Billy went at the tune again, crashed after eight or ten bars, said, "No, *fuck*, keep it running," and started once more and crashed again, then placed his hands together in front of his lips, supplicating, then played the piece through, grunting with the syncopation in the fast section, coming up off the bench like a dirt biker, averting his face at the legato, cheek to shoulder, then suddenly a modulation, then another and another, ending in the improbable key of B flat. A tune called "Caughlan's Condition." The grunts remained audible on the finished track, like Glenn Gould's wayward humming on the *Goldberg Variations*. Billy Caughlan was no Glenn Gould, but Fanning admired him, he did, and no more keenly than this night when he'd risen to the occasion, when he'd not yet known he was done with Kyra.

Their first autumn, the Canadian Rockies:

They'd soaked in the hot springs. They'd made love and slept. She'd stood before him reconstructing her braid. It had been necessary then to make love again. Now they were dressed and seated in the hotel's dining room. Light lapping on a concrete balustrade, fir needles dropping to the deserted walkway outside. The high white ceiling with its fretwork.

They were a little more dressed up than was called for, Kyra in a black sheath with two fine straps at each shoulder, Fanning in a soft charcoal suit, his favorite.

"I like how I am with you," she said.

"How's that?"

"Not so——" She folded the panels of the menu and stared at him directly. "Like I'm in a race," she said.

"You never seemed that way to me," Fanning said.

"You make me feel calm and capable."

"Not too calm, I hope."

"No, not too calm."

Later she said, "I've neglected parts of myself."

Fanning assured her he'd neglect no part of her.

Kyra smiled. She said, "That's a promise, is it?"

"I want you all the time," he said.

Thin strips of veal in a dark sauce, Belgian endive with walnuts, merlot.

"I'm sorry," he said. "What have you neglected?"

Kyra said, "If a person's always asking, *What's next, what can I get out of this*——"

"We're all like that."

"Not you."

"It's only that I'm older maybe."

"No, you have this——"

A miracle that Fanning could be taken for a man with inner peace.

The Fanning residence: 2448 Weymouth Street, on the upslope side of the block, not a flashy neighborhood—for the most part, single-family houses from the 1920s, some barely modified except for the replacement of siding and roof slates, the hacking out of blackberry and arborvitae, the installation of security devices, though Weymouth wasn't considered a high-crime area. Others, like Fanning's, were so remodeled they might as well be new—angular decking, walls of double-pane glass facing the canal. It was a house in the shape of stacked boxes, airy, yet the traffic sounds were virtually nil. Four levels in all, if you counted the slender, no-longer-functional garage and half-cellar bored into the rocky hillside below, the master bedroom forming the highest layer, a cedar-shaked roost fronted by a skinny balcony lined with clay pots. Fanning had acquired the place from a realtor friend only months before Billy Caughlan's breakup with Kyra. He seldom cared to remember his time there alone, the newly sanded floors smelling of sealant, the walls largely barren as he moseyed from room to room like a hound. He'd gotten word his old flame Bridget had married—he sent a card wishing her well, but found himself wondering again whether she hadn't been right after all, that he was too private a man, his cool surface arising from a blankness within. It was an old fear, dating to his days at Griffin, or earlier, to the windy yellow-clapboard house he'd grown up in, with its hayfield and pine woods where Fanning spent great quantities of time by himself. But then Kyra had approached him and he'd responded. She'd moved from Billy's bed to the bed at Weymouth Street, and Fanning's old insecurities went dormant again. He seemed to thrive.

Pick a Saturday morning, early summer, the hemlock branches sidling lazily. There was Kyra's bare leg glossy with sweat, heel on the wooden railing outside the kitchen, foot pointed, toes curled, the upper body folded along its length, a posture she could hold indefinitely. Fanning slid to his right for a better view. What a marvel of nature. His own tendons were tight as guy wires.

Long in the shank.

Inside, peeling off the T-shirt, *Havelock's Creamery,* the sports halter, accepting coffee from Fanning, holding it away from her a moment as he placed a mouth to her nipple, wide and brown, flattened from its confinement. "Oh, I'm salty," she said, head thrown back. She was.

Weekdays, she woke instantly, strode to the shower, dressed without deliberating. Dark tailored suits, skirts a light wool or linen by season, low heels, gold circle pin, or pearls. One earnest kiss on the lips, a waft of Cinnabar, and then she was into the silver-gray Accord and across town to the mayor's office, where she was guardian of the appointment book, flourishing amid the chaos, adept, forthright-friendly, sufferer of no fools. An early observation of Fanning's: that Kyra was a woman without incongruities. Then how could he find her so *erotic?* That itself was a mystery. She gave freely, with a simple carnality. She panted, laughed in whoops as if on a carnival ride, often told him, "Boy, are you a lucky man." But even this was guileless, a statement of fact. He *was* lucky. She liked pleasing him with her body, exhausting him, estranging him from whatever made him brood, made him go briefly ill-tempered, or for longer periods, self-absorbed—he knew that, he surrendered to it. She pleased him very well, but nowhere was there the least whiff of wickedness or shame, no sly complicity or teasing, no reservoir of the ironies that ordinarily fuel desire.

In Fanning's desk, scratched on a torn strip of legal tablet: "There's just not much hidden about me, Miles. I'm right out where you can see me." The handwriting Fanning's, so he'd recorded it from a conversation, saved it for some purpose, since forgotten.

Was it true of Kyra?

Of anyone?

San José del Cabo. Cozumel.

Florence, San Gimignano, Venice, Lago di Garda.

You, nine other adventurers, and our licensed naturalist will sail by yacht to explore more islands than any other Galapagos expedition. Macchu Picchu option.

Or, as it turned out, none of the above.

One year, though, Fanning booked reservations for the festival at Montreux, lakefront room at Villa Toscane. Business-related, it was true—he'd hoped to sign a duo called Rives & Cork, wanted to hear how the international crowd responded to them, and was on the lookout for others who might be scruffing about unmoored, hungry. Beyond that, he wanted to be out in the greater world with Kyra, to walk a new city with her, their shoulders brushing, to drink coffees with her where they had not previously drunk coffees, he wanted to follow her up long flights of marble stairs. Then, two days before lift-off, an AP report citing malfeasance in Public Works, allegations of double-dipping, kickbacks. The mayor circled his wagons. Fanning flew to Geneva by himself.

Quarter past three in the morning, exhausted, overstimulated, he called Kyra and she wasn't yet home—after six their time. He left a message, but it struck him as disjointed, as demanding when he'd only meant to ask how she was. He waited up to try again, woke later in shirt and trousers, with ashen light at the curtain. The next afternoon, on the terrace overlooking the water, he began a letter, which he knew he'd beat home. He and Kyra had no history of absence from one another, of committing things to paper. *I don't feel like myself,* he wrote, stopped and watched the tacking of white sails, then added, *without you,* though he hadn't really meant that—what he'd started out to say was how self-conscious it made him, reporting the minutiae of his day for her, how he couldn't find a natural voice for sharing these mundane observations.

Then where *did* they go?

Down I-5, and west on Highway 6 to Tillamook, where Fanning was granted the pleasure of seeing Kyra among her brothers. Tow-headed men, square-jawed and affable, robust like her. Todd who ran the orchard with their father, Keith and Jimmy who owned an excavation business, Terry who worked for the phone company. He witnessed how fond of her they were, how accustomed to admiring her: the youngest, the prize, holder of the state record in the 800-meter hurdles (since surpassed), page in the Oregon Legislature, winner of the prestigious DeVoto Scholarship. The one who got away. Fanning memorized the names at last, began to connect kids with parents, to track the references to old injuries, grudges, bailouts. Fanning was treated with respect, deference. They didn't have to like him especially, he thought, it was enough to be Kyra's husband. He spoke this aloud to Kyra. She made one of her faces, said, "Don't be weird, Miles. They like you just fine. Relax. *Please.*"

One fall morning, Todd and Jimmy took him bird hunting, lending him the father's Remington. Fanning said he hadn't fired a shotgun since boyhood, but found the swing of the barrel, the release, was second nature even now. He dropped two pheasants in the first half hour. A look passed between the brothers. Todd said, "Well, that answers that." Fanning told them, to be honest, he'd only ever shot clay pigeons, from behind a bunker in a neighbor's field, he wasn't sure what to do with the damn birds, dressing them out, and so on. Jimmy said, "Now that's where the art comes in, any fool can blast them out of the sky." Fanning let himself be ribbed and the three men walked along peaceably, discussing the foibles of Roy's retrievers, and the father's hip joint, which had deteriorated to the point where he was going to need a replacement, and when the conversation touched on the virtues of the Reagan presidency, Fanning chastely held his tongue.

They parked the truck in the dusty grass outside the barn at the main house, and Fanning followed them in through the mudroom, and there in the kitchen were Kyra and her mother and Jimmy's wife, Starla, and Roy's moon-faced wife, Gail, and they uncapped bottles of wheat beer Gail had made, which was a little sweet, but not bad at all, potent as hell, and that night on the screened porch they ate pheasant breasts swimming in sour cream and onions, arguably one of the happiest meals of Fanning's life, looking back on it, but as sanguine as Fanning felt all evening, as blessed by marrying into a big noisy family, when his own had been, though loving enough, so thinly populated, so decorous, he never quite got over feeling like an outsider. Invited, but a guest.

For their fifth anniversary, a portrait in black-and-white, shot by Fanning's friend Ryugi, who'd done cover art for Sun-Break, his signature style being still lifes in extreme close-up: the bubble in a carpenter's level . . . the two tapering points of a steel caliper forming a tulip . . . the raised letters on a wood clamp, *1500-Pound Test,* which became the name of Billy Caughlan's last album for SunBreak, before Fanning released him to sign with ECM. The "toolbox covers," Gloria de Santos called them. Too severe, she said, altogether too male. She went for the gaudier stuff, the grease-crayon drawings, the folk art, girls on stilts, blood-flushed faces, lips on lips. But Fanning very much liked how plain Ryugi's pictures were, how empty of ego. He'd watched people handle the jewel cases in stores, holding them transfixed, taking a chance on an unknown artist by virtue of Ryugi's work. And Fanning liked the man himself. He was in his middle fifties, wiry, quizzical, an ex-gymnast, ex-opera company carpenter with brown ropy forearms. Fanning sometimes met him for drinks at Lombardi's around the corner from Ryugi's second-floor studio, or, on rare occasions, joined him in the darkroom, craning over his shoulder while Ryugi talked: "I love this new Czech paper, luscious skin tones, very creamy . . . but *slow slow slow.*" Fanning took solace from Ryugi's utter lack of sourness, the way, ruminating along without embarrassment, he could ask, "So is beauty enough of a consolation?" Expecting an answer, not putting up with Fanning's hesitance to talk about art head-on. And maybe a knuckle in the ribs, "What do you *think*, Miles?" "A consolation for the world?" Fanning answered. "If someone's not too far gone, too sick or distraught. Sure, it helps. Otherwise, why do it?" "But," Ryugi asked, jostling the prints in their bath, "is it for them or for ourselves?" "I think it must be different for you," Fanning said. "In my case, it's always other people's music." Ryugi produced his rapturous lopsided smile, ruby-red from the safe-light. "All the same, you love getting in there and making the artifact, try and tell me you don't." "No, I do," Fanning said. "Sure. It's only that——" Ryugi shushed him. "Listen, Miles, if it weren't for you, half your people wouldn't have an audience at all. It's an honorable thing."

In any case, now it was the night of the portrait—a September evening because he and Kyra had married on a September evening, not five months after her overture toward him at Billy's session. Such an uncharacteristic plunge for Fanning. Now he waited out back on the flagstones at Weymouth Street, lost in thought. The light was coppery, benevolent. Kyra finally appeared, late, caught in Seattle's ludicrous traffic. She waved, called out that she was taking a quick shower. Fanning nodded. He gave her a few minutes, entered the house, climbed the spiral stairs, found her wriggling a cotton sweater over her head. "What?" she said, catching his eye. Fanning asked if she still had the black outfit she'd worn in Canada. Yes, she thought so, would he like that? Fanning said it didn't matter, she could wear what she liked. But Kyra flapped through the clothes on the bar and found the black sheath, in plastic from the cleaners. She removed the sweater, let the wraparound skirt fall, fished a strapless bra from her drawer and cupped herself into it, and then the dress Fanning liked, turning her back to him so he could do the hook and eye. "Better?" she asked into the mirror. "Very nice," Fanning said. She began switching her earrings, still watching him in the glass, almost bemused, *Since when are you sentimental, Mr. Fanning?*

In distant times, Ryugi's had been a barber shop: eight porcelain chairs, eight stations each with its glass box of barber tools and hanging strop, garish gold script on the avenue-facing window, R. E. ADAMS, HAIRCUTTER. Since Fanning had been here last, Ryugi had removed a false wall, exposing fifty feet of original plaster, spidered with cracks, stained by smoke and rusty dripwater, spattered with the silver backing where mirrors had hung. He positioned Fanning and his wife against this polychrome, set the lights, the cloth bounce, gazed at them through the Hassselblad.

"Not too *stern*, Miles," he said.

Fanning said he was only registering the sober nature of the occasion, taking posterity into account. He meant this as a joke. Three-quarters of an hour earlier, Ryugi had met them at the door with a beaker of martinis. The gin turned Ryugi puckish, infused Kyra with a glow, a huge confidence. But gin sent Fanning down another path.

"All right, okay," he said. He made his face less stern, and Ryugi began clicking the handheld plunger, but relaxing the muscles seemed to loosen Fanning's grip on the moment. His heart skipped, a toxic sweat dribbled inside his shirt. Though he loved photographs, he hated pictures of himself, his freckled forehead with its sprigs of hair, his mouth. While there on the contact sheets would be dozens of Kyras, the braid hugging one shoulder, her hand curled about it at the breast, the clean jawline, the eyes round and serenely *there*, and not one sappy expression in the lot. But worse, for Fanning, was confronting *old* pictures of himself . . . or of, say, Walter Fanning as a young buck, holding an oyster-white fedora, one foot on the running board of someone's roadster.

Ryugi stopped to change film, and now he put Kyra on a stool in front of Fanning, and while they waited her head rolled softly against his stomach, back and forth. She said, "We should do this every year, don't you think?"

Fanning ran his hands down her bare arms.

And who would gaze at such a gallery, Fanning was thinking. Posterity?

"Honey?" she asked. "Miles?"

But didn't she want her *own* children?

She assured Fanning it was enough to be Aunt Kyra, who remembered all birthdays, who sent Baskin-Robbins coupons or Mariner tickets or a backstage pass to Soundgarden, whose cards descended on the eight nieces and nephews out of the blue. *Shannon, I was thinking of you this morning. You are absolutely the COOLEST kid.*

Was it true, was this enough?

There's not that much hidden about me, Miles.

And what of Fanning? No, no burning need in him, either. Shouldn't it be a burning need?

So why would he not get himself cut? Why horse around with contraception ad infinitum?

He was squeamish, superstitious.

She said, "I'll do it, then."

"What if you change your mind?"

"Are you going to change yours?"

In December, the mayor's staff party downtown. Fanning had a head cold for which he'd swallowed a dose of decongestant that left him ethereal. Seattle lay in a trough of air from the Gulf of Alaska, and the late afternoon mist had begun to congeal on windshields, side streets. Kyra asked if he wanted to stay home, she could give his regrets. But Fanning believed he should make the effort for her sake. Plus he took an eerie pleasure in observing his wife's finesse among these bigshots.

"We don't have to linger," Kyra said.

The mayor had the same lousy cold, as it happened. He and Fanning stood commiserating, emptying flutes of champagne. "Tried that zinc?" the mayor asked. "Comes in lozenges?" Fanning said he hadn't. The mayor pressed a square of handkerchief to his face. "This is one bugger," he said. "What I get for being out in public—whatever's making the rounds it finds me." The two men watched the mayor's youthful, very pregnant second wife navigating her way toward them, a barge of red satin parting the well-wishers. "Did you tell Miles how much we liked the *music?*" she said, and the mayor said no, he hadn't gotten to that yet. "That acoustic sampler?" the mayor's wife said. "I've been playing it in the *tub*, very re*laxing*." Fanning said he considered it an honor to relax the mayor's wife. He hardly knew what he was saying. Then Kyra was steering him onto the parquet. Fanning felt the squeak of the crepe dress against her stockings as their legs met, the pressure of her fingers at his collar. He abandoned himself to the slow box-stepping. But after a while, he asked her if he felt hot, and she said maybe a little, they could go if he wanted. Her voice sounded impatient, distracted. Fanning said he didn't mean that, he wasn't rushing her, he knew how she liked these affairs.

Outside again, later, she asked for the keys. "What is it?" Fanning said. She said she didn't think he should be driving. Fanning disliked being the passenger, but put up no fight. "Slippery?" he asked after a few blocks, and Kyra said not bad. Fanning said, "Why don't you stay on the arterials." Kyra said the streets were okay and she was a good driver. Fanning sat back. "I know you are," he said. He rode with his hot temple against the side glass. He asked if everything was all right. Kyra said, "Everything's fine, Miles." Fanning nodded. He let his eyes drift shut. "I wish—" he said, and it was then Fanning's head erupted with light, a single tentacled burst, for he had cracked skulls with Kyra as a van plowed through their Honda's rear door, rocketing off the glazed hill at 36th, and then there was the sensation of being sucked backward as if in a whoosh of drainwater, and then the tires on Fanning's side met the curb and the car popped onto its roof and slicked through a planting of ground cover, with the

sound of a banner snapping, whipping in a gale, then their
bodies were suspended by the belts, blood inflating their
faces, Kyra's braid hanging like a bell rope, he saw that
indelibly, and he may have gone out briefly, for next thing
Kyra was saying, "Miles, Miles, I'm releasing this, can you
brace yourself?" and then they both stood upright in the wet
grass, panting, Fanning beginning to brush the kernels of
safety glass from his eyebrows, his scalp, abruptly turning
Kyra's cheek up to the arc light, and looking mutely at her
features, which were fierce and soiled, but intact, not cut, not
punctured as far as he could see, squinting, for his eyeglasses
had vanished, he realized, and her jacket was gone also, still
trapped by the belt possibly, so that now he was looking at her
bare shoulder, which was like rosy marble, at her bare
expanse of chest . . . she must be freezing, he thought, but her
whole body seemed to be giving off steam. Fanning said,
"Your coat—" and she grabbed at his shirt front, bunching it,
and said, "Don't go back there. *Don't.*" Fanning stopped
where he was, breathing in longer drafts, staring at the
undercarriage of the Honda, hearing the engine ping as it
cooled, and it was only then that either of them remembered
the other vehicle, the blue van they'd seen only as spears of
light in the corner of the eye. Fanning broke into a run,
aware of a searing in his right side every time his lungs filled,
and crouched into a low, loping stride. The van was inert,
flush against a wedge-shaped pier of yellow-striped concrete
where the roadway turned, an old Econoline with the motor
housed beneath the cab, Fanning saw. The windshield had
come out entirely, and the driver was upright on the seat, hat
over his eyes, a boy, skinny in the chest, starkly underdressed.
Fanning thought for a moment he might be all right, only
collecting himself. He tried the door, found it jammed, put a
foot up and yanked with both hands, wincing. This produced
enough of a rocking motion that the boy tipped forward
through the window socket, striking the concrete post with

his head for what Fanning realized was the second time, this one almost gentle. He turned to keep Kyra from seeing, but was too late.

If there was to be a consequence, for *them*, once the flulike muscle aches had departed, the twin knots on the sides of their heads dissolved, and, in Fanning's case, the ribs healed to where he could breathe, he thought it would be that Kyra's confidence might be blown, that she'd find the world a flukier environment, its hazards less avoidable. He thought she might flinch. She did seem quieter, less *busy*, unless he was inventing that. They replaced the Honda with a newer model. One day as they drove toward Weymouth Street, Fanning bypassed their usual cutoff and Kyra said, "You don't have to do that, Miles." Fanning said, "I just thought, for now——" and Kyra only gave him a look, which, for once, wasn't quite fathomable, and then, routinely, they began passing that intersection again. The blue smudge on the reflector strips, the swath through the brittle ivy leaves. It was after that, a week or two into the new year, Kyra announced she'd changed her mind about kids. This was the last thing Fanning expected.

His *own* hadn't changed.

He started referring to the accident as Kyra's "conversion experience."

She told him not to say that, she didn't like it, it sounded cruel somehow.

"I don't mean it that way," Fanning said. "I just don't get it exactly, I don't see how it follows——"

Kyra failed to argue back at him in her customary fashion, scoring debate points, she didn't say, *It doesn't need to follow, Miles,* but instead, forearms in an X across her chest, not a customary gesture, either, "It was seeing him like that, only a few seconds afterward, I don't know——"

What could Fanning say against this? He'd felt it, too. Kyra had stepped around Fanning's arms, outstretched like a barricade, she'd crossed the remaining few feet of slick pavement and looked at the boy. Fanning had come and stood with her. The boy was broken-necked, unquestionably dead, yet it seemed a third presence was with them. Fanning had the palpable sensation of being watched, *entreated*—he almost said to Kyra, "Do you *feel* that?" but held back, and that quickly it was gone.

"I thought we were together on this," he said. "On children."

"I'm not trying to put something over on you, Miles."

Fanning said he wasn't implying that.

"Will you think about it?" she asked.

She'd been sweet with him when his ribs were howling, got him the codeine, helped with the shirt buttons, promised to tell no jokes so long as laughing sent him through the roof—this itself being a joke because Kyra, for all her fine points, wasn't much given to displays of humor. In any case, Fanning had no desire to pick a fight. He wished to be generous, yet couldn't help saying he didn't believe in sudden changes of heart, just distrusted them.

Kyra said, "But you were the one who didn't want me getting my tubes tied."

"I only meant if something happened to me, you might still—"

So there they were.

"But you have to think about it," Kyra said.

Fanning wiped at his mouth. "All right," he said.

She looked at him, and he could see she was about to become Kyra the Persuasive, Kyra the Enumerator of Reasons Sensible and True, then saw her lips close again, saw that moment of discretion, or perhaps it was a foretaste of resignation. Though resignation was not a mood she often visited.

They used to meet for lunch sometimes.

Not so often anymore.

In the evening, if one or the other wasn't busy downtown, a little communal television: pretzels, Wheat Thins, Kyra's stockinged feet in his lap. *Frontline, Seinfeld, Law & Order.* Otherwise, she was in the study with her clip file, the prospectuses, newsletters, annual reports, or at the computer, Fanning in the other room under a cone of light, reading, hearing the keys tap, nothing for a while, then a clatter, stones in a backwash.

Not so often those spirited talks that rose out of nothing, Kyra saying, *I'm sure I've already told you this,* Fanning encouraging her, *No, I don't think so, keep going.* Tales of Tillamook, Tales of City Hall, Kyra on the sectional, cheeks flushed, saying, *And see, that was it exactly, she was trying to . . .* Fanning borne along, listening with an awe-tinged pleasure. Or maybe it was a night *he* did the talking, when he tried to explain why a particular work got to him, its audacity or flukiness. He might get up, almost shyly, and play passages for her, so she could hear what he heard, but he was never sure she did. There was a blandness to her reactions, he sometimes thought—despite her having dated Billy, the mechanics of a composition didn't seem to interest her much. Still, it hardly mattered—those were good evenings, the talk eventually subsiding, midnight or later, then he and Kyra would close up shop and get into bed, still not finished with each other.

Instead, those months before he took up residence in the Hospitality Suite, he might go for a walk along Weymouth by himself, hands jiggling pocket change as he went. Sometimes he gave himself over to a Mariners game on TV, Junior Griffey with his knifing uppercut, his momentary pause to admire the ball's arc before his slow trot toward first.

Maybe Kyra would stop halfway up the spiral stairs: "Aren't you coming, Miles?"

"In a while," he might answer.

*   *   *

Why was it that what attracted you later seemed to be the trouble? Kyra's very flesh, her vibrancy and directness, her need for immediate remedy. Or, in Fanning's case: the vague air of culture and dissolution, his living in the well of his thoughts, his customary *reserve*.

"But you are thinking about it."
"Yes," Fanning lied.

Then, one evening early this October, Kyra at her most reasonable: "No, I think it would be good if we tried separating."

A bad week, in a string of aimless and contentious weeks. In times past, Fanning refused to take such talk at face value. He stalled, he temporized: *It's come to that, has it?* Palms up in the air. Or turned it back on her, reasonable himself: *You expect too much, Kyra, people don't get along every minute of every day, honestly. Things go in cycles. We'll—* And he was right. The moment passed and before much longer they were in each other's good graces again. But now, unaccountably, he felt dull and stingy, he succumbed to this scheme of hers, suddenly unwilling to speak against it.

Kyra said, "And if we're going to separate we should be *separate*. What good will it do otherwise?"

And so the terms hammered out over the next minutes: four months without contact, no chance encounters, no chatting on the phone, no reneging.

"What if I need something?" Fanning asked.

"From the house? Come when I'm at the office, or leave a message and I'll go out."

"What about the holidays?"

Kyra said she'd be going home.

"What if we decide it's a crappy idea?"

Her hands on his shoulders, arms straight and locked.

"Then we'll see. But let's let it work, Miles."

It wasn't her desire, this separation. She was only its agent, the one able to take steps. He understood, didn't he? That she loved him, but couldn't sit pat? Didn't he know her well enough to know that?

Yes, yes, yes.

"I do love you," he said.

But love wasn't the issue, was it? Not as far as Fanning could see. Nor love of another. There was no third party. Unless the not-baby was a third party.

"Is it all about that?" he asked.

"You know it isn't." She had a certain chin-squared way of gazing at him that vaporized whatever advantage his age conferred. She said, "You're not here anyway, Miles. Be honest."

Fanning shook his head.

"You look miserable," she said.

Fanning denied it.

"Go look in the mirror," she said.

Fanning wasn't looking in any mirror.

Another half hour of this, not so long, really, and then they undressed and slept in the same bed together as always, and in the morning he was out of the house, and that whole conversation, and the days leading to it, seemed beyond belief. How had he let things stray that far, how was it he couldn't say what needed to be said?

4

FANNING APPROACHED his e-mail with trepidation, but found no further communiqués from Carly Lamoreaux's sister. Thank God for small favors.

And, of course, nothing from Kyra.

Let it work, Miles.

He rooted among the books beside his chair for the one with the marker in it, began reading:

I followed Marek's broad back up the passage. Gradually it grew light enough to see without the lanterns, and then we burst out the entryway into full sunlight. It was blinding. I stood panting, my eyes shielded, overcome by a glorious sense of relief to be back among the living . . .

If so inclined, he listened to demo tapes and scratched his reactions on a clipboard. Some nights there were performances, some nights sessions in one of the studios. Time melted away. If he didn't still love hearing sound, notes struck and blown, the playbacks, the endless trial and error, the breakthroughs, he might worry about himself.

Another week, another.

One night, late, the phone. He'd kept the number unlisted and no one he'd given it to had called him here. Four bleats and voice mail took over. After a while, he flipped his book onto the hassock and dialed in to see if he had a message. There was Julia's voice: "I wish you'd have picked up. It wouldn't have killed you. Anyway, it's me. I'll try another time." Fanning listened again, hit 7 for delete and stood staring. Not five minutes later it sounded again and he grabbed it up.

"Can I ask how you got this number?" he said.

"Don't panic, I won't share it around. Look, about the other night, I need to ask you to accept my apologies."

"That's all right," Fanning answered without conviction.

"Well, no, it's not all right," she said. "I get like that, I can't snap out of it . . . I probably could, but sometimes I'm just unwilling, feels like too much of a sacrifice. The thing is, I wanted you to know I can be a perfectly regular person."

"I'll have to take your word on that," Fanning said. He dug out his watch and held it far enough away to read. Quarter to twelve.

She said, "I didn't even get into what I wanted to talk to you about."

"And what was that?"

"You weren't asleep just now?"

Fanning said no, he was still up.

"Fresh as a daisy?"

"Close enough."

The clack of an old Zippo. Unmistakable.

She said, "I take it the wife kept the lodgings. So where's it you're holed up?"

Fanning experienced a brief irrational fear of telling her. He let it wash through him and dissipate, leaving a zinclike tang on his gums. He explained about the Hospitality Suite, but she knew nothing about SunBreak, so in bare outline he described his work life, citing a couple of the better-known names in the SunBreak catalog, on the chance they'd ring a bell.

Julia said he'd have to forgive her, she didn't keep up with music much. She asked him to describe the Hospitality Suite.

Fanning eyed his quarters, gave a sketchy tour. The industrial shelving, the hot plate. The shirts dangling from an iron bar.

"Heartbreak Hilton," she said.

"It's nothing," he said. "Just a few months of—" He toted the cordless across to the sofa and lay down. "Can I ask what this is about?"

"Told you, I wanted to redeem myself."

"I meant the whole, you know, flying up here and all that." The more he'd gone back over it, the odder it had seemed, the more marginal.

"Call it an irrepressible desire."

Fanning let this pass.

She said, "What I wanted was to hear you say what you liked about my sister."

He told her he didn't know if he could.

Julia said, "Yeah, well, it was another lifetime ago."

Fanning received the same little zap of chastening he had at the hotel, the shiver up the skin of his neck.

He said, "I was *attracted* to her, Julia."

"Sexually."

"Yes, all right, sexually. Why not? But that wasn't the main thing. She had this aura, this confidence—people wanted to be around her. But without seeming saccharine, or taken with herself. That's my memory."

He paused a moment and Julia waited him out.

"I tended to feel beaten down sometimes," he said. "Your sister absolved me of it."

Now Julia would ask what in God's name he'd had to feel beaten down about. He couldn't have said precisely, then or now. The spells of feeling *separate*, of feeling—compared to boys like Sully—so unsure of his talents, afraid he didn't add up to an entire person.

But Julia backed off, so maybe she was trying to ingratiate herself. Not that he trusted her. He said, "What your sister got from me, I couldn't tell you."

"Must have been those big ideas."

"Yes, I was a major brain," Fanning said. "I could sling the hash in those days."

"You don't sling it anymore?"

"Not so much, no."

"Well, that's a pity."

There was a wind off the bay tonight. The tall windows knocked sporadically against their sashes.

"So tell me about the trip to Wells Beach," she said.

"Never happened."

"I get that. Tell me anyway."

Fanning shut his eyes. After a moment, he said, "Sully's aunt had a house on the water. I think she was a great-aunt, his father's aunt. His mother had been more or less bedridden for years, a cardiac cripple we'd call her now . . . she'd passed away our sophomore year. I don't remember what the story was with his father, but he'd been out of the picture a long time. The aunt was devoted to Sully, and he spent his summers with her in Maine. This was your typical old beach house, vaguely yellow. No insulation. Flowered linoleum, rag rugs, enamel basins full of shells. Somebody painted watercolors. Sully's aunt and her sister-in-law were usually there when I visited, but sometimes they stayed home in Arlington and we had the place to ourselves. So that was the situation: Sully and his girlfriend and Carly and I had cooked up this plan to spend two or three days there alone."

"Cozy," Julia said. "And how was Carly intending to get this past the old man?"

"I don't remember," Fanning said. He didn't. Maybe he'd never known, maybe Carly had spared him. Certainly, some deception would've been involved. He found this humiliating, even now. To be under such scrutiny, to have had so little say over their lives.

"Okay, assuming you pulled that off. And that's a whopper of an assumption."

"That's all there is."

"Come on, don't bail on me now."

Fanning kneaded the loose flesh along his jawbone and lay still. What did she *want?*

"Tell me about the car."

He told her about the car. A black Ford Falcon, red interior. Station wagon. Shift on the column.

"Yes, I rode in it," she said. "Not that you'd remember."

True. Fanning drew an absolute blank. But didn't it make sense, that they'd have been detailed to ferry the younger sister somewhere? The city pool, say.

She said, "Okay, so going to Maine you'd have taken Route One. What were the towns?"

Without blinking, he listed them: Portsmouth, Kittery, York, Ogunquit, Wells.

"Stop on the way or bull on through?"

"We'd have wanted to get there."

"Sandals and cutoffs for Carly? Feet propped against the dash?"

Jesus, why was he putting up with this?

"Polish on her toenails?"

"I don't know," Fanning said.

"Pink or coral."

"No, darker."

"Like an oxblood?"

"All right."

"What was this other girl's name?"

"Don't remember," Fanning said. But, no, he did suddenly. Sandy Costello. A townie. Raucous, always laughing, huge squared-off teeth. He remembered the three of them—

Sandy, Sully, and himself—outside on the concrete steps leading to the sand, later that summer, August it must have been,
Sully mouthing in a stage whisper, *Glorious tits,* and Sandy
Costello in a red two-piece, arching her back, hefting them in
her hands for Fanning's benefit, repeating, *Glorious tits,*
mocking, haughty.

"The girls would've cooked you two dinner," Julia said.
"You'd have acted like a couple of princes. Maybe a walk up
the beach afterward. There a breakwater?"

"If you went far enough."

"Beacon at the end of it?"

Fanning said there was.

"Now, the bedrooms. Your friend Sully could've taken the
front room, which faced the water, but I'll assume that was
where the great-aunt slept. He stayed in one of the back bedrooms, and it didn't make much sense to switch now, so you
and Carly got the premier spot."

A quick exhalation, a clearing breath audible against the
mouthpiece.

She went on, "This was June, nights could be kind of
nippy still, so some blankets. Let's say a fraying quilt. They
had one stingy little bathroom, and it was downstairs, right?
So Carly would've changed into a flannel gown, at least to
walk around in. Now let me ask you, what about a joint?"

"No."

"No you're not telling, or no you didn't have any?"

"Carly didn't care for it."

"Why do you think?"

"She just didn't want to have it around. She was afraid one
of us would get caught and ruin our lives."

"And you?"

"I used to like it."

"I'll bet. But that night you were both straight. Maybe
you'd had a couple of Budweisers. And there was someone to
buy for you?"

"Sully's aunt kept the icebox stocked."

"Bless her heart."

How progressive that had seemed. But more likely, the two old women couldn't be bothered about any drinking age. They treated Sully like a younger brother, doted, yet deferred to him as the last of the Sullivan males. It occurred to Fanning that Sully would've simply explained the situation to his aunt, and she'd have said, *Yes, I see, that sounds like fun*, and the two women would have remained in Massachusetts.

Julia said, "I imagine sounds carried up there, maybe the walls were only partitions, open at the top. You lay talking and Carly tried to keep her voice down, but that only made it easier to hear Sully and his friend, which you wouldn't have minded, you'd have just as soon clamped your ear to the door, but Carly, no. She was perfectly happy to be there, more than happy, but she was shy about her body, or let's say *private*, and this must have bugged her, because it was a good body, after all, limber, loaded with energy, never given her a lick of trouble before now, and as you said, she was so on top of things otherwise, and let's also say you were just what she wanted. She had the desire. It must have bugged the holy hell out of her that she hadn't been able to let herself go through with it . . . and not really understanding why she was saddled with this particular hangup, *that* must have bugged her worse. I imagine this was a topic of discussion for some weeks. Am I right?"

"Look, Julia," Fanning said, "I really think——"

"Your position would've been you were in love and it was only natural, and everything would be okey-dokey. She said she knew all that, she agreed a hundred percent, except you'd have to give her just a little more time. Certain of her girlfriends had slept with boys, and she'd have felt squeezed from that side, too, except, as you say, she had this way about her. No one thought ill of her, no one thought she led anything but a charmed life. Now you were torn, you didn't want it to seem like you were giving an ulti*ma*tum, you weren't the demanding type, though, true, you could go a bit sullen on her, and she'd have to say she was sorry and try to jolly you out of it. Meanwhile, you felt this chagrin, this scratch of doubt. Maybe it was something in you, a lack, maybe if you were more *forceful,* more compelling in a masculine sort of way. So when you were together that spring, when you'd kiss and whatever else you allowed yourselves, it was a huge relief, but there was this nagging subtext. At long last, though, the trip to Maine appeared on the horizon, and Carly told you yes, she'd go, she would, she'd find a way. And that drained off some of the tension, at least outwardly. So, all right, Sully and what's her name were in the other bed——"

"Sandy."

"Okay, Sully and Sandy were down the hall, and you could hear them laughing and so on. Carly had taken off the flannel gown and folded it on the chair. She'd put a dark-colored beach towel down over the bottom sheet, and now she was beside you, up on one elbow, rubbing your chest, and let's see, you had a stub of candle burning, wavering."

Fanning found himself standing, looking down at the wet street. "This is too gruesome," he said.

"I want to know what was she saying."

"No, I'm done," Fanning said.

"See, because it could have been, *Thanks for being so patient with me, Miles,* or some reference to earlier in the evening, *Wasn't it funny what Sully had said at the table about blah blah blah,* in order to normalize the situation, to keep her bearings. On the other hand, maybe she'd had enough of that, keeping her bearings, pleasing Simon, and so forth, and now she was trying to be sexy for you, a little wanton in the manner of this Sandy character, she was trying to get that bad-girl sound in her voice, even if it took a concerted effort, even if she thought, *This isn't me——*"

Fanning waited to see if there'd be more. His chest rose and fell.

She said, "But that was supposed to be the night?"

He said nothing.

"Tell me and I'll get off."

"I can't believe you're so *fixated*."

"But the trip to Maine was about sleeping in a bed together."

"Okay," Fanning said. "All right."

"Tell me about the next morning. Tell me about the light in the curtains, the sea air. Did she tiptoe downstairs to clean herself up?"

"What's *wrong* with you?"

"Let's not rake Julia over the coals, okay? I would just very much like to know if you were lovers. Is that beyond your capability? It's a simple question."

"You know we weren't," he said.

"Not in that sense."

"Not in that sense, no."

The Zippo again.

She said, "You still fresh as a daisy?"

Fanning cleared his throat. "What do you think?" he said.

It was after one before he managed to get her off the line. He went to the sink and broke an Ativan in two and felt it dissolve on the back of his tongue, a bit of ash. Minutes later, he took the rest. He was accustomed to being at SunBreak at all hours, but the studio space was densely soundproofed. In the Hospitality Suite, he heard the noise the building gave off, dark unidentifiable rattles and slippages.

5

FOR THE PAST three nights, Fanning had left the phone on voice mail but there were no messages, nor had *julamo@netrisys.net* visited his screen. Yet, the way you know things, he'd known all day a call would come tonight and he'd take it. And now she was asking was he a religious man.

Fanning said not particularly.

She asked if he meant in the sense of not believing at all.

"I can't say I'm a believer, no."

"But you worry about it."

He denied this.

"I don't buy that. A man of your sensibility."

"I don't dwell on it much anymore."

"You used to, though."

"Okay."

"So would it have been one big disillusionment or more like an erosion?"

"I don't remember," Fanning said.

A small note of exasperation from Julia. "What about your worker bees? Where would they stand?"

"Can't we leave them out of it?"

"Let's say I'm taking a survey."

Fanning sighed. "Gloria goes to mass," he said. "She's office manager. My engineer Aaron's Jewish, I'm not sure how practicing. Martina I don't know about . . . we're a pretty secular—"

"What about your buddy Sully?"

"Sully's Episcopalian," Fanning said. "Sings in the choir. And he's on the board, or council, whatever it's called. Involves fund-raising, fixing the roof leaks."

"But you don't get into it with him, questions of belief."

Fanning made a brief effort to remember if he and Sully had ever talked of such things. He said, "In Sully's case it has more to do with the music. Plus I think he genuinely goes for the ritual."

"But if you sat him down and said, *Do you believe God's got his eyeball on you, do you believe in the life everlasting, amen?* I realize you wouldn't, but hypothetically?"

"Hypothetically," Fanning said, "you wouldn't get a straight answer out of Sully."

Fanning had recently wrestled the sofa over by the windows, so he could sit with his feet on the sill.

"Skip Sully, then," she said. "What about your lovely wife?"

"I'd have to say Kyra's fond of the here and now," Fanning answered.

"You two have that in common."

"All right."

"Rational beings."

Fanning ignored this.

She said, "You run into couples where one's a believer and the other not, but I can't see it."

"They must connect in other ways."

"But it's so basic," Julia said. "Because only one of them's right. If there's the big God, then there's the big God, and if there isn't, where does that leave the believers? They're *dupes*.

No? Let's say you and your mate have agreed you're going to have different views, you're going to *connect in different ways*. All well and good. But back there you're thinking: Jesus Christ, I'm married to someone who's completely delusional."

Fanning stared from his perch. Outside, a mist fell, foreshortening his view of the city. "What brought this on?" he asked.

There followed that lag time he'd come to associate with lighting up or stubbing out. He pictured the narrow torso hinged at the waist, flopping back against some padded surface with barely a sound.

She said, "I wanted to tell you about Simon."

Forty-two years old, Fanning was, and hearing the man's name still ran a current up his hackles. There was no use in saying he'd rather not listen to this. The Fannings had been recent interlopers to Massachusetts. Fanning's father had emigrated from Ashtabula County, Ohio—after the war, he'd taken a position with one of the paper companies along the Nashua River. A diligent, equitable, sweet-tempered soul. The first time Fanning laid eyes on Simon Lamoreaux, he seemed, despite the French-Canadian surname, the embodiment of old Yankeedom: flinty, rail-thin, with great unruly brows. A man of grave assessments, just the man to make you feel like an arriviste. Carly's wavy chestnut hair, the light-olive skin and compact body, these were the mother's. Mitzi was small and brisk, easily a foot shorter than her husband, and she'd come from elsewhere, down the eastern seaboard, was it Maryland? She had a residue of accent, a gracious and animated way of greeting Fanning, he remembered. If there was anything of Simon in Carly it was the broad, almost-masculine forehead, the sharpness of the jawline. Naturally, he'd been struck by how different the parents seemed from one another, naturally he'd favored the mother over Simon. Yet he'd never stopped to think how unlikely a union it was, not until just now.

"He was a pietist, Simon," Julia said.

Fanning had but the dimmest notion of what that was.

"No one stood between him and his Savior, that was the gist of it. They weren't high on clergy. And they were pacifists, from way back."

"What about the war?" Fanning's father had remained in the States, assigned to the Third Service Command, a liaison to steel plants and copper mines taken over by the War Department.

"Noncombatant," she said. "He drew blood. During Vietnam he tried to get appointed to the draft board. More power to him, but can you imagine thinking they'd let that happen? He tried to take them to court, but I mean there was no way. Talk about delusional."

Had Fanning ever been told any of this? Not by Carly, not that he recalled.

Fanning himself had missed Vietnam by sheer accident of birth. It was a calamity that befell older sons. Ed'ard Stowe, for one, who often did jobs for Fanning's father, digging post holes, or sawing up sugar maples that had come down in a hurricane. Fanning must have been in the seventh or eighth grade, still at home, when Ed'ard was killed in a mortar assault. Fanning's mother wept at the sink, Fanning's mother who never wept. At dinner, she held her husband accountable, *Walter, this is the most sickeningly pointless thing, I could just*— Fanning's father numbly recited the rudiments of the Domino Theory, but his heart wasn't in it.

Julia said, "This was the Messiah Church. It was the main reason we were in Clarion, I suppose. I feel sure Carly took you by it."

Fanning did remember this: a white structure of board and batten, on a hump of grassy earth, not so different outside from the two plain-white church buildings planted in the center of his own town, the one Methodist, the other Congregationalist, except it was without steeple, without colored glass, and had its own cemetery in back, shadowed by blue spruce. A day in late fall: their breath showed but the ground was still bare, so it must have been the Friday or Saturday after Thanksgiving, when Fanning had driven down to surprise her. They'd known each other by name since junior year—Moorcroft and Griffin being, informally, sister and brother schools—but it was only this October he'd begun calling her, amazed to hear she wasn't seeing anyone else, a girl like her, and only a week or two since he'd realized how necessary these calls had become, how reluctantly he hung up. So it was his first time in Clarion. He didn't know what to make of her leading him through the churchyard, passing among the Messiah dead, *Ernst, Gustavus, Juditta,* unless it was to say, *This is where I come from, know this about me.* She took his arm, not flirtatious because Carly wasn't flirtatious, but matter-of-fact, maybe understanding that, casual as he tried to act, the stones spooked him, and maybe to reassure him that he wasn't off base to think the two of them were at the start of something.

"Actually, it was across the line in New Albany," Julia said. "Were you ever inside?"

Fanning said they'd only peered through a window.

"Well, it was quite plain. No *representations.* No Jesus with the rays streaming from the clouds, no crucifixes. There was a raised area with a low altar, and a speaking platform I guess you could call a pulpit, but no pews as such, just chairs and short benches that weren't nailed down. The main part of the meeting was personal testimony so everyone needed to face each other. We all had the Inner Light. During our time, there were maybe twenty-five families left on the books, some on their last legs, if you want the truth. Kind of a skeleton crew. Once in a while a new member joined—it was rare, though. We did have the occasional spectator, dropouts from your standard churches. They found our simplicity 'refreshing' or 'authentic.' It 'cleared their heads,' etc. But they'd be history after a few weeks. We got another sort, too—people who'd been through the meatgrinder, and some of these just needed a safe haven, but others were kind of glazed or wild-tongued or just *wrong*. But they didn't last long either. Anyway, not many months before Carly's disappearance, Mitzi had stopped going to meeting. A massive disappointment to Simon, but she was a grown woman and entitled to her own choices—needless to say, personal choice was a big deal at the Messiah Church. If she'd allowed the spirit to quit her, he couldn't browbeat it back into her. He could only set an example. She said don't be silly, it hadn't left her, she was only taking a breather from the Sunday service, making it sound as if she'd return at some unspecified time in the not-distant future. I think the whole operation was too bare bones for her. Simon was a good dozen years older, and when they were first married I think she viewed his religion as something of an adventure. Simon had a charisma, a raw power, you have to admit. I can see her getting caught up in it, believing she believed, I can see how she couldn't separate this from Simon. But the austerity, the week-in, week-out practice . . . I think she finally just told herself, no more. That's my personal theory. Of course, Carly and I weren't exempted, we were still front and center, and this had a consequence I don't think Mitzi foresaw—that we'd be allied with Simon from that day forward. We'd be Simon's girls. And Carly was good at it, being Simon's girl. She didn't idolize him, but she loved him, despite the restrictions, despite his peculiarities. She went along with the program, gave her testimony. It was like another school subject—and when was that any sweat for Carly? But what did it mean to her beyond loving her father, did she consider herself *Redeemed,* capital 'R'? Did she feel a presence in her hour of need? Excellent questions, Fanning."

*　　*　　*

She said, "Anyway, Simon. He struck most people the way he struck you. Mitzi tried to keep up their social life, but you can imagine what a trick that was. Here was this throwback, this dour, humorless . . . the thing is, he wasn't entirely humorless, I have to say, he did laugh, things seemed funny to him now and then, not jokes, or TV—he barely watched anything except Huntley-Brinkley. But they had a catch phrase at the Messiah Church: *Every day a revelation*. Simon subscribed to it whole hog, and the form a day's revelation took might squeeze a laugh out of him. We had a steel drum we burned trash in, and once I watched him head out there to see if the fire was still lit—picture those long scissory strides across the crabgrass. Then he stepped on a garden rake and it sprang up like a cartoon rake and bashed him in the snout. This he found utterly hilarious, where another man would've flung the thing against the side of the barn. There he stood laughing, studying the smear of blood on his fingers, reenacting the event in slow-motion for my benefit. He'd been raking plums the night before when Mitzi had called him in to the telephone—he'd dropped the rake and not thought of it again. So the day's revelation was about the swiftness and symmetry of God's justice, etc., and underneath that revelation was another urging humility, and underneath that, one more that said: *Wake thee up, Simon Lamoreaux* . . . it was always nesting boxes of revelation with Simon. But as I said, by and large people took him for a severe and unfrivolous man, an uncompromising man, and that's the irony, because it was totally at odds with how he saw himself. His whole *life* was compromise. Now, the Messiah Church recognized that a man had to make a living, that we'd come a long way from the days of the yeoman farmer, the honest smithy. Simon worked in the casualty insurance business. He was middle management, and he liked it, liked his yellow tablets, his dictaphone, liked conducting *business*. His own father had delivered milk, and he was something like forty-eight when

Simon was born, this ancient figure with a big burl of Adam's apple, up in the dark every morning, God-fearing and taciturn to a fault, a product of the Messiah Church himself, and his father before him. So here was Simon, been to college, had himself a very decent job, and part of him was pleased as hell to be mucking about in the modern world, part of him was delighted by how far he'd come from the rattling bottles and the coal oil . . . no, you weren't expected to renounce the world, but you weren't to get too enamored of it either. Then there was Mitzi."

Fanning heard himself say aloud what he'd been thinking minutes earlier, that it was hard to see how they'd ended up together, Simon and Mitzi.

"Yes, well," Julia said. "Picture two sturdy old families on adjoining streets in a town along the Chesapeake, the Roushes and the St. Pierres, son of one scheduled to marry daughter of the other, everyone tickled pink. Excellent blood lines. But the daughter begins to feel a little claustrophobic, a little of the never-been-anywhere, never-done-squat, so next thing, unbelievably, she's in Boston in nursing school. Peter Roush is crushed, but vows he'll wait out this spurt of independence. Naturally, he has people's sympathies. Good-looking boy, affable, all primed for law school. He calls, he ventures up on the train. She relents, they set a new date. Then it turns out no, she can't go through with this one, either. So, who can blame him, Peter finally moves on, and there's a bit of a breach between the families. Mitzi's awarded her nurse's cap and decides going back to Maryland's not a viable option. She takes a flat with a pair of other graduates for a year or so, then accepts a job working for the Red Cross in a city where she doesn't know a solitary soul, and eventually, blah blah blah, crosses paths with this rather serious, rather intense and inward man, and she sees the effect she has on him, how she burnishes him, how susceptible he is to her when she's just being herself, not playacting, not chirping away, and the Red

Cross has her thinking in terms of utility now. *How can I be useful?* It was clear that Simon needed her, that her challenge was to haul him back from the abyss. She was the leavening. Despite the fact he worked in an office downtown, despite his natural savvy, he was capable of appalling lapses in social comportment. So she covered for him, she took over that end of things. Imagine his relief, to be nearer the mainstream, nearer ordinary life. You have no idea. All the same, it was a surrender. God didn't mind him having fun, savoring his wife's flesh, or watching his older girl canter across the pasture, hair tossing with the horse's gait. No, it was that pleasure was nothing but hollow sensation unless he knew in his bones it was God having the pleasure *through* him. Sometimes he could manage that, much of the time, let's say, but sometimes, I'm sure, he just wanted to chuck it, and not have to be so goddamned *mindful.* Naturally, that was a sin. So all in all he was torn, Simon was."

She let up again and Fanning, briefly, felt his own jaw unclench.

She said, "Then there was the day the school called. Had Carly come home, perhaps gotten a ride, some mix-up in the arrangements? Believe it or not, this was the second call Mitzi'd gotten that day, because my school's nurse had sent me home after lunch with a sick headache. Mitzi was working part-time on blood drives, but she was off that Friday, or at least the afternoon, and so I was on the couch in the front room with the blinds pulled and the radio playing in the kitchen just loud enough to drive me crazy. I was surprised she'd come for me. Her attitude was always, *See if you can push yourself a little, Julia, see if you can't just rise above it,* not to make her sound heartless, but there was no conning Mitzi. I think she worried I was going to be one of those girls who went down with migraines all the time—she wanted to nip that in the bud. But

she'd given me two green capsules of something and I was
under a cotton sheet, trying not to let my brain meet the walls
of my skull, hoping not to need the plastic pail. Much later, the
telephone rang, out through the double doors in the front hall.
Well, confusion. But she didn't even call Simon right away. She
did come to me, though, saw I was awake, asked had Carly
talked to me that morning about after-school plans? I said no.
She said, *What about Miles?* I said, *Can't help.* But she was
already on yellow alert. She said, *I know you don't feel good but
think about it, Julia.* I said, *She wouldn't tell me anything like
that,* which was only a partial truth. Carly had never much confided in me, didn't trust me to keep my mouth shut . . . she
thought I'd use these confidences against her if I needed to, not
an entirely erroneous reading of my character, I have to say.
You'd be forgiven for thinking there was constant friction
between Carly and me, that I couldn't take her goodness, for
lack of a better word, and that she found me a royal pain in the
ass, never satisfied with anything. But it wasn't that neat and
tidy, I'm afraid. We were at the verge of some new appreciation
of each other, I think. In fact, she *had* started to tell me about
you. I was grateful to hear it, greedy for this new relation, and
there was no way I'd have betrayed her. Simon was home when
I woke again, and they must've discussed the situation because
now Simon was on the phone, then Mitzi, then Simon again.
Friday was our night to eat fried clams from the stand out on
Holcombe Road. Carly usually drove and lately I'd ridden shotgun. But that night Mitzi finally fixed a supper and she and
Simon ate in the kitchen. I drank a ginger ale and went
upstairs. It was a still night, cooler. The headache had vanished.
I lay atop my bedspread, still in a convalescent mood, when it
occurred to me I felt all right—more than all right. I still had
an acute sensitivity to sound and touch, but it didn't *hurt* now.
Eventually Simon came to interrogate me. He left the light off,
but I could see his long expanse of white shirt. What had
Simon's attitude been toward me before this day? Another good

question, because it speaks to what happened later. So let's say Simon loved me because I was his daughter, and God fills the righteous man's heart with love for his offspring, each in equal measure. But was Simon not fonder of the first-born, who, as you yourself explained the other night, had this undeniable glow, who was a testament to good nutrition, who did what was expected of her as if it had been her own idea, etc.? Or, to turn it around, was he not less taken with the younger girl, whom his wife sometimes referred to as *The Little Engine Who Won't*, who was known by teachers to be mouthy, possibly devious, and, frankly, even at age fourteen, less of a treat to look at, could he help it if he had a natural preference . . . but, I'm sorry, we need to turn it once more, because didn't the church instruct him to walk the stonier path? What test of character was it to let his love flow where it flowed of its own accord? If the younger girl's Inner Light came from a dimmer bulb, shouldn't he . . . all right, well, you get the pitch. So he stood over me, and he said, *Julia, we're concerned about your sister.* His voice was solemn, but businesslike, without tremor. He asked the same questions Mitzi had asked, and I replied, as I had to her, though not so gruffly, that I had no insight into Carly's intentions. He asked me to please think about that morning, had Carly been her usual self, and I said, *She was running late*— He asked what else. I said she seemed happy about having rehearsal instead of school. He asked if she'd talked about meeting you, and I said yes, she was supposed to see you there, but she hadn't told me anything concrete. He looked down, his hands laced together at his belt. He and Mitzi both tended to assume they weren't getting the straight goods from me, so I saw him trying to decide how hard to push, but I was in a strange way myself, post-headache, no motive but to float on the skin of the bed as light as a waterbug. I told him, *She gave me a look in the bathroom mirror.* He asked what kind of look. I described it, the flaring of the eyes, the lips clamped briefly between the teeth, a look I'd describe now as complicit and sexual, a look between sisters, accompanied as it was by a little adjusting tug on her bra, but all I said then was she seemed excited about being with you. *If you thought about it longer would anything else come to you?* he asked. *No,* I said. He thanked me and left, closing the door with just enough force to make the latch click. Later, I eased up the receiver of the hall phone upstairs and heard his voice and another man's, and not long afterward Simon left in the car, and didn't return until well past one o'clock. I was still awake. I heard the tires crunch on the gravel, heard his door, and foolishly thought I'd hear the second one—two near-simultaneous thwacks bounding off the barn wall, then footsteps, cries of relief downstairs. But there was none of that. It was almost daylight before Mitzi began to crack. She hadn't slept, as you might guess. I don't imagine Simon had, either, but he was telling her she had to try, she couldn't be sensible if she went without sleep. She kept saying, *But where is she, Simon? For God's sake.* The lighter it got—another hazy, sticky day—the more the host of reasonable explanations scuttled away. I'd slept a few hours myself and woke desperately hungry. I realized that both conditions I'd been in the day before—pain-constricted, then weightless, thrumming with reprieve—that both were unnatural, not to be trusted. I realized I hadn't addressed the issue myself, hadn't really thought, *Carly's not here*— I don't mean to make this sound like a giant thunderclap or anything, it was just that I understood what we were dealing with in a way I hadn't during the night. It was *real.* I felt no rush of sadness or panic, not then. It was more like a sick confusion, and instinctively I knew I had to fight it off, had to stay vigilant, keenly on guard. The sadness was much longer in coming—it was a virus in no great hurry to multiply because it was immune to treatment and had all the time in the world."

She said, "I'll say one thing for the Messiah Church, it wasn't lethally patriarchal. A faithful heart was a faithful heart, sister or brother. They turned their backs on the women-as-unclean strain of thinking, nor was there talk about the man's duty, the woman's duty. The distinction was between the drowsing and the watchful, the self-satisfied and those who, let's say, swam upstream. So Simon didn't have *that* baggage, at least. It wasn't a question of reclaiming his rightful spot as ruler of the roost, it was that an extraordinary task called for greater concentration. And that's a good word, because, as I was saying, regardless of what a spook he seemed to you, to most outsiders, he believed he was leading a life that had gotten soft, or *diffuse*—his relation to the Messiah lacked the single-mindedness he ascribed to the elders of his father's and grandfather's generations. Are you with me?"

Fanning murmured yes.

She said, "So he called us to prayer."

And why should Fanning quail at the sound of this—wasn't it where she'd been leading him for the past twenty minutes?

She said, "Not that he stopped grilling the police or the school people, because he didn't let up in the slightest, and later on hired an investigator who'd done work for his company, and this guy was a bull terrier, let me tell you, a man named Quinton—"

"Quinton," Fanning said. "I talked to him. He came and found me."

"Yes, I know," she said. "But, anyway, Simon took it upon himself to direct us in prayer. That was how it was done at the Messiah Church, you stepped forward, you were *imbued.* That first Sunday, the day of the concert—" She stopped abruptly and asked if he'd gone ahead and sung in it.

No, he hadn't, Fanning said. "My father brought me home for the weekend. I had a long session with his lawyer." And Monday his father had driven Fanning back to Hartford for his confab with the authorities, and later back to school—long hours in the car, his father no doubt offering a word of encouragement now and then, but all Fanning remembered now was the blur of budding leaves and the sight of his father driving off alone after their handshake, and the split-second, before his waking mind kicked in, when he thought, *Need to go call Carly—*

Julia was quiet a moment. Fanning pictured her cheeks caving in, the ash brightening.

She said, "We hung around the house that first Sunday, couldn't stray from the phone. Word must have circulated through the school community by then, but Simon and Mitzi weren't really *of* that, out in Clarion. They hadn't informed what friends they did have, and Mitzi had forbidden me to call anyone I knew. I never thought of her as an innocent, but she must have believed she could keep this trouble contained. She had a horror of approaching people and saying, *Can you tell us anything?* Naked supplication. At the start, I mean, those first days. It was strange, I have to tell you, for once I felt no driving urge to buck her. You'd expect me to want to blab it around, to take a certain cachet from my situation, but I simply waited as they waited. And how odd, I thought, it was Carly's basic trustworthiness that made the wait so grim."

She said, "The Messiahs believed prayer was a silent instrument. You were to play it constantly, as you were engaged with the world. Climb from the lake shivering, and you'd think, *Thank you for this dry towel, thank you for the sun on the dock.* Like that. Constant awareness. Prayer was strictly improv at the Messiah Church. Simon was contemptuous of the canned stuff. Anything memorized he considered 'going through the motions'—those sing-songy graces at the table, for instance. Vapid, worse than pointless. All that amounted to, in his view, was asking for things. What about praise? What about owning up to your shortcomings? What about sharing your day with its Maker? But there were times you

needed to offer your petition, and routine prayer built a relationship where a plea for clemency might be acceptable. So
Simon directed us to pray for Carly's safe return. We were in
the kitchen at the trestle table. The leaves of the Virginia
creeper had just opened, making the window light greenish,
wavery. Simon sat at the end, Mitzi and I across from each
other—I was holding Mitzi's right hand, Simon's left. He
spoke a few words, still firm of voice, and then we com-
menced our silent requests. I heard a bird up in the kitchen
chimney, sticks or soot falling on the flue. I didn't want to be
the first to break away, so I prayed and kept my head down. If
Simon was at war with himself, Mitzi was just beginning her
own fight. She was proud and skeptical by nature, but also, I
have to remind myself, not a gloomy or vindictive sort—she
was upbeat, blessed with energy. She liked her work, liked
mixing with people. Her marriage was no picnic, but she'd
chosen it, the way she'd chosen nurse's training. You could say
that was one thing she and Simon had in common, disdain for
the easy road. She believed in her own resolve, believed that,
despite her size, she didn't rattle easily. But it was Mitzi who
pulled her hand back first. She said, *Simon, I'm going upstairs.*
The skin around her eyes was papery, blue. I was left in the
kitchen with him. Forty-eight hours had gone by. Outwardly,
there was no change, no word, but the situation kept evolving
regardless, acquiring its own history. Simon covered my hand
with the one Mitzi had vacated. Had he been strict enough
with Carly, or too strict? He couldn't have said. The 1970s
made no sense to him. He understood he couldn't shield Carly
from the times she lived in, he understood it was no good just
amassing an arsenal of injunctions. How did that promote the
free love of God? But he couldn't turn his girls loose, either,
he couldn't abdicate. So he was still picking at Carly for symp-
toms of rebellion, of deceit. Not very fertile ground, I have to
say. But hadn't she been less forthcoming since you'd been on
the scene, somewhat impatient, secretive? By now, he'd been

told you were as much in the dark as we were. I don't think he bought it, not at first. The simple fact was, were it not for you she'd have been home, among us. Now, Mitzi liked you, I don't suppose you remember that, but she thought you were a decent sort, not brought up in a barn. She thought you had a nice way with Carly, and she was relieved Carly had finally acquired a boyfriend, that she was seemingly in love, because I think Mitzi worried Carly was turning out a little too diligent or one-sided or *something*, possibly because she was a product of this odd duck of a marriage. So when you appeared she read it as a good sign. Even if Carly was, arguably, a bit touchier, a bit more teenagerish, Mitzi was nonetheless your defender. I hope you appreciate that."

She said, "But back in the kitchen, Old Post Road, Clarion, Simon Lamoreaux and his daughter Julia Isabel. Simon said, *Your sister might change her mind but be afraid to call, she might be ashamed.* He asked me if I thought that might be true. I said I didn't know. He stared at me. He said, *She might think that no one else has ever felt these things.* I said yes, she was like that. He nodded. The skin of his hand was cool and shiny. By the following Sunday, we were in church again, Simon and I. Mitzi would no more go now than she had for the past several months. She said, *I'm sorry if they think we're a house divided,* and if Simon had previously tried to set her straight as to what the Messiah Church did or didn't think about the Lamorcaux family, now he only nodded and asked me to please get in the car. Beginning that Tuesday, I'd been expected to go to school as if nothing were amiss, except Mitzi drove me now, and otherwise kept me under quarantine. She made an effort to put food before us and we ate, and as soon as possible, I fled to my quarters. All week, we'd had that same gummy weather, curious for May, a sky the color of mothballs. The upstairs was stuffy as hell. At twilight, Mitzi switched on the attic fan, ordinarily reserved for high summer, but it had the virtue of drowning out all human sound. I knelt at my window as the night smells were sucked into the house. Carly's room was shut off. It'd been gone through, to the point of having the bottoms of drawers examined, the linings of her winter clothes. You hadn't proved to be much of a correspondent, so there was no great archive to pore over—a birthday card, half a dozen typed letters, some song lyrics and cartoons you'd annotated. None of it that juicy, I guess. Maybe you'd assumed other eyes might see them, or maybe you saved yourself for those phone calls. In any case, everything had been meticulously searched, and Mitzi had picked up and vacuumed and told me to keep out, but I didn't so much as turn the door knob, which should tell you I wasn't myself. That second Sunday, Simon and I left Mitzi and drove to New Albany together. By now, there'd been a piece in the daily paper, plus a follow-up, WHEREABOUTS OF CLARION GIRL . . . people called, they stopped by, Mitzi received them on the porch, not asking them in, all but the Shaskys. Jessica Shasky was the closest pal she had, another nurse, and she'd had her own sorrows. So, people were aware, but Simon got to his feet at meeting and spoke his news formally. Standing in his summer suit, exposing one detail after another, saying, *But she failed to appear,* and so on, his voice grinding along, painful and stately, referring to Carly now as Carolyn, and when he said, *our daughter,* I could hear he meant the daughter of every adult in the room, of which there were twenty-odd, and no one shirked from this weight. When he reached the end, he asked the congregation to offer its prayer on her behalf, and it did, running to some minutes. Imagine the sound of the folding chairs, the wincing, noses snuffling from spring colds, the clearing of phlegm, but there was another sound, as if you could hear everyone's circuits humming. Later, I became aware of the rain. A man I didn't know went around closing windows. When the meeting was done, we stood in the foyer waiting to see if it would let up, but it was a drenching, vertical rain now. Simon's bony arm lay on my bony shoulder. A few others waited with us, as afraid to dash into the storm as they were to leave Simon and me there alone. Any other week, somebody would have said, *God's will,* in reference to the downpour, joking but not. Finally, Simon reached into a tin stand and withdrew an umbrella. He aimed it under the dripping overhang, jerked it open, and out we went, the two of us."

Fanning had been listening as if in a trance. He saw them splash toward the car, the wet shoes, Simon's shoulders bunched as he held the umbrella low enough for Julia. Saw the rain battering the lilacs, splaying the clumps of blossom, the runoff cutting grooves in the slope of the gravel drive. It was as vivid as if he were there in the doorway with the others. Her memory was merciless.

She said, "As you'd expect, this church of Simon's took the Bible at its word whenever feasible. For instance, the Gospels they accepted pretty much verbatim: crucifixion, empty tomb, Jesus's appearance to the disciples. If you didn't believe that you'd boarded the wrong bus. Where the accounts didn't mesh—the Annunciation delivered to Mary in Luke, but to Joseph in Matthew, items like that—whatever it was, they discussed it vigorously, took joy in their disagreement. Then again, some passages they thought made more sense as stories illustrating a truth. They most certainly believed God created heaven and earth, but not that it happened any time recently, didn't believe, as a woman out here once swore to me, that God planted fossils in the ground to test the power of our faith. At meeting, people were always trying to lay bare what things meant, and the irreducible nut they were left with they called God's Mystery. It pleased them to exercise logic and faith both. As dead earnest as they were, they took a surprising degree of pleasure from daily life, you have to admit.

But here Simon was faced with a conundrum that brought only anguish: God knew where Carly was and wouldn't tell. Heretofore, Simon had thought of God's silence as magisterial, as a tool for quickening the organs of perception, for instilling patience. Now it felt malign. When we returned the following Sunday, the fair skies restored, the air so clean you could make out the fish scales on a weather vane at a hundred yards, when Simon reached the church door, and other members sought him out, asking, as you would, if there'd been developments, and how he was bearing up, etc., he returned a look that shrank them back. I couldn't fail to notice it. They turned to me then, they said, *And Julia* . . . as if they'd never taken proper account of me until now, and even if they only were by default, because Simon had given them the first glimpse of the tar collecting in the neighborhood of his heart, I didn't care, I saw my opportunity. I shielded my face from the sun, and said, *This is a difficult time*, and though it was far from untrue—after all, we were swimming in bafflement— the way I said it, aware of my audience, aware of my spot at Simon's side, made me feel like a fraud . . . or not a fraud so much as someone capable of more complex motives than I'd given myself credit for. When we went inside, Simon made no direct reference to God's silence. He was virtually silent himself. He kept looking about, stretching his neck as if the vertebrae had begun to fuse. God replenishes our strength when it runs out, someone said. This sentiment was seconded. I'd heard such talk all my life—Simon himself often said things of that nature, but I'd always let them blow by. Now I wondered was it literally true, or illustrating a truth: that an adult had no choice but to beat back grief and move on. Simon gave a curt nod, blinking, his brows ruffled into peaks. Or were these remarks just *hot air*? Was it just what people said when they couldn't say *nothing*? What an interesting idea, I thought, what interesting possibilities that raised. We drove home. Simon's long straight back was cantilevered over the wheel, his hands at nine and three. We rolled along, in and out of leaf shadow. Convertibles passed us, music whumping. Simon signaled and pulled over at an ice cream stand he'd never, so far as I knew, even noticed before. He killed the ignition. *Would you like a Coke?* he asked. I said I didn't want anything. He stared at me. He said, *I'm just parched.* I said, *Have a drink then.* He got out and bought two Cokes from the machine. He came to my side of the car and said, *Why don't you get out?* I said I was all right where I was. He lifted his chin and drank with his eyes shut. I don't think I'd ever seen him drink a Coke. Now his lips were tacky with sugar. He looked at me again, holding the two cans. He said, *Why don't you get out and have this other Coke, Julia?* He nodded toward a wood-slatted table anchored in an island of unmown grass. He secured one can against his suitcoat and opened the car door for me. I didn't budge. It was second nature to resist, to throw up my roadblocks. But then he offered his free hand, and suddenly I took it. We sat on the same side of the table, our backs to the road. I was in a cotton dress Mitzi had sewn, blue, with lemon slices, sleeveless. In the field beyond us, a man was pounding stakes, the sound of the blows reaching us a beat late. Simon said, *Thank you for sitting with me, Julia.* This solicitude was new. He said, *This is a long siege, isn't it?* I said yes, and I understood he meant not the past sixteen days, but the time ahead of us. *There's no predicting when you'll be tested,* he said. *But you will be, Julia. You can count on it.* I understood he was talking about himself. His voice was measured, conspiratorial. I said, *I know.* Well, I was fourteen. How could I have truly known? But I sensed that certain tests were in the offing, yes, I had an inkling. We watched the sledgehammer falling on the green stakes. Wouldn't Simon have loved to break down and sob on behalf of his beautiful daughter, like an ordinary man? Wouldn't he have loved to blame random catastrophe? But he couldn't, he couldn't. He was a man undergoing a test, and it was this:

How long can you stand God's silence? Slowly, I downed my Coke. When I finished he carried the two cans to a receptacle. He turned, his eyes sought mine again, he started to speak but held off. He didn't have to say it aloud, though. I knew. I'd been handed my own test: Could I not forsake him, come what may? This I couldn't answer, not yet. He ushered me back to the car and we drove home without speaking. That was the third Sunday, and now we were into June. School got out, and not long afterward Miles Fanning made his famous Visit of Condolence to the Lamoreaux household."

She stopped here, as if daring Fanning to add his two cents' worth.

She said, "I'd been scheduled to start Moorcroft that fall— they'd already sistered me in, despite my grades. But no mention was made of it all summer. Mitzi had evolved a double standard about me. She was a fanatic about keeping me on the property at first. If I was reading in my room, she wanted the door open, wanted to see me from the hallway. If I was out communing with the pigeons in the barn loft, she'd come on the pretext of bringing me iced tea. There wasn't a trip to the supermarket I didn't make with her. I gave out Tang and deviled ham on white at the blood drawings. Gradually, she began to let me off the grounds if she trusted the supervision. But no swimming, no driving with anyone's older brother or sister, no diverting from the agreed-upon plan. Ordinarily, I'd have chafed mightily at this, I'd have planted myself in front of her and had it out. Instead, I lay low and let myself be watched over. On the other hand, this was hardly the future she'd expected either, marooned with Julia Isabel who was not her sunbeam. It was irrational to blame me for being the one left, and irrationality itself offended her, but she was raw, short-fused. The sight of me *was* a letdown, she couldn't help it any more than I could.

And don't think she couldn't sense the new commerce between Simon and me. Anyway, late August, I made some reference to Moorcroft. Mitzi looked at me in panic. *But you don't still want to go there,* she said. This was one of the summer's most enlightening moments, because I saw she really hadn't given it a single cogent thought until now. I'd assumed I'd trot along in Carly's footsteps at Moorcroft, the way I had at the Turkey Hill Middle School. I'd pictured the head-shaking, the *Gee, she's not much like her sister, is she?* Vaguely, I'd turned my mind to plotting a response. But then I thought: No, no Moorcroft. I announced I wanted to go to the high school in Clarion. They let me. It was that simple. But there still remained the question of how we'd speak about Carly. Mitzi began to say, *When we know more, when we have the truth about your sister,* and so on. Never anything so brazen as, *When Carly comes home.* No, she couldn't manage that, but neither would she ever say, *your sister's death.* Because it was still theoretically possible, as you and I discussed the other night, that some virulent and unanticipated strain of wanderlust had seized Carly. Not likely, yet not beyond conceiving of in the year 1973, if you were a parent, say. So she tried to stake out this middle ground. By early fall, she could see that keeping Carly's room like a shrine was folly, too, and one day she opened it up, and though I wasn't hot to poach Carly's things, Mitzi encouraged me to borrow the navy sweater, the nail clippers, to use the room as I'd use the room of a sister away at college. Meanwhile, Simon—"

But here she suddenly asked Fanning what the time was.

Fanning said late.

"How late?"

"Twelve forty-two."

She said, "You've had enough for one night, haven't you?"

Fanning waited perhaps one click too long to reply.

She said, "You're such a pussy. *Miles.*"

"I'm listening," Fanning said. "You have my undivided

attention. I don't care what time it is. You want to talk all night, be my guest."

"No," she said, "I don't think so."

"You were saying, *Simon*—"

Fanning heard the Zippo.

He waited.

It took him some time to realize she'd deadened the line.

6

WITHOUT PREMEDITATION, Fanning left work and drove midafternoon to Weymouth Street. A Friday. Kyra's car was gone, as he'd expected. He parked under the mountain ash and climbed the twenty-six concrete steps and used his key, entering through the utility room. He punched in the alarm code. Mercifully, the light went to green. There lay her workout bag, three pair of gym shoes, a croptop hung to dry. He went up a flight. In the kitchen: a glass plate with English muffin crumbs, hardened marmalade. He watched the tap drip, turned suddenly and read the grease board: *Quiklube, disks, card to Annemarie.* He opened the fridge, stared in, touched nothing. He passed into the living room, which looked benign enough: corduroy-covered sectional, hassock, pages of stapled photocopies, a highlighter minus cap. What had he expected to find here, Pompeii? He climbed the staircase to the sleeping loft. The blinds were drawn, the bed disheveled. On the rug: a half-slip, a pair of black tights, a damp towel. He counted five of their white mugs. What a temptation to gather them up and carry them to the dishwasher. A light burned in the bathroom. He left it. He went to the glass door, parted the louvers with one finger and eyed the little redwood balcony, and thought he'd step out onto it, but what was the point? He returned to the main floor and ducked into the workroom to grab the insurance folder that was his nominal excuse for coming. There, aslant against a glass bowl, a square white envelope marked MILES in Kyra's block printing. Fanning picked it up, saw it was licked shut, put it back. He stood massaging his cheekbone, listening to the air. Now he lifted the letter again thinking there might be a mark in the dust to say how long it had awaited him, but he couldn't tell. He put it back again. In the kitchen, he took an orange from a paper sack on the butcher block, cut a nickel-sized hole from one end and sucked out the juice, then split the skin and ate the sections, watching the slow change of light outdoors. There was a whole raft of oranges in the bag, too many to keep track of. He tucked the peel inside a napkin and dropped it into his pocket.

Fridays, Kyra often went for a drink with other staffers, and so he didn't expect her for some time, but the truth was he didn't know her schedule for certain anymore. It was nearing seven weeks since he'd been in this house, not quite half the four months. Fanning supposed he could just slip off his jacket and wait for her and announce that his sojourn in the wilderness had come to an early end. They could go to Buscemi's for crablegs. Maybe that was all it needed, a declaration, nerve. *I can't stand this anymore, Kyra. I want you.*

Do you?

I absolutely do.

Make me believe it, Miles. Because this half-light we've been—

Fanning wiped his hands and looked about. No, he thought.

He turned his back on the kitchen and walked down the lower staircase, hand on the rail. He was tempted to descend the final flight and inquire after his tools, his broken cane-bottomed chairs, but he passed the door and activated the alarm. Outside, the hemlock gave a wet smell in the near-dark. In the street a car's lights stuttered along the iron fences, but it was no one.

Exactly the wrong time to be crossing town, a Friday yet, so he kept to his secret routes through the neighborhoods. He rolled along in second gear, swung into the wire-bound lot behind SunBreak, and shut off the ignition. He undid the shoulder harness and sat with his hands loose on the wheel. A moment later, he started the engine, backed out and drove to the bottom of First and down under the expressway among the antique dealers and parked again.

The steel tables outside Lombardi's had been stowed. The place had the look of an off-season refuge as Fanning crossed at the light, collar up against the lofting grit. He swept into the heat, bought a draft of Henry's, and moved to the rear, scanning faces through the tops of his lenses.

There was one he knew, and another. Fanning raised a hand.

"Hey," the first man said. A lithographer pal of Ryugi's named Nye, very black droopy eyes.

Fanning asked if Ryugi had been about.

"Gone," the other man said. "Left town."

"No."

"Fell in with a gal up in Port Angeles," Nye said, mock-solemn.

Fanning shook his head, dumbstruck. "When'd this all come about?"

Nye shrugged.

The other man, whose name Fanning couldn't recall, had once had them laughing here, hard coughing laughter, a story concerning his mother and her sybaritic boyfriend, but Fanning could remember no more of it than that. He was bigger than Nye or Fanning, bigger around and heavy-faced, wearing an aging sport coat too short in the sleeve.

"You expecting him back?" Fanning asked.

Nye said he imagined it might go either way.

Ryugi had been party to two marriages Fanning knew of, plus how many liaisons? No matter the discussion, it led obliquely to Camille or Natalie or Kyoko or the one on the houseboat or the one with the neck painted by Botticelli, and nothing but praise for each, succulent memory.

Nye said, "You've been scarce yourself."

True, Fanning hadn't been to Lombardi's in ages. He'd gotten sort of reclusive since relocating to the studio—actually, he thought, it dated back into those last months with Kyra, this reluctance to mingle. A tiredness had enveloped him, unrelated to sleep. Only his work seemed to bring him out of it these days, brightened his mind, gave him a shot of affability.

Nye and his friend said they were going up the street for mussels.

Fanning said another time.

Nye said then maybe one more here.

Fanning ordered another draft.

"How's the recording business?" Nye asked.

Fanning said not so terrible.

The bigger man said, "I could stand Chinese if you'd rather."

Fanning said thanks, but he had to run. He laid a bill among the bills on the tabletop. He turned back to Nye. "What's her name?" he asked.

"Lydia," Nye said. "Runs a bed-and-breakfast. That's the sum total of what I know."

Fanning nodded.

"Old Ryugi," the other man said.

On the way to his car, Fanning picked up a package of butterscotches and a *Weekly*. He drove back to SunBreak, climbed the two flights, and let himself in. Nothing was scheduled for tonight, but Aaron was in the control room, head down, phones on, bald dome casting a waxy sheen. Fanning let him work in peace. His own office was dark. He flipped the switch, inspected for sticky notes from Gloria. He'd been thinking he would at least clear the paper from his desk, but was in no mood now. He passed through the outer office and down the hall to his living quarters.

The smell of wilted cardboard, steam heat.

Fanning washed at the sink, took the *Weekly* to his sofa, and folded it open to the movies: a glum Scottish picture at the Harvard Exit, a tale of warring sisters at the Seven Gables, a miscellany of fare at the multiplex he and Kyra frequented. The allure of the dark room.

He tossed the paper aside.

Not quite half the four months and what had been gained? Was he "letting it work," or just camping out like a hobo, as Gloria had said? Waiting, passing time? His hunger for Kyra had come back after a few days, the physical hunger, but when he hadn't fed it, it had leached away again, leaving him as he was now.

His genial father, years ago: *You off your game, Miles?*

On a sudden urge, he dialed Sully's number. Nine-thirty on the East Coast. He got an adenoidal baby-sitter. Did he want to leave a message for Mr. Sullivan? "No," Fanning said, "that's all right. I'll try him another time."

He unwrapped one of the candies, slipped it onto his tongue. After a minute, he rang Ryugi's, not that Fanning disbelieved the account he'd been given. And there was the impish voice, but it was the old recording and yielded nothing of Ryugi's changed fortune. Fanning stood the cordless in its housing and lay his head back.

And *julamo*?

Unlike the other evening, tonight he had no conviction his own phone was about to ring. Nor did he expect word from her in the computer's in box were he to check, which he had no intention of doing, but, later, did anyway.

He sat for a time, hand on mouse.

Friday night in the big city.

He could have eaten with Nye and the other man, what harm would that have done?

He wandered over to the control room. No Aaron, but the lights were on, so maybe he'd only stepped out to clear his head. Like Gloria, Aaron had been with him from the out-set—SunBreak wouldn't have survived without Aaron's wizardry, his fine discriminations. Fanning reminded him of this constantly, but Aaron waved it off as flattery. *It's all collaboration, Miles, group process.* He was six years younger than Fanning, half a head shorter. Around the perimeter of the bald spot was a thicket of blackish ringlets that lifted and fell when he walked in a breeze of any strength. The summer before last, he'd dodged a scare with testicular cancer. Sometimes, now, Fanning found him up on the building's roof, leaning on the low wall facing the water, or bounding a tar-dulled tennis ball against the ventilator housing. One afternoon, Fanning slid over and stood beside him, stared off where Aaron was staring, asked if he knew the definition of "perfect pitch"? Aaron turned to him, squinting, holding his hair down. Fanning said, *It's when you throw an accordian into a Dumpster and it lands on a banjo.*" Aaron gazed back out across the rooftops. *That's a four,* he said. Fanning said it was a six at least. Aaron said the one about God's girlfriend wanting to sing with the band, that was a six. Fanning said, *This one's better.* Aaron shook his head. *Besides,* he said, *I took accordian for years back in Bronxville. You didn't know that, did you?* Fanning said he didn't remember hearing about any accordians in Aaron's job interview. *I don't remember you asking,* Aaron said. *But it would've been an interesting moral dilemma—I needed the work.* Fanning looked at a long banked stretch of off-ramp. The air up here smelled like the air inside a tire. After a while he said, *Things are okay though? You feel good? Your checkups?* Aaron told him he was fine.

Fanning nodded. They talked a minute about a work-in-progress, then Fanning said, *You're sure?* and Aaron said, *To the best of my knowledge, Miles.* Fanning nodded again, said okay, that was great, he'd leave him alone, catch up with him downstairs.

Tonight, Fanning collapsed into one of the control-room chairs and waited, but Aaron never showed. Finally, Fanning rewound the tape and let it play: two female voices, soprano and alto. The SunBreak catalog was 80 to 90 percent instrumental—its niche, if it had one, was a strain of jazz and piano blues and string music sometimes filed under "New Age," a term Fanning resolutely banned within his earshot. His fond and subversive and commercially suicidal hope was that SunBreak be impossible to pigeonhole. He and Aaron had once excitedly driven the van to Portland, and recorded Nella Randolph in a club the dimensions of a streetcar where she'd fetched up in her dotage. A humped figure at the piano bench, shawl-wrapped, gazing through immense square lenses, no more than wetting her mouth with tea between songs to avoid having to be helped back to the facilities. She'd last cut an LP in 1959. *Gravy Train*, for Fantasy. Back in Seattle, he and Aaron mixed the two nights down into fourteen tracks—Nella's voice had lost some oomph, some range, but her phrasing was still wicked, and her playing had acquired a steeliness, a willful withholding of notes that gave Fanning the chills. What a coup, locating her, but despite Aaron's work and, in Fanning's opinion, a classy packaging job, sales were blah. A shame, considering. And there was the traveling boys choir from Krakow they'd recorded in the chancel of St. James. Palestrina, etc. How many copies of that goddamned thing did he still have in boxes? Fanning didn't care. Well, Jesus, he *cared.* It was his business to care. But what he heard now wasn't singing, as such: it came as a coda after the last notes of a sixty-seven-minute piano composition, two voices entering the dead air without warning, moving laterally, a fourth apart, a syllable like the *oo* in *proof.* A modal, lost-in-history sound. Fanning ran it back, played it once more, head down, then again. Out through the glass, he saw the two microphones still positioned where they'd been that morning, and the disembodiment of the voices brought him, suddenly, to tears.

7

ROOM BY ROOM, Fanning moved through his childhood house, as if on a camera dolly. Inspecting, withholding judgment. Record jackets flanked the hallway, as they once had, face-out on thin shelves, held in by fish line. Harry James, Nat Cole, Cannonball Adderley, Count Basic. The smell of violets from the half-bath. A humidor. Odd lights left on. A sense of trespass dogged him tonight . . . though in other scenarios he'd be greeted by the current owners, handed the keys— inexplicably, as if negotiations had been conducted without him. Often he got no closer than the hayfield. He'd be walking up from the woods in the first light, the powdery tire tracks along the hedgerow dew-damp, the wooly sumac heads tremoring, the wild grape leaves like hammered pewter.

Fanning woke to the phone.

He worked the cordless down among the covers. Instantly, he realized that he was relieved to hear her voice. He couldn't imagine what advantage knowing this would give her, but it seemed not to trouble him so much anymore. "I thought you'd thrown in the towel," he said.

"Me? You must be kidding."

The long windows were still opaque, but he understood it to be near morning. He said, "It's early."

"Early, late."

Neither spoke.

Fanning thought of the neighbor's tractor crisscrossing the field, laying the cut hay into windrows. He thought of the red fox he'd seen one evening in the stubble, its muzzle upturned so it appeared to smile. He thought of the sea shells that worked their way out of the dirt and, eventually, into his hands, flat and chalky, mute. Kyra slept so heavily she claimed not to dream at all. "Everybody dreams," Fanning said, but didn't pursue it. If he happened to describe one of his, she listened indifferently, pulling on stockings, dressing. Fanning scarcely trusted the effluvia of the dream world more than Kyra did, except that a dream's mood often leaked into his day, staining the first hours with its peculiar dye.

"You were telling me your mother passed away last summer," Fanning offered.

"*Died.*"

"All right," he said, noncombatively. "But she couldn't have been that old. Mid-sixties?"

"Sixty-five on the button."

"Still in Clarion?"

"No, the Clarion place went years ago," Julia said flatly. "She was up in Cambridge. She had the top floor of a house. Not a bad setup, really. She could take the bus to work."

Fanning remembered the constricted, hardwood-shaded back streets of Cambridge, which he'd once known well enough to navigate. When he flew east now, it was to New York, or to visit Sully and Pascale at Lake George in the summer, to speak with their music-camp students. But renting a car, driving to his own town, where he knew no one now, he'd not succumbed to that.

"She stayed with the blood banks?"

"Yes."

"I've never given blood," Fanning said. "Never seemed to come up."

Having said this, he remembered his own father, and several others in the loose community along Gilchrist Road, going into town to donate for Lucas Tate's father, who suffered from a condition that suddenly required constant infusions, and soon afterward, Mrs. Tate was widowed, and she and Lucas and his two brothers moved to Haverhill and Fanning never saw them again. Lucas Tate with his strawberry birthmark. Fanning would've never thought of him again. "To be honest," he said, "the sight of blood makes me woozy. Even in plastic bags."

"You get over it."

Fanning didn't argue. Then, it only now sinking in, he said, "But didn't you tell me both your folks drew blood, Simon in the war—"

"One of life's little oddities," Julia answered, the *oddities* accented, the way, at the hotel that night, certain words betrayed her, *the bawx . . . maybe you'd have gotten to carry*— She could produce it at will, it was for his benefit. Beneath the covers, Fanning found himself infected by a smile.

"What's it, about five?" he said.

"Twenty-eight past."

Fanning asked if she'd been up all night, a dumb question, but not unkindly meant.

"I shouldn't've called."

Fanning said, "Five-thirty, you can almost get up and make a run at things. My mother'd have the Cryptoquote done by now. You at home?"

She said yes.

Fanning asked where that was.

She told him, not a name he recognized. He'd get the map book out later. "The Bay Area," she'd said before.

She said, "I have the top floor of a house myself."

"Not a bad setup."

"No. I'm gone half the time."

"For work?"

She said yes, for work.

Fanning didn't pry. He said, "I am sorry about Mitzi."

"There's no need."

"You were out there?"

"When she *passed away*?"

"You know what I meant," he said. "It's awkward with the distance. And if you're the only one——"

She said, "I'll tell you one thing, it was goddamn *fast*. You remember Jim Henson? Muppet guy? Like that. Raging strep infection. Complained of a scratchy throat on Wednesday— I'm told this after the fact—scratchy throat, then stone dead before midnight the following Tuesday. Might as well have been Ebola."

Fanning made a noise of commiseration.

She said, "Naturally, I didn't check my messages until first thing Monday. Naturally that was the weekend I was *chilling out*, willfully incommunicado."

"You can't guess these things."

"They had her pumped full of Cipro, Rocephin . . . nothing touched it, nothing got near it. I mean, believe me."

Fanning said he'd read of these superbugs.

"I don't think she knew," Julia said.

"No?"

"I don't think so."

"That she wasn't going to . . . fight it off."

"Right."

Fanning said he wasn't sure what you gained from knowing.

"That's one theory," Julia said.

"You'd *been* out there, though," he said.

"Not for a while. Not for quite some time, to tell you the truth."

Fanning tried to sit up but his shoulders were bare and then he was cold.

She said, "Though, honest to God, why things should be any different with her, anything less than totally fucking *up in the air*."

Yet her voice lacked momentum this morning, the marbles-down-a-chute sound of the other night. If he wanted more it would need extracting.

"Where was it you were chilling out?" he asked.

"There's a motel up the coast."

"Your safe house."

What passed for a laugh. "Okay, like that," Julia said.

"Under an assumed name."

"You think I'm that far gone?"

"Fifth Amendment," Fanning said. "You smoking?"

"This instant? What's your guess?"

"If you're not I can't picture it," he said. "What were you doing before you called me? Or do you lie there and keep trying?"

"No, I was up," she said. "Reading papers on the Net."

"Newspapers?"

"The *Irish Times*, if you want to know. Gerry Adams, all that."

"The lure of current events," Fanning said. "What about at the safe house?"

"No, not up there."

"What do you do?"

"Pretty much *nada*."

"How long since you'd been east then?"

"A while."

"But *when*?"

"1991."

Fanning took this in. Six years.

"Were you two completely . . . I mean had you given up talking?"

"No, we talked. After a fashion."

Abruptly, Fanning swung his feet to the floor and stood. He drew his half-buttoned shirt from the chair back and slipped it on, switching the phone from one shoulder to the other. Then pants, yesterday's socks. He went to the fridge and ran the last two inches of juice down his throat, gazing back across this apartment. The light was the consistency of vitreous humor.

"Would you rather not get into this?" he asked.

She said, "You want to hear about our last encounter? I'll tell you. I don't mind. It was the day before Thanksgiving. I had to switch planes in Cincinnati. We came down through the muck and it was snowing . . . before we could get out, they lost their ceiling. Imagine how congenial people were. Wasn't a blizzard, they announced, just ground squalls, the airport was staying open. Then they closed it. I called Mitzi. Not home. I'd told her I'd catch the shuttle, but she'd felt obliged to pick me up personally and so had driven out to Logan, then someone rear-ended her in the tunnel. That was the tenor of the visit. I didn't reach Cambridge until early afternoon, and we were due at a party in Waltham in half an hour. I was feeling exceedingly ratty. I told her I had to at least wash my hair. *Take all the time you need, Julia,* she said. But she seemed fidgety. I stood under the shower like a zombie and it occurred to me she hadn't seen my hair since I'd dyed it—"

"That . . . eggplant?"

"I don't know as I'd achieved this exact degree of purplitude yet, but right. So I came out in my finery, such as that was, an actual skirt, not hideously wrinkled, pumps, and I asked what she thought of the hair. Stupid, I'll grant you, I absolutely knew better, begging her to find fault. But she barely gave it a glance. She handed me my coat. I wanted to say, *Look, I'm making an effort here.* But I got the idea she didn't know these people who'd invited us terribly well, that it irked her to be seen as the one with no place else to go, the charity case, and then to pull in late, the car's trunk taped down with duct tape, and who could predict how I was going to comport myself, the unmarried daughter. She'd only accepted because I was coming, she'd have been happier letting the holiday tiptoe past without her. Really, she was the one making the effort. That's what I thought, watching her drive out Route 20, chapped knuckles on the wheel. She was working at it, keeping up the bond between us, but I wondered if she was just going through the motions. I remembered how Simon felt about gestures made with a less-than-full heart. The Cincinnati storm hadn't reached us yet, but the sky was streaky, with this little punk-point of a sun, bare hardwood branches, brakelights popping on nervously . . . I was just at the edge of hysteria myself. The Chases had a divorced son in attendance, a realtor out by your way, Fitchburg or someplace, so it became apparent this was another subtext, throwing the two of us together. Merritt Chase. A beefy guy, pewter-haired already, though he couldn't have been more than thirty-five. I said, *What do they call you?* He said, *Merritt.* I said, *Do you merit a chase?* which struck me as the height of wit, nothing he'd already heard ten thousand times. He said, *Oh, yes. I would think so.* It turned out he was named for a distant relation, the painter William Merritt Chase. We went outside onto this brick walkway and had a smoke. He said, *Actually, they call me Kit.* The grass tailed away to a marsh full of cattails, then pinewoods, already inky black. I said, *So what's with the divorce, Kit* . . . you know, because I really didn't care, here was some doofus I'd never see again, not my type, I hope I've made that clear. He said, *Inconstancy.* No, really he said that. *On whose part?* I asked. He said, *On the part of all concerned.* He knelt and touched his cigarette to a dimple of standing water and we went back inside, into this wall of odor and conviviality. There was Mitzi clutching a wineglass to her chest, trapped by Mrs. Chase's sister and Mrs. Chase's geriatric mother, both of them dwarfing her, chatting away. I saw what it was costing her. And this was the former Mitzi St. Pierre, whose social skills had been honed at an early age, who used to love to get out among people. I felt this wave of——"

Waiting, still listening, Fanning squatted and twisted the radiator valve, then gingerly wiggled the window up, propping it with a chopstick.

She said, "Well, never mind what I felt. He called the next afternoon. Merit-the-Chase. Would I consider an early dinner and a movie, or vicey-versey? I said, *Oh, man, you realize this is going nowhere.* He said, *You're not my type, either,* which I have to say caught me the slightest bit off guard, and was perhaps the one thing he could've said that would pique my interest. *The thing is, Kit,* I said, *the whole point of this expedition was to spend some quality time with Mitzi.* And he said that was admirable, far be it from him to interfere, but I'd be around through the weekend, would I not? Yes, I said, I wasn't flying until Monday. In the meantime, Mitzi figured out what was going on and mouthed, *Go ahead, go on,* making these sweep-sweep motions with her fingers, so all at once I stopped examining the facets of everything, and said, *I'm not that hungry, Merritt, but why don't you pick me up and we'll just whatever . . .* and so he did."

She said, "We never did see a movie. I said, *You know where you can take me? The planetarium.* He couldn't decide if I truly wanted to go or was in fact goofing on him. I managed to convince him that the thought of lying back and watching the firmament, however contrived, appealed to me just then, so he acquiesced, and there wasn't a single *Beam me up, Scotty,* out of him, nor any furtive quasi-accidental contact in the dark. When the show was done, he said he was starving and wanted to take me to a place in the North End for calamari. I said, *Jesus, I'm sorry, no squid.* He said, *It's an Italian place, you can*

have rrrrravioli . . . well, I can't do it, but he really did roll his
r's very proficiently. So off to the North End. He had his calamari and I picked at a platter of four-cheese rrrrravioli, one
being goat, I was reasonably sure—had a certain barnyardy
tang—and meanwhile we whistled through a quantity of
wine. I said, *So why aren't I your type, Kit?* He said forget it, he
hadn't meant anything by that. I said, *No, really.* He was trying to be a decent guy. I said, *What about the person, or persons,
you were inconstant with?* He said that didn't bear discussing. I
said, *Is that what you'll be saying about me, I don't bear discussing?* He said, no, he didn't expect to say that about me. I
said, *That's a load off. But getting back to this woman, I'm
assuming it was a woman—* And he said with a perfectly
straight, though by now somewhat shit-faced face, *Of course it
was a woman,* and you could see the next thought blip across
his eyes, that possibly I liked girls myself, which might explain
my demeanor, and he was afraid he was going to be the butt of
a another joke. I hadn't meant him to feel that way, exactly, I
was only, you know . . . so I said, *Tell me about her then, the
straw that broke the camel's back. Let's start with her name.* He
blinked like a fourteen-year-old. *Loretta,* he said. *And your
wife's?* I asked. Kit said, *Her name is Loretta, also.* So it was my
turn to feel toyed with, but, no, he was being entirely genuine.
Wife and girlfriend both named Loretta. How could a man be
so blessed? *What did Loretta have that Loretta didn't?* I asked.
There's the billion-dollar question, he said. I could've stopped
right at that point, I suppose."

Fanning said that seemed unlikely.

She said, "Yes, well. I asked, *Was it thrilling?* Not a word
he'd have plucked from the ether on his own, but it struck a
chord. Considering that the original *frisson* had gotten a bit
buried, a bit discredited. Kit said, *I was a wreck the first time,
but the next time, oh, Jesus—* and blanched, hearing himself
talk so nakedly. I said, *Objectively speaking, who had the better
chops?* Well, he had to draw the line at that. I said, *C'mon, Kit,*

it's just the two of us here, and he actually threw a look over his shoulder, a reflex. This was a neighborhood place, close quarters, clattery, overlit, but then he shrugged. There wasn't a living soul within miles of here who gave two shits about him one way or another. He said, *My wife Loretta was better-looking, to tell you the truth.* I said, *But that wasn't what I asked.* He said, *I know.* So, without further coercion, he described Loretta Number Two's chops for me, in some little detail, nor quite as chastely as I might've predicted, mentioning certain nuances of technique, and then went silent. I held out my wineglass for him to fill. He poured. *That wasn't so tough, was it?* I said. He took this to be a rhetorical question. He rested on his elbows, assessing me. Could I, in some perverse way, be hitting on him? You'll have to believe me when I tell you I wasn't in the hitting-on-people business at that juncture in my life, but despite that, and despite the fact that he was so big, *thick*, you know, big hands, I could almost feel myself thumping against his chest, being sucked into his gravity, and suddenly I pictured him at work, filling the front doorway of some house, then standing aside for his clients to pass, ushering them in cordially, one hand out . . . and at the same time, as I said, he was regarding me from across the tablecloth, wondering if he could conceivably get a charge off me. But I said, *The two Lorettas, did they know each other before?* He breathed out heavily and said they did. I said, *Well, that's a complication. And you said she had her own inconstancy, but that was later?* He nodded. *A payback*, I said. He said yes. I said, *And this was also someone you both knew, someone you'd considered a friend?* He stared at me as if even his thoughts weren't safe. *Just a guess,* I assured him. His eyes had a beleaguered quality. I was on the verge of saying, *Monogamy's not for everyone*, but I didn't, I just let that one rot on the vine. Kit pulled out his napkin and stood. He knew another place we could go for coffee, not far, walking distance. Outside, it had started to snow. The goddamn sidewalks were slick and about as wide as a gangplank. We kept bumping, and finally I put my arm around the sleeve of his coat, which I hoped he wouldn't read too much into, other than my need to stay upright, but I had a reprise of that sensation I'd had in the restaurant, being drawn up against his bulk, his solidness, and so we went along like that, not talking, then we had our coffee, and Kit wanted me to try the bread pudding this other place specialized in. I said, *Oh please, I'm carbo'd out, honestly*— but he took a clean spoon and nipped off a corner and held it for me, his other hand underneath where it was ready to drip. I was expected to lean in and let him feed me. I did. He said, *See, that's something, isn't it?* I said I couldn't think when I'd had bread pudding that tasty. He more or less accepted this at face value, which is good, because I had no desire to mock him now, not in my heart of hearts. Then he asked what about me, meaning had I racked up any messy divorces myself, or their equivalent? I said, *I've been out of circulation.* He frowned. How could I stonewall after what I'd run him through? I said sorry, nothing to tell, nothing in recent memory. He considered this. He said, *You know, Julia, if you'd only*— I said, *If I'd only what? Lighten up? Give it a rest?* Well, he was sorry he'd waded into these waters. I threw back my coffee and, in the interest of moving things along, I said, *You know what, Kit? Let's drive before the weather gets any shittier.* And so we did, we drove, and I could tell he was longing to speak a bit more about the Lorettas, but sadly we'd drifted beyond that port of call. He didn't know how to act with me now. There was nothing to do but drop me at Mitzi's. Before he could attempt any final speech, any fumbling at my person, I touched his shoulder, I said, *You take care of yourself, Kit, huh?* I got out and listened as he rolled away in the snow."

She said, "It was like the city had been soundproofed. There was a light on at the foot of Mitzi's stairwell, but up at the landing, nothing, dark as a knothole. It dawned on me I didn't have a key. A doorbell was mounted in the middle of her door, the old-fashioned kind you twist and it makes a godawful ratcheting. Overkill, I thought. I tapped with my knuckles, then had to resort to this bell, and still no response. I sank onto the top step and thought, *Well, isn't this ludicrous?* I felt leaden, like my head would snap my neck off, also, a little queasy, which I ascribed to fatigue. What was I going to do, curl up there for the night? I stood and brushed myself off. I started grinding the holy hell out of the ringer, smacking the door panel with my open hand. Was she even *in* there? I had these rather childish, *Twilight Zone*-ish thoughts. I walked outside and tried to see the upstairs windows, but didn't have an angle. The snow was coming straight down, wide wet flakes, and, of course, no hat for Miss Julia. I squeezed through a wire gate and stood in back looking up, but the windows were uniformly black. Anyway, what did I think, I was going to fling pebbles? I hope you can picture this. I have on a long dress, a jacket lined with like crepe paper, and little flat Rockports—"

Fanning distinctly remembered her toes flexing inside the suede shoes in the Queensbury's lobby. Briefly, then, he thought of the toes themselves, long, knobbed, nothing like Kyra's.

She said, "Four or five blocks over, there was an arterial where I found a pay phone, and believe it or not I had her number and a quarter, but she'd set the machine so the first ring activated the recording. I told myself, *Okay, enough.* I called a cab. I told this cabbie, *Find me a decent hotel.* Was this a Pakistani gentleman, a Rooski? No, this was an Eddie Guheen, whose name I remember because there was an Eddie Guheen in my class at Clarion. I squinted at his picture in the plastic holder. We came to a light and I said, *Turn around and look at me.* He did, somewhat warily, I should add. I couldn't tell if this was the Eddie I knew or not. *Shit,* I thought, *now you're hallucinating.* Again I got a distinctly not-right feeling—speedy, clammy. Well, miracle of miracles, this Eddie Guheen found me a room, and I was in it exactly long enough to flip my purse on the bed before I was heaving in the bathroom. I'll spare you the blow-by-blow."

"Thank you," Fanning said.

She said, "And then it was morning."

"Saturday."

"Yes. I stood at the window in my slip. The streets were wet and the sun was trying to come out. Whatever'd made me sick—the goat cheese being the likely candidate—it had departed. I felt human. I ran a tub. Later I got another cab and had myself delivered to Mitzi's. The door was open. She'd been at the kitchen table, writing in a spiral notebook. The look she gave me, it was like: *I don't presume to tell you how to live your life, Julia, but honestly, it makes me—* I said, *You locked me out.* You could see her weighing this. I said, *He dropped me off around twelve and you had the place shut up like Fort Knox.* I was trying not to go overboard, trying to show I would wrest a little humor from this, but she'd already persuaded herself I'd stayed out all night with a man I barely knew. She said, *But I gave you a key.* I said, *Not to my knowledge you didn't.* Suddenly it was imperative to establish the truth. I said, *No, here,* and I took her sleeve and led her toward the landing, hoping to God I'd left some evidence behind. There on the varnished boards alongside the top step, quite clearly, you could see my two palm prints in the dust. Still, she hesitated, as if I might've planted them on my way in just now. She said, *I really locked you out? How could I have done that? And I didn't wake up?* I said, *It's a mystery, that bell would raise the dead.* She said, *Oh yes, it's dreadful, isn't it.* We went back inside. She'd roasted a turkey breast so we'd have the appearance of leftovers. She asked if I wanted a sandwich. I said, *What were you writing?* She said, *That's nothing* and flipped it shut, and still didn't like the look of it lying there, and so she stuck it up among the cookbooks. She said, *Do you want a sandwich, Julia?* I didn't want to get into the throwing-up portion of the evening, but, amazingly, I had an appetite, so I let her fix me a sandwich. She said, *I'll reimburse you for the room.* I told her she didn't have to, money wasn't the issue. She said, *I'd be happy to,* and I said, *No, it's all right.* She dropped it. I said, *Aren't you having anything?* She said she'd already eaten, had been up since the crack of dawn. After a while, she said, *What should we do today?* I didn't know what I wanted to do. I had no idea whatsoever. Neither did she. She said, *Make sure you have a key if you go out tonight.* I said, *I'm not going out.* She said, *Well, if you do.* I said, *Trust me, I'm not going anywhere, okay?* She stared at me. I said, *I don't mean to be difficult.* She had her hands on the back of the chair as if it were a ship's railing. But suddenly she went, *I'd like to buy you something for work . . . an outfit.* Oh, Christ, I thought. She hated shopping as much as I did. Neither of us saw the sport in it, yet I knew perfectly well we'd go through with this. She said, *I think we should take the T, I don't want to have the car to wrestle with.* So then we were on the train, crossing the river, the two of us seated, and this gang of five black boys sidled over and stood in front of us, and why we were selected I can't tell you, but they were jostling each other, smiling sly smiles, sharing a secret. The four turned to the one who was the main man. He had a Nefertiti aspect to him, like Scottie Pippen, you know, and he opened his mouth and out came this *note,* and then they were all singing. It wasn't like rap, more doo-woppish . . . close harmony. Is that what you'd call that?"

"Sure," Fanning said. "Close harmony."

"They sang until the next stop, the doors swooshed open, and out they went. *They didn't seem to want money,* Mitzi said. *No,* I said. I'd been riding with my eyes closed, mesmerized, flooded with an extravagant . . . like *hope.* The cars jerked ahead. I saw the boys trot down the platform stairs like a pack of young coyotes. *Well,* I said. Mitzi's hands were in her lap, one swiveling inside the other like a ball and socket."

"You shopped?"

"Oh, we did," Julia said. "Please be assured. And the stores were insane. Christmas Countdown. Next thing, I was trying on suits, standing in front of Mitzi for inspection. Her fingers were inside the waistband, she was going, *What is this, a six? It's too loose,* suppressing the urge to say, *Don't you eat, Julia?* Where do people get the idea I don't eat? I mean, I *eat.* Mitzi was no butterball herself. Well, I tolerated the fingers, the pinching and tucking, the critique of my alleged figure. I avoided the temptation to lure the salesgirl into my camp, no rolling my eyes at her, none of that. I took what I considered to be a suitable amount of interest in the suits, because, to be honest, my wardrobe could've stood some upgrading. I didn't quibble, didn't turn up my nose, said nothing about the scummy, fraudulent feeling that visits me in changing rooms. When we skinnied it down to three, I was fully prepared to go with the one I thought she favored, a rayon and wool, one-button, like a teal or jade, easily the most expensive choice, even if I couldn't picture myself wearing it to work. I said, *You know you don't have to . . . isn't this kind of pricey*— But she said, *It's my pleasure, Julia.* So I put my head down, went back and changed, and that's when I saw the jacket was mis-stitched, had a bunched-up place behind the shoulder. How had we missed that? I asked the salesgirl for a different one in the same size, and naturally they had none. She said she could call another branch of the store. I said I was from out of town. She said they'd be more than happy to ship it. I said I guessed that would work. Mitzi's lips were fixed in a certain way. I said, *Or I could just keep this one.* Mitzi said, *Don't be silly, Julia. We'll have it sent.* She took the MasterCard from her wallet and gave it over, touching just the edges. Then we rode the escalator down, empty-handed. The whole outing seemed to reek of futility. The middle of the afternoon and already the day was losing light. We caught the train back across the Charles. No serenade this time."

*   *   *

She said, "That night after Mitzi had gone to bed, I remembered the notebook she'd been writing in. I debated going in search of it. It was entirely possible this had nothing to do with me, as she'd insinuated, or if it did, was a scab better left unpicked. And, of course, there was the issue of Mitzi's right to privacy. I kicked all this around a full ten seconds and then proceeded to the kitchen in my stocking feet. I told you I'd seen her wedge it between the cookbooks, on this long green shelf? I'm wondering if those cookbooks struck you at all. That they had to be *relics*, from when she had people to cook for? Or that the Lamoreaux household wouldn't have gone in for haute cuisine even when Simon was alive? But Simon did appreciate his evening meal, and not just presiding over it. This was part of the doctrine of Paying Attention. Nor did he see why you needed to eat the same staples week in, week out, another thing that distinguished him from the older generation of Messiah elders. Anyway, the cookbooks accumulated, Mitzi experimented, she paid attention in her own way, annotated the pages, *Simon likes* or *Drain BEFORE adding the cream!!* So I flipped on the ceiling light and went for the notebook. Not there. I checked to see if she'd stashed it elsewhere in the kitchen. No dice. Out in the other room were a pair of glass-fronted cabinets Simon had bought when the library in New Albany was remodeled. I made a cursory inspection of these, then her desk. The cubbyholes were wadded with warranties, tax records, pages of ancient mimeographing. I concluded that the notebook had accompanied her into the inner sanctum. Along the bottom of her door was a slit of light, but most certainly, I thought, she was asleep by now. I entertained the idea of slipping in on a reconnaissance mission. I could say I was only turning her lamp off."

"But you didn't," Fanning said.

"No."

"You sat by an open window and had a smoke."

"Lucky guess."

"And you slept?"

"That might be putting it a little strongly," she said. "But you want to know the joke? Monday afternoon I caught the shuttle back to Logan. My flight was overbooked. They could possibly squeeze me on United to O'Hare at six-thirty, and so on . . . I was thinking, *Okay, just one good deep breath here, Julia,* but I must have been giving off this serious squeaky-wheel vibe, because then it was, *Or, we could put you in First Class.* I said that would be perfectly adequate. Next they were offering a blanket, champagne. Well, I didn't think it would behoove me to take a pass on these comforts. We weren't twenty minutes out of Boston and I was curled up on the leather, out cold. Hours later, there was a hand on my arm, the woman in the next seat. *I'm sorry,* she said, *you were whim-pering*— I couldn't squint her into focus, I couldn't figure out where the fuck I was. *Whimpering?* I said. *I was whimpering?* She leaned and drew the blanket over my shoulder and went back to her reading. She had this wonderful patrician hair, bronzed, defiant of gravity. The plane was purring, the win-dows black. My eyes fell shut and I was gone again. I didn't wake until we were on the ground, trundling toward the gate. Believe me, I'd never done that in my life, slept through a landing. Anyway, I got my car out of hock. The sky was mist-ing, and a waterlogged, Novemberish smell wafted off the bay. Having slept, I knew I'd be up all night. I zipped through my meager clutch of messages, entirely work-related, urgent schedule changes and etc. I was running on fumes by now. I undressed, turned back the bedcovers, then couldn't stomach getting in, and found myself dragging the duvet out to the recliner, not something I succumb to often, I should tell you. In minutes I was down inside this decadent sleep again. I roused a couple of times, half-believing I was still on the plane, sensing that vibration under me. I thought of a line I'd read and copied out: . . . *the cream pies were so thick that sleepers had baked them in their dreams,* and it seemed gloriously profound as I hovered, not quite awake, and when I did come around, toward dawn, the chair *was* humming. We were in the midst of a temblor. The blinds rattled and twitched, a spoon jittered about in my coffee mug. Any other time I'd be bolting for the street, but this one I just observed. I seemed to know I wasn't going to wind up buried in rubble. When it stopped, a very odd state of mind overtook me. I was hyper-alert, as empty as if I'd been scoured out with a wire brush. The trip to Mitzi's seemed weeks in the past, and I saw it with fresh eyes. She hadn't once mentioned Simon, I realized, not the mildest passing reference. Nor my sister."

Fanning placed an open palm on the window glass, and aimed the tops of his lenses at the street. It was just light enough to see the slash between buildings. A gull sailed by on fixed wings, mouth ajar.

Julia said, "I saw how complete the change was from the mother I knew as a girl, or even the woman who seemed so duty-bound to keep up the semblance of family life while I was in high school. I rethought that scene at the department store. I'd convinced myself she was thinking: *If only this was Carolyn here in the mirrors,* because even if Carly wasn't much of a clothes horse, things fit her, they hung very nicely on her, you surely remember that. Even just a plain blouse and kilt. She had a waist, hips. Wouldn't Mitzi have craved to see the adult Carly, to have her right there trying on suits? What a joy. But that wasn't it, she was thinking: *Is there no statute of limitations? Do I have to keep on with this mothering for the rest of time?* Did these thoughts make her a monster, or were you entitled to whatever you felt, even if it was a hunger for detachment? She didn't know. I had to drive out to Merced that day, and in the car I thought, *All right, I can accommodate you, Mitzi, I can pull back—* I wasn't sure if it was true. I've never been real good at leaving things be."

"No," Fanning said.

Julia was still for a few moments.

"But you pulled back," Fanning said.

"It didn't seem so senseless at the time," she said, and went into another short silence.

"Her notebook ever show up?" Fanning asked.

"I'd managed to forget about it until I was cleaning out the apartment, then remembered how I'd been all in a lather, camped outside her bedroom door like that. *Oh, man.* Anyway, there it was, back among the cookbooks."

"What didn't she want you to see, if I can ask?"

"I don't know if she'd been to some therapist . . . I find that kind of hard to swallow, frankly. Maybe it was just something she'd picked up from her reading, but the notebook turned out to be a dream journal. It started a few months before my visit, ran for maybe a year."

"You read through it, I assume. You were in there?"

"Oh, we all made our appearances, Simon, Carly, and me, friends from Clarion, people I'd never heard of, maybe coworkers or figures from her childhood. But you know how it is to listen to other people's dreams . . . and Mitzi's accounts were so clinical. She'd go: *Section aboard the boat quite vivid, no trouble reconstructing on waking.* It was an experiment of some sort and she went after it zealously for a time, then stopped cold. You want to know what she had to say about me . . . it was like: *Julia and I seated at a long table in what seems to be the basement of a church or community center, not a place I recognize. We're stuffing envelopes with folded papers, perhaps mimeographed letters or flyers, sealing them with a wetted sponge. A large woman is passing around marzipan on a silver platter, urging us to keep our strength up. It's quite stuffy and Julia sticks out her lower lip in an exaggerated way and blows up at her bangs, then there's a commotion outside and we all dash up the stairs and a whole string of antique fire trucks goes by, but now it's a street in Baltimore, and I'm with my mother's sister, Helena.* I mean this isn't word for word, but that was the flavor. It always seemed on the verge of being illuminating, but never quite was. I guess her keeping it at all was the illuminating thing, plus hiding it from me."

She said, "You know, a minute ago I thought I wanted to tell you about sorting through her things, but what's to say? You hang on to some, the rest you have hauled."

"What did you keep?" Fanning asked.

"What did I keep?"

"It's none of my business."

She said, "No, it's okay. Small items mainly. The furniture I couldn't deal with. I thought I'd have it stored, but I pictured getting the bill ad infinitum, and I just thought what's the point? I discovered a room in one of the gables, where she'd stacked several packing boxes. I slit into the top one and it was lace bedspreads and mothballs, and below were photographs in frames, the glass crisscrossed with masking tape. Under them was a brown accordian folder, also containing pictures: Simon in his orderly's jacket, a packet of ripply-edged snapshots from a day the three of them had spent on Cape Ann before I was born (sandcastle genus), Carly seated atop Bailey, that reprobate of a horse she rode one summer, and lots of others taken in the grassy patch behind the church. The Messiah people were peculiar about having their pictures taken, too, devoid of vanity and self-promotion, supposedly. At any given moment you manifested your Inner Light, so they rather enjoyed the camera, or maybe *enjoyed*'s putting the wrong spin on it—let's say the camera was duly welcome at church functions, box cameras, those old Brownies, nothing showy, nothing with a screw-on lens. So here were the white shirt-fronts and the stalwart chins, everyone *man*ifesting like crazy, and, like a motif, you could see a section of the railing around the graveyard, the wrought-iron spear-points. I put the pictures away and hoisted this box to the floor and sliced into the one below. All belongings of Simon's. His shaving kit, his deerskin driving gloves, the penny bank from his office, a cherrywood box with a silver dollar and six or eight brass collar studs, which must've been his father's because *he* wouldn't have needed collar studs, another of those brown folders, this one bulging with typing paper, including his correspondence with the Selective Service, and so on. Why these things, and not, for instance, his hacksaw or his ice skates or things from the *barn?* I had zero desire to imagine Mitzi assembling such an archive, but it was unavoidable. This was a Mayflower carton, so it dated from when she'd sold the Clarion house. He'd been dead four-plus years, and by then her sentiments must've undergone an adjustment, the fury cooled. Or maybe not. I remember my own reaction to the objects that had seen fit to outlast him. It was the week after his service, and I was staring at his suits on the wooden bar in his closet, thinking: *Here they all are, Simon's suits, but there's no one to wear them.* It seemed like a brain teaser I should be able to get."

"Is it light yet?" Fanning asked.

"Here? Let me see."

Fanning waited. It seemed to take longer than he'd have guessed.

"There's a kind of a sheen," she said finally.

"What are you looking at?"

"It's hilly, the street drops away," she said. "It's roofs, aerials, dishes. TV tower on the next ridge, five red lights. On-off, off-on."

"Fog?"

"Nope, not today. Usually though, we get buried. We go around like sleepwalkers."

"Or not-sleepwalkers, in your case."

"Or not-sleepwalkers," she said.

"You're looking out the front?" he asked.

"Yes."

"Bedroom?"

"Actually, I'm at my work table."

Fanning nodded to himself.

"You went to college," he said.

"I did."

"Do you mind saying where?"

"Ann Arbor."

"You were in Ann *Arbor*? When?"

"Left in '83."

Fanning did the math. "We overlapped by a year," he said. "You knew I was there?"

"I don't know, maybe."

"But it must've come up," he said. "It was an *issue*, because your sister——" Carly had been accepted at Wesleyan, been offered scholarship money by B.U. and one other place that escaped him now. But she'd refused to apply anywhere beyond a half-day's drive from Clarion.

"Maybe it did, then," Julia said. "I don't remember."

Fanning filed this away. When had she forgotten *any-thing*?

"What department?" he asked her.

"J. School."

He asked so was that what she did, wrote for a newspaper, magazine work?

She said no.

Fanning let out a long, unfresh breath. He asked, "What is it you do do?"

She went, *"Do do?"*

Fanning found himself grinning like a simpleton. "There's one of the joys of being up at this hour," he said.

"They're in great supply."

After a moment, she said, "I was doing technical writing for an outfit called Lomax Telemetry, three brothers . . . the middle one, Gregory, had a heart attack at forty-two, and after that they threw their energies into medical diagnostics. Their main market had been in transponders . . . well, I'm condensing this, you understand." And so she explained her metamorphosis into representing this company, now devoted to portable heart monitors, and other devices, not precisely a *sales rep*, Fanning gathered, more demonstrator and spokeswoman. Could he imagine Julia glad-handing and schmoozing? It was a stretch.

"You don't need to sound so stunned," she said.

"Just wasn't what I pictured."

"And what would that be?"

"Never mind."

Fanning waited to be goaded, taken issue with. "You in a stare?" he asked.

"I'll let you go."

Fanning said he didn't have to be anywhere, not for a while. He asked if she was on the road today.

She said today was an office day.

"Which is better?" he asked, knowing perfectly well she'd say *road days* without hesitation.

He said, "You were going to tell me about the other carton?"

"Was I?"

Wasn't this where they'd been aimed for the past ninety minutes? And wasn't it what had possessed her to click on *Who-Where?* or *Four 11* and type out his name that first night, "Miles Fanning" being just distinctive enough—imagine the futility of looking up a name as common as Sully's.

She said, "It was just stuff, Miles."

"But you went through it, the same as Simon's."

"I gave it the once-over."

"And brought it back with you?"

"What do *you* think?"

"I think it's on the shelf in your closet," he said. "I'd bet the farm on it."

And I know why, Fanning thought, suddenly getting a fix on Julia's chain of logic: that ditching the yellow box marked *Carolyn* would be too blatant, too ceremonious a snubbing of nostalgia. Better to let the box slumber in the next room, so she could test herself when the urge struck, as it did still, as it still, from night to night, unflaggingly did, so she could tell herself: *It's just stuff, Julia. It's just a beaded belt that reads MOHAWK TRAIL, it's just a bundle of odd-sized envelopes and tri-folded binder paper, just a plastic case of twenty-five-year-old Cover Girl blush, hard as pottery to your thumbnail. If she's gone it's because she's gone, it's because that happens to be the system we're operating under here, take it or leave it.* And Julia took it, Julia had no intention of leaving it, Julia Lamoreaux wouldn't grant the Powers That Be the satisfaction. Then he thought: *But took it under protest,* her objection renewed daily, hourly, the way certain monks are said to pray without ceasing. This last understanding hit him like a hand between the shoulder blades, forced a burst of air from his lungs.

"What?" she said. "What's funny?"

"Nothing."

She said, "You can't *do* that."

Fanning went, "Can't do *what?*"

"Okay," she said. "Okay, okay."

He said, "It was just . . . I was just, you know, laughing," to which he heard no immediate response, beyond the metronomic Zippo.

She said, "I need to get in the shower."

Fanning stepped back from the window, free hand bristling up the hairs at his neck. He said, "All right, I'll say good night, then."

She said, "I didn't mean this exact instant."

Fanning thought back to the night he'd laid eyes on her adult incarnation, recalled how supremely uninterested he'd been in considering the body beneath its lank coverings.

After a moment, he said, "How did you know I'd listen to you, that I wouldn't just blow you off?"

"I didn't," she said. "How could I know?"

8

A FRIDAY NIGHT, mid-December. They'd been recording in the back studio: synthesizer, electric bass, three percussionists. Young guys, the bassist still in school. The demo tape had come over the transom, unheralded. You never knew. About midnight, the keyboardist digressed into a tune Fanning recognized, but hadn't heard in years. Loosey-goosey, joyously syncopated. "That's Abdullah Ibrahim, isn't it?" he said. Yes, yes. Fanning said he'd seen him in the Village once when he was known as Dollar Brand, and later in Ann Arbor, two nights running. "You want to work that up?" he asked. No, they were just screwing around, hadn't practiced it. But Fanning was buzzed. "It's got this sweet stuttery thing," he said. Give it a few minutes? Humor me? So they did a few takes, and by the time Fanning found his way to the Hospitality Suite, it was nearing two o'clock, Ibrahim's beat still juking about in his limbs. He ran water into a saucepan, set it on the hot plate. He stripped off the rancid oxford-cloth shirt, tossed it, drew on a sweatshirt. Then, spur of the moment, he knelt at the computer table to leave a short message for Julia.

She'd beaten him to the punch:

Date: 13 December 1997 23:24 (PST)
From: julamo@netrisys.net
To: mfan@juno.com
Subject: The ongoing ongoing

MF:

Out riding my circuit these last days, intended to call then didn't. You miss me, Miles?

Had a very fair sleep last night, no idea what to ascribe it to, but not complaining. Feeling kind of all right. Before the mood evaporates I'm going to subject you to the rest of the Simon Lamoreaux story.

Buckle up.

In the fall, I started school. Sophomore year. Most mornings, Simon drove me. The high school was on the far side of Clarion, where the ridge drops off toward the river. Not precisely a dungeon, but old by then—had these nice deco-ish touches out front, so I imagine it dated from the twenties. It had been built onto willy-nilly, but was beat-up and overcrowded. They had to run two shifts, so Simon dropped me before seven A.M., then doubled back along the Post Road and into the city. After the time change in October, it felt like the middle of the night. The wind blew, oak leaves skittered through his headlights. "You'll work hard today," Simon said. He used the plainest language, and he meant the plain things the words suggested, but more, the way a Bible verse might unfurl endlessly. I said I'd work hard that day. At first it was all pro forma, same as I'd always gone, "Uh-huh," when one of them said, "Be careful, Julia," or "Please don't stay up so late, Julia," but then one morning I found I was answering him truthfully, nakedly. Simon was double-parked outside the Cleghorn Street door, his foot jammed on the brake, Cleghorn being insanely steep, other lights glaring in our back window. Not a moment that could drag on, in other words. He didn't expect a kiss, but gave his free hand for me to squeeze and I did and then got out.

What do I mean by "answering him truthfully"? I was beginning to get a new take on schoolwork, a new answer to Carly's record of accomplishment. Before, it was always: "Julia is an indifferent student, Julia has shoddy work habits." Can you picture me copying Brazil's exports out of the *World Book*? I admit to being resistant. I admit to having the point elude me. And across the hall at home was Carly, who could sit still with the best of them. I have this distinct memory of watching her type on the blue Smith-Corona, never a flurry of keys but a constant clack-clack like an all-day rain. Now and then she'd back up and calmly insert a sheet of correction tape and retype the mistaken letter. Later, she'd sit cross-legged on the bed, proofreading, her shiny knee protruding from the chenille robe. Can you see that knee, Miles? Catching the overhead light? If you'd asked her why she was doing a particular assignment, she'd have said, "Because it's due Friday." It was just an ordinary truth she seemed to tolerate, the way you tolerate a regimen of medication. Things were expected of you, you were asked to have five double-spaced pages worth of opinion about Mistah Kurtz he dead, you were asked to walk onto a riser in front of a couple thousand people and sing your head off. This was the Messiah Church again, this attitude. This was Being in the Moment. You know those pukey evangelistas on the tube: What does Ja-ee-zus ask of you? It was never ever like that at the Messiah Church. If you chose to acknowledge God's Light . . . I was trying to explain this before with regard to Simon—that, ideally, you just gave yourself over. They avoided the word "surrender," had the wrong coloration entirely. No, you were just there in the moment, bathed in grace, in the zone, you might say. Then again, maybe it was only Carly's nature, her disposition. Maybe it simply pleased her to stay on top of her homework, to bask in Simon and Mitzi's approval, maybe she couldn't stomach loose ends, or contention.

Had no gift in that one area.

Anyway, I gave Simon my promise to work hard and he let off the brake and rolled solemnly away, turning left onto Maynard Avenue at the base of the hill and proceeding to his office, and don't think I didn't have some little appreciation for the irony, even at that age (I was now fifteen)—his going off to labor in the insurance vineyards morning after morning. Not that he'd have viewed it as ironic. No, if things appeared incongruous it was strictly because you were blind to the larger picture, or that's the line he'd taken until now. I won't bore you with much more of this Messiah claptrap, but let me just say these people weren't keen on the God of Wrath, nor do I remember any bone-shriveling depictions of damnation. Not their M.O. Don't get me wrong, when a person fell away from God, it was the gravest of disappointments. And a deep shame was attached to fucking up, especially with regard to self-control. If your comportment was bad enough, a "shunning" took place, a holdover from the church's German roots, I imagine, though watered down by our time. By losing "self-control" I mean serious drinking, womanizing, wife-beating, infractions of that nature. There was a man named Harold Minor in the church, and he'd repeatedly gone after his wife, Pris. She was a straggly thing, wan and awkward, and, some Sundays, purple-eyed. Finally, the members wouldn't abide his pathetic excuse-mongering any longer. Pris and her two daughters went to live with Harold's brother in Sturgis Mills and the two families arrived at meeting as a unit then, minus Harold—a recipe for more virulence from Harold, you'd expect, yet no further harm came her way. As humiliated and out-of-control as Harold had to feel, the shame of betraying the group must've been worse.

But what about Simon? What had he done to earn his estrangement from the Messiah? He couldn't stop ruminating on it. Did some poisonous vein of hubris run through him, was it his work, was our mundane concept "insurance" too gross a tempting of fate? Or was it something else altogether? For once, Simon didn't know what to believe. He was bereft.

But more on that in a minute.

When he left my sight, I stood in the cold air, gathering my wits, then went in through the double doors and up the wide frayed staircase to my locker on the top floor. As I said, the school was old, old. They tried floating a bond that November. It failed, but squeaked by the following April, so our class was the last to graduate from that building. Something about it appealed to me, though. The rust-red ceramic tile lining the halls, the clatter, the look of hard use. Seemed to inspire me. I'd had girlfriends in the middle school, but it had been a hard summer on friendships, and LouAnn Colter, my chief partner in crime, had been shipped off to Emma Willard. The others, I don't know, we were dispersed in the high school, I saw less of them. It was as if the earlier friendships were insupportable here, but more likely it was because I had changed.

People seemed to know about me, about our "situation"—this was not, after all, a big-city high school, this was still only Clarion, CT. But ours wasn't the only sad story. Weren't there fathers with lung cancer, hadn't two cousins on the cross-country team been creamed by a locomotive down in New Britain? I refused to talk about it, to fuel the fire. After a while, people forgot what they were supposed to bear in mind about me. And, remember, Carly had never set foot in this school. For the first time in my life, I had no wake of hers to contend with.

The windows were pitch-black until the end of second period, and even when the light went ashy, then brightened to the semblance of day, I felt like a night worker, on special assignment. Those first weeks in September I'd turned in my usual half-assed efforts, collected my C-minuses, spaced out vocabulary quizzes, etc., but now it was November, and all I can tell you is I had a change of heart. That morning, my lab partner in biology was a goofy, pug-faced girl named Sylvia Wojcik. We were dissecting cows' eyeballs, and Sylvia was going, "Oh, this is fucking gross, there's no way I'm doing this," making a real show of it, and I just took the scalpel from her hand and made the cuts the way we'd been instructed, slid out the cornea, drew the diagram, and so on. I was sick of being a screw-off, I was sick of associating with screw-offs. I bought myself a black date book and started writing down deadlines, I used the library, I checked my answers. This was not rocket science. If anybody had asked me why I was doing an assignment, I'd have given the same answer as my sister: "It's due Friday." But this had nothing to do with pleasing people, this wasn't Being in the Freaking Moment. I was going to be a competent person. I wasn't going to let anyone sit in judgment of my work and mark it down for stupid and blatantly predictable reasons. I refused.

Our shift was done by twelve-twenty and I rode the bus home. Mitzi had gone back to half-days. She had a sandwich waiting for me. That was the fall I ate liverwurst on black rye. It's hard to picture Mitzi watching soaps, so unlike her, but she'd gotten herself hooked on *General Hospital* and we watched together, but for the most part I did my work, and if I had time I took a walk off the back of our property to an abandoned gravel pit where I poked around for salamanders, or just sat among the pine needles until the light began to fail. We had an early frost and the hardwood leaves had given up the ghost one rainy weekend. Whoosh, stripped bare, then winter hadn't come, just a gray still time, a hiatus, to use one of your words. I didn't mean to imply above that Mitzi and I had become buddy-buddy. Not the case. Her easy affection for Carly didn't suddenly transfer to me. Nonetheless, she was my mother, and as different as she was now—emotionally bludgeoned, her sociable side gone into eclipse—she seemed equally driven to keep what was left of the family intact. So my attitude shift vis-à-vis school didn't go unnoticed, though it wasn't discussed outright. Maybe she thought my character had taken another lurch, inspired by motives that were, if not ulterior, at least inscrutable, not what they appeared. She'd have been correct, of course. I routinely posted test scores, etc., on the fridge, and Mitzi made noises of assent, normal-sounding words, she'd say, "Your father will be extremely pleased to see this, honey." But there was nothing on earth Simon would be extremely pleased to see. Other than the obvious.

As I say, though, Mitzi endeavored to keep us going. We took our suppers together in the dining room. We had "conversations." We talked about the President, who had his own troubles—he was scrapping with the Senate over his secret tape recordings. He looked so frazzled and twitchy on the news. I thought he was a horrid man, but Simon was uncharacteristically slow to judge. Nixon was, after all, a Quaker.

And then we had our "outings." It was a good year for ice skating, a hard cold then nothing but dry spits of snow. I'd outgrown my skates. I debated how to handle this, then just dug into the window seat in the vestibule and found Carly's, and was prepared to tell Mitzi I was "borrowing" them, that I didn't think Carly would care, and I'd state this matter-of-factly, because that was the protocol we were following. But Mitzi took no notice. Now before you picture my inelegance on the ice, let me tell you I'd made the same decision as at school. No more klutzing around, no more ankle-flopping histrionics. The pond was in a gulley behind the Forchettes': long, skinny, floodlit at the end nearest the road, and often there were fires along the far shore where the outlet spilled into the woods. Simon wore what I suppose were ancient racing skates, black, long-bladed, sharpened with a file in the barn. Typically, he skated for exercise, up one side, down the other, bare-headed, neck wrapped in a thin worsted scarf, big herringbone strides . . . you could hear him coming, the ice parting under the blade, the honking lungfuls of God's air. This year, none of that. We skated as a threesome, Simon coasting along, Mitzi on one arm, me on the other. He noted the texture of the ice, asked were we warm enough. We stopped at the fires, and sometimes Simon exchanged a word or two with people, but often he said nothing. Sometimes, it was just kids parked beside these fires, smoking, clowning around, sometimes they knew me and I said hey, but there was no staying behind with them. Mitzi wore a squarish hat with earflaps, her eyes ran in the cold, the tears froze to her cheekbones. "I should've brought us chocolate," she said when we approached the car again, as if she'd not said the same thing the week before. I undid the skates and returned my feet to my moon boots and clomped up the embankment, telling myself that having a sister "disappear" was a thing that happens, was one thing from the vast array of possible things, that it didn't need to annihilate me as well. Again, I remember this specifically, the skates thumping into the Dodge's dark trunk as if into the hold of a ship, my sleeve reeking of wood smoke as I brought my hand to my cheek. Thinking: Didn't need to erase me.

Eventually, Cleghorn Street became too glazed to drive down. Simon let me out on the flat, and one morning after I gave my daily assurance that I'd work hard, and was ensconced in the auditorium for an assembly, I thought of him in his office. I saw him, not in the generalized way you picture people absorbed by their lives when you're away from them. This was a hell of a lot more vivid, this was CinemaScope. He was coming from the lavatory in his plain gray suit, his hands still damp from washing, his gait no different from usual except for the wordless way he bypassed his secretary and took to his desk. I was convinced if I hissed, "Dad, Dad," he'd look up, fierce-eyed, trying to pin-point the source of this bodiless voice. It occurred to me he might automatically assume it was his first-born's. My impulse was to spare him that . . . myself, too, I suppose. I scooched down in the seat and clamped my mouth shut. I saw him heft a bundle of manila folders into his lap, flap open the top one, then the one beneath, hunting some germ of data. It dawned on me: his injunction about hard work was only incidentally about me mastering school sub-jects. It was his own survival strategy, work as balm. He was handing it down to me as his heir. I watched the stony con-centration as long as I could stand it, then told myself, No more of this, enough, and scattered the image as if it had been floating on water. Moments later it was back: Simon at his desk, Simon disregarding his "enigma" for a few minutes, a few hours. I admit to panicking then. What if I couldn't shut this vision business off, was I flipping out? I had trouble breathing. I wiggled my way to the aisle, then up to the foyer, then the girls' bathroom opposite the choir room where no one would be. I stared myself down in the mirror, hands on sink. Julia Isabel Lamoreaux with her very attractive bangs, her blade of nose. But, no, I looked all right, I didn't look crazy exactly. I jimmied up the frosted glass window and the cold air rushed at my skin. In the top branches of a hickory tree were the remains of a plastic streamer. I watched my breath, awaiting discovery. There was always that fallback line, "I don't feel well—" Vague, possibly menstrual. I vowed not to use it, but no one came. At the sound of the second bell, I decided I was calm enough to resume my day.

One morning in the car, Simon cleared his throat and said, "I've had a report from Mr. Quinton. He feels that all avenues have been exhausted." I hadn't heard this name in weeks, not since late summer, I'd ceased to think the man had any relevance to us. But apparently Simon had believed—had persuaded himself to believe—that information was still forthcoming, not "resolution" necessarily, but something that would lead to something else, that the case remained "active." You remember how take-charge Quinton was, never say never. We were climbing Ridge Street in the dark, passing those mammoth old places with their turrets and their granite gate posts. Simon's driving gloves gave a dry squeak on the wheel. "Maybe Mr. Quinton's wrong," I could've said, or managed some mumble of consolation, but Mr. Quinton was not wrong, and Simon didn't want consoling. Short of vanquishing the 11th of May from the History of Time, he wanted to be told in plain words what had happened and why, why our family, why him. Short of that, he wanted relief from waiting, from thought—it was wearing a steep-walled channel in him. As I said the other night, for months I'd known that it'd fallen to me to be his comrade-in-arms. I'd known the collusion he'd expected from me, but not its degree, nor what it would require of me. Do you see how it was, Miles? I couldn't help being flattered, craving his attention, wanting to measure up to it. At the same time, I was horrified, stuck fast, wished like holy hell none of this had been thrust on me.

Fanning let his eyes break from the screen, and as he stared off he became aware of the low rumble behind him. He rose and went to unplug the hot plate, then burned his fingers on the handleless saucepan, dropped it, splashed scalding water up his pants leg. He ripped open his belt and kicked off the trousers and stuck his fingers under the faucet until they numbed a little. Jesus, what was he doing, grabbing it like that? He tucked the hand in a dish towel and stood in his boxers, his temples sweating in the cool air.

Then he was back at the screen, kneeling bare-legged, reading: *So okay, Christmas.*

Never a spectacle of wretched excess in the Lamoreaux household. Still, we'd celebrated. There was a wreath. Mitzi graced each window with a single white-bulbed candle— Simon claimed to like seeing them as he wheeled in off the Post Road each evening. His house, respectfully festive, ungaudy. Simon wasn't, by nature, a stingy man, a spoilsport. There were presents. For instance, that blue typewriter of Carly's had come from Simon, also her saddle. But this year: imagine how sick it made him when the thought "something for Carly" would ambush him, and be replaced a millisec- ond later by "No, she's—" And then an emptiness. This year we still honored the conventions, we ate Mitzi's oyster stew, the brown bread, the cranberry tarts, Simon and I put on our heavy coats and drove to church. Not a joyous occasion, it goes without saying, though Simon made a supreme effort not to look glum. He stood in the entryway breathing in the scent of wax and pine boughs, he greeted people, but as we settled into the benches and folding chairs, it so happened that a seat was left vacant to one side of him. We listened to the readings, we gave our sponta- neous testimonials on the Messiah's birth. By "we" I mean the others—Mrs. Mathay, the Gutschenritters, Mr. Parmelee, Mr. Eich, even Pris Minor and her older girl. I said nothing the entire time, and when everyone dove into prayer I failed to follow. This was new. Until now, I'd assumed my lack of success in the prayer department was traceable to my lack of success in other arenas. Why should this be a horse of a different color? I had no gift for clearing the noise from my head. I'd never felt "connected," but assumed the fault was mine. I'd never stopped trying, by which I mean talking in my mind to an Outside Party as if the Outside Party were listening in, on at least a token basis. Despite my reputation as "difficult" or "contrary," this Messiah Church business ran pretty deep in me—in a way, I'd always been Simon's daughter. But that night I just thought: Fuck it. This was not my ritual. I'd go it alone. Could I possibly have known what that meant, to "go it alone"?

Maybe I had the first glimmer.

I stole a look at Simon. His eyes were wandering, the fingertips of his left hand were grazing the curve of the empty seat beside him, back and forth, back and forth. All at once, he stood, wobbled perceptibly, then strode out between the bowed heads. I recognized his singleness of purpose from my own recent fleeing of the auditorium at school. I waited for a time. Maybe his trouble was only abdominal. Eventually, I got up and checked the anteroom. The bathroom door was open, the light off. I went outside and waited on the stoop, arms folded against my chest. After another ten minutes or so, chilled, I crossed the gravel to Simon's Dodge. It was possible he'd locked himself in, but the passenger door gave when I tried it. I slid onto the seat. Simon was at the wheel, his two fists pressed together, obscuring his mouth, but I got the distinct impression he had recently vomited. Neither of us spoke for a while. Finally, Simon looked my way, and said, "If there were a place to drive, Julia, I'd drive there."

The first anniversary of Carly's disappearance arrived without fanfare. We had a slow, foggy spring. May 11 was a Saturday, milder, but overcast. The ground had never quite dried from winter, and still gave off the stink of mulch. Simon was at work in the barn. You may remember that the barn roof had a cupola—eight-sided, copper lightning rod on top? Several of its window panes had been broken over time. I don't know by what, birds maybe, or unripe plums flung by kids. Anyway, Simon claimed he couldn't stand the sight of them in that condition. Not that they were such an eyesore I thought, not that there weren't other repairs awaiting his attention. The cupola was accessible from the inside—a ladder of wooden slats had once led up into it, but Simon had prudently dismantled this when Carly and I were little. Now he needed a monstrous extension ladder. He'd nailed a cleat to the loft floor to brace its feet. I watched him climb, the ladder's middle section swaying in and out, watched his shoulders disappear into the opening, his long gray pant legs, his boots.

Meantime, Mitzi was up on a ladder herself. She'd removed everything from the kitchen cupboards, canned goods and crockery, codfish poachers and so on. They lay across every flat surface, awaiting her scrutiny, and she was atop the stepladder, on tippy toes, going after the shelves with a sea sponge dripping ammonia water. Likewise, she'd stripped the windows of curtains. The light in the kitchen had an odd sourceless glow. I'd made a halfhearted offer of help, which she'd ignored, or failed to take seriously, then I'd migrated to the barn. Simon descended from the cupola, the shoulders of his workshirt dusted with pigeon droppings. He seemed unsurprised to see me. I followed him downstairs to the tool room. He retrieved a flat square package wrapped in brown paper and drew out a sheet of glass. Heavy gauge, slightly greenish. He flipped open a palm-sized steno pad and gave it to me. "Read me those numbers, Julia," he said. "The short side first." "Eighteen and three-eighths," I said. He measured with a tape then lay a long T-square across the glass and scored the surface with a glass-cutting tool. The sound, I couldn't help but think, was like the blade of his skate on the ice of Forchette's Pond. He scored it again, tapped along the line with the knobby end of the tool, snapped the piece off. "Now the other one," he said. I read it. "Why such screwy sizes?" I asked. Simon looked at me, blinking. "I don't know," he said. "Someone's idea of proportion." He measured and scored and broke off the glass. "Two of that dimension?" he asked. I nodded. He made another like the first. As he worked, I found myself studying the windows of the shop itself, the cobwebby glass, the sashes, bare water-stained wood. Outside, of course, they were layered with generations of black barn paint. That's when I realized how a window is glazed—that the putty's applied to the outside. How did Simon mean to install these panes he'd cut? He explained that one of the eight faces of the cupola was hinged. "You're going out on the roof?" I asked. He dropped a packet of glazing points in his breast pocket, wriggled a tack hammer through a belt loop. He beat a pair of work gloves together and handed them to me, along with a red tin of putty. "You can help," he said.

Simon sent me up the ladder first, following one rung back. Up in the cross members of the barn was an array of antique hardware, pulleys and giant rust-pitted hooks and brackets. It occurred to me I should be scared, but I felt no scrap of fear, not for myself. My head poked up into the milky glare of the cupola. Around the inside ran a wooden ledge, and it was evident from the debris that birds came in and out of the barn here, though it wasn't as foul (sorry) as you might expect. I brushed off a spot with the gloves and sat, making way for Simon. He sat on the ledge opposite. Our legs dangled into the hole. We looked out at the house, saw down inside the mouths of our two chimneys. A very peculiar vantage point, in my opinion. Simon pried open the putty and dug out a glob and began softening it between his fingers. "I can do that," I said. He let me. The hinged panel he'd referred to swung inward, and it was stuck, badly swollen. For all we knew, it'd never been opened, not in a hundred-twenty-some years. Simon extended his arm through an empty window socket and began tap-tapping with the hammer, really too lightweight a tool for the job. He reached up as high as he could, awkwardly braced, but without impatience, increasing the force of the blows until I was sure the remaining glass would come raining in on us. All at once, the stuck part gave. Simon let out what I took to be a sigh and made ready to climb out onto the roof.

As I said, it was a wet spring, and though it hadn't rained

in several days, the shakes had a filmy, saturated look. Simon's boots were rubber-bottomed, but the roof pitch seemed too steep for safe footing. Even Simon hesitated. I said, "What if you tied a rope around yourself?" Ordinarily, Simon's first reaction would've been: "Well, I don't think that will be necessary, Julia." Instead, he stared at me. "If you'd like," he said, almost bemused. He asked if it would bother me to wait there while he went for the rope. I said no. He told me not to move around. I said I wouldn't. He disappeared. I rolled the putty between my palms. It warmed and softened. I indulged in the sentimental thought that whoever had first glazed these windows was long dead, along with his children and grandchildren. I looked off into the treetops—they'd finally budded out, the maples. If I screwed my head around to the left I could see the gravel pit, and, beyond, a twist of smoke, someone burning apple branches. I felt the ladder twitch, saw the top of Simon's head as he secured the rope to one of those iron hooks. A rope thick enough to tow a car with. He asked me to hold it while he got situated. "This needs a bowline," he said, drawing out a loop big enough to fit over his shoulders, tying it off and snugging it without the slightest uncertainty. "As opposed to a slipknot." Where he'd come by such expertise I had no clue.

So Simon trussed himself up in this improvised safety harness and crawled outside, all arms and legs. He wiggled loose the still-attached sections of broken window and handed them through to me, cleaned the channels with a putty knife, then with the bristles of a dry paintbrush. I passed him the new panes, and he tacked them in and glazed them with the snakes of putty I rolled out, no pane not fitting, none getting away from him and sliding down the roof onto the retaining wall, nor did his balance falter. He worked with deep concentration. In this fashion the day was spent, and no reference to what day it was. Could I be the only one to notice? That evening Simon and Mitzi were scheduled to go to the Shaskys' for supper. I'd been invited, but assumed I could beg off. It was only then, by the vehemence of Mitzi's reaction, I saw how I'd misperceived things. She was absolutely not leaving me at home that night. "And I want you in decent clothes," she said. "It's just the Shaskys," I was about to protest, but I went upstairs and changed and managed some eyeliner. As we waited for Simon to bring the car around, Mitzi lifted my bangs and examined the skin on my forehead—it was a little oily and graced with if not outright blackheads, then a rash of fine flesh-toned bumps. "Oh, Julia," she said, both sympathetic and put out with me. "You've got to let your hair grow. You've got to pull it back with barrettes." She let the bangs fall. I said nothing. And then we piled into the Dodge, the doors slammed and off we drove, a party of three.

9

FANNING ROLLED BACK from the computer table, rotated his head. His neck made that granular sound it had taken to making. He closed his eyes, still seeing lines of type. After a while, he thought to check his hand. Not blistered, just angry-looking. He got up, kicked his shucked-off pants in the direction of the laundry, dug around for sweatpants and hauled them on. More of her message remained—the scroll bar wasn't halfway down the side of the screen, but Fanning milled about his apartment, the Ibrahim now replaced by the cadences of Julia's voice, *burning apple branches . . . in this fashion the day was spent . . . managed a little eyeliner*. He saw her head through the dust-caked glass of the cupola, as if he were hovering in the air.

He read:

There's a term hospitals use with newborns, "failure to thrive." Do you know it? That's how it was for Simon, born to a new condition, and withering, though it took time. I'll get back to that, I promise you the denouement, but first some other matters. For starters, what went on between

Simon and Mitzi behind closed doors? Didn't they let down when they were alone, were they no sanctuary for each other? You might well figure them for a couple who seldom touched, but Simon used to come up behind her when she was at the sink, or the south window, watching birds go after the suet in the feeder—he'd rest his hands on her shoulders, or cup her hipbones in a companionly way, and she'd grip his hands with her own, tipping her head back against his collarbone. It didn't matter if Carly and I were around. Even in public they sometimes stood like this, at the fireworks, say. But what about their sex life? Kind of appalling to speculate, but obviously they had one, despite Simon's having to square his lust with the church's precepts, and Mitzi, I suppose, keeping hers fresh by viewing Simon as a man like no other, an exotic. But was that aspect of their life finished now, was it another casualty? Did each want the other to make the first move, did each want "special consideration"? They certainly seemed more separate. For the first time, I realized that marriages are constructed things. I saw how ungainly and provisional this one was. Despite whatever was left sloshing in their reservoir of good will, the sight of one another constantly reminded them of Carly, whom they missed for all the normal reasons. Her absence made them no less gut-sick after a year's time, and it had spawned a rabble of further questions: Why were the daily comforts Mitzi provided no comfort to Simon—the suppers, the clean sheets? Was she paranoid, or "uncharitable" to think Simon had commandeered our loss, redefining it as a "spiritual crisis" ... did Simon have a brute selfishness she should've heeded long before children were involved? Or was the failing hers? Was she small-minded, or, at heart, too secular a woman for Simon? And what to make of his leaning on me, this "alliance" of ours? Was she wrong to feel excluded, to resent us? Maybe, after all, Simon was only trying to assure me I hadn't been lost in the shuffle. For his

part, as I've said, Simon believed unremittingly that he'd
been singled out, denied not only his oldest daughter's presence, but her story. He felt rudely turned-away-from. His
assignment was to wait. All would be unveiled in due time.
But what if it wasn't? Then that became the assignment, to
take it without complaint. Nothing escaped the purview of
The Messiah's Plan. If Simon continued to believe under
such conditions, he was the righteous man he'd always
sought to be. That or a sucker.

So there we were.

A second year came and went. Not a year grossly different from the one it replaced. Snow and melt, a few scant
weeks of puffy clouds and heat. I got my driver's license.
There'd been talk of Simon engineering a summer job for
me in the lower reaches of the Travelers, but nothing came
of this. Did Mitzi put the kibosh on it? No explanation was
given. I did begin working late afternoon/evening shifts at
that same dairy stand where we'd once routinely, inno-
cently, bought our fried clams and cole slaw. Ingersoll's, on
Holcombe Road. Simon chafed at this. It wasn't as dignified
or healthful as Carly's employment at the stables. But can
you picture me dealing with a bunch of sweaty horses? No,
thank you. Ingersoll himself was an old poop, something of a
grabass, but I liked twirling out the soft ice cream, refilling
the porcelain reservoirs of syrup and so on. I liked the
scraps of inane conversation that blew my way, liked being
away from the house during those fragile hours. And you'll
be pleased to know it was back of Ingersoll's, on break, I
took up the fine art of the cigarette.

One night a school friend of Carly's came in and sat at
the counter. Lizzie Gould, you might remember her. Ethereal
type, pale as pale. She was by herself. She'd have no memory
of me, I thought. I left her alone with her coffee and lemon
pie and a paperback book. But later she was still there, and I
approached her. She startled at her name. She lived in the

city and obviously believed she could pull over at a roadside place out in Clarion and be anonymous. I said who I was. She returned the book to her straw purse, and asked, circumspectly, if there had been any "news." I said there had not been. She volunteered that she'd shared a seat with Carly on the bus to the Civic Center that Friday morning. I admit it, for a split second I thought this was a preface to some little revelation, but of course it was only a stray fact recollected. She said she'd been among that earnest delegation of Carly's friends who visited our house the weekend before graduation. "Do people stop by?" she asked. I shrugged. "Not that much," I answered. She said maybe she would sometime, maybe even this evening as long as she was in the vicinity. If it wouldn't be an intrusion. I said as far as I knew Mitzi would be open to seeing her. We talked a minute more, she said she'd finished two years at Wesleyan, and was going to Amsterdam for the fall semester. She gave my hand a squeeze by way of summing up, withdrew a couple of ones, and exited. About ten, I got a ride home from a coworker. I scuffed up the drive in the dark. I'd worn a blister into my heel and my hair reeked from the fryer, as per usual, but still, I thought, it was a pretty night, moonless, cloudless, the plum leaves rustling. I had the feeling Mitzi'd been waiting for me on the front steps, but had gone inside at the whap of the car door. I found her in the kitchen running tap water over a tiny crop of raspberries in the bottom of the colander. "Anyone come by here tonight?" I asked. She said no, why? I said just curious. She said, "Well, no one did." I went upstairs and showered. I started to comb out my hair and wandered into the hallway and loitered in the draft under the attic fan, still combing, letting the water trickle down my shoulders. I didn't know what to do with myself. It was too early to sleep. I threw on jeans and a T-shirt and lay on the bedspread, barefoot, stir-crazy, but at the same time, struck by a ferocious lassitude, from the heat upstairs in part, but also from my encounter with Carly's friend. She'd told me she intended to study international law. I'd just gaped and gone, "Really, huh—" But she was so blithe about it, and the way she glided out of Ingersoll's, so erect and untouchable I found myself thinking, "Don't worry, Liz, you'll get your turn." It was mean to blame her for having a life, but I couldn't summon up much charity just then. I lay on the bed, half-paralyzed, and I realized, as Simon had suggested the day we drank Cokes together, this was going to be a long haul. I'd barely begun, barely gotten my first look at it.

I came to later and told myself to undress and get in bed, but now I was stone cold awake (you'll have no trouble believing). I went downstairs and poked around the kitchen to no particular end, went back upstairs and retrieved my smokes from their resting spot (in the breast pocket of Carly's blazer, inside the garment bag, inside her closet) and took them outdoors. Gingerly, still barefoot, I crossed the turnaround with its sharp stones, then the wet grass, and strayed into the deeper shadow where the yard light was blocked by the barn.

I sat on the retaining wall, lit a second smoke from the first, then a third, getting zingy from the nicotine—I was still a novice, after all. It was a nice night, but I felt edgy, and I thought, what's so wrong with appreciating a summer's night, why can't I just— Soon I became aware of a figure moving slowly up out of the field. It was Simon, in his white pj's, the top mostly unbuttoned, flapping. He was wafting toward me like some wraith out of Dickens. I had plenty of time to ditch the pack of Benson & Hedges. Doesn't it seem insane to have obsessed about such a thing, cigarettes, to have stashed them where Mitzi refused to go, but I'd wanted to postpone that fight as long as possible. Yet, as I watched him approach I did nothing, kept smoking, not defiantly, not fatalistically—it was more like, if Simon was out strolling through the long grass at two-thirty in the morning, then the ordinary rules of life must be suspended. So Simon stood before me. We were eye to eye. His hair was cropped into fine metal-gray bristles and his temples had beaded out in sweat. He said, "It's so stuffy inside," as if this alone might be adequate explanation. I said yes. "Can't sleep?" he asked. I said no, couldn't sleep. He said not one word about the smoking. After a moment, he put his hands on the rocks and hoisted himself up and sat to my left.

He said, "I don't see much of you these days, Julia." I said I guessed that was true, but I'd wanted to have a job, needed the work experience, etc. Simon looked at me in such a way I knew he was really asking if I'd been keeping my distance on purpose. The easiest solution was to deflect him with a quick falsehood. It was such a reflex, protecting myself—but not with Simon, not anymore. I shook my head yes, as if to say: Been staying away by design. Simon accepted this. In fact, he seemed gratified I'd chosen not to weasel out of it. He said he understood. A girl my age had to establish her independence, there were places outside the house I'd want to spend time, it was to be expected. He knew perfectly well he was asking a lot of me. All the same, he said, I should try to understand that he was only stating things as they were, that there was a teaching to be gleaned from our trouble even if it was thus far impenetrable, and that even given what he'd said above I should try my hardest not to abandon him altogether. He reached his hand across my back and stroked my arm with a soft downward motion, almost hypnotically, but not long, not long enough to make me squirm. He was a chaste man, Simon.

I lit up again.

"It's like she was swept overboard," I said. "I see her bobbing in the water as the rest of us sail away." Well, I was astonished to hear myself say this out loud—it was an image that'd come to me while I lay upstairs thinking about Lizzie Gould and Carly's other friends (including you, let me add). A waking dream, with shockingly profuse color. Carly's mouth was open wide as if she were panting, her lips an otherwordly shade of plum. The lights from the boat left trails across the seawater like gold leaf. I'd wondered at this picture, feared it was "melodramatic," and, boy, that was one thing I was determined not to be. Nor could I stomach the idea of my subconscious boiling and bubbling away when I wasn't looking. And yet this little scene seemed no less than accurate. We were all leaving her. Simon nodded sagely. He said, "Your sister always loved the water." I think he realized how starkly inappropriate this response was, but it was already out of him. He stared off at the sumacs. I ground my cigarette on the rock and deposited it into the now-empty pack. After a minute, I asked was he coming in to bed. He said no, he didn't believe so, not just yet. And then he turned a look on me I can only describe as one of gross neediness. I said I had to go. "Must you?" he asked. I said I was sorry, I'd made myself dizzy and was cold and couldn't stay. I slid down onto the grass and walked off, leaving him there.

Since before my birth, Simon had rented us a house on Cape Ann for ten days in August. It was brown-shingled, drafty, built atop an outcrop of bare granite. Carly and I shared a gabled room upstairs, two narrow metal cots. When we returned from swimming at the cove, we took turns standing inside a canvas-walled shower affixed to the side of the shed, Carly exhibiting her customary modesty, then clothespinned our suits to the line. In two or three days, her shoulders and arms would have the makings of a rich tan. Carly did love the water, seawater. She swam headlong into the frigid waves, while I horsed around in the shallows or hid among the rocks, sometimes spying on her. In the evening, Simon usually made a fire on the rocks and we all sat around it, Simon in a tall-backed wooden deck chair with wide flat arms. It was the most at ease I ever saw him.

Often, after Mitzi and I went inside, Carly stayed out with Simon. I could hear their voices from my cot, but not what they said. If I got up in the night I smelled the woodsmoke on Carly's clothes where they hung on a hook.

The summer she disappeared we hadn't gone, of course, nor the following summer. Simon had taken days off, but he'd had no vacation as such. What would he do with himself on Cape Ann for two weeks? No one even mentioned it. The days he didn't go to work were, I think, days he woke and simply couldn't manage it. You can imagine how it would appall a man like Simon to miss work on grounds as nebulous as "not feeling up to it." Didn't Mitzi ever say, "Simon, you've got to give yourself a break. It's not healthy like this. People need to get away, you'll never heal"? She must have, but not within my hearing. Apparently, too, concern about Simon surfaced at the company this third summer. Had the quality of his work eroded? Had he become touchy, demanding, morose? Did he make remarks as stunningly ill-considered as the one he'd made to me as we sat on the retaining wall? Again, I knew nothing directly—it was in the air, is all I can tell you. He was instructed to use his accrued time in a block, and should more prove necessary, there was talk of a leave of absence, which must've terrified him, the mere mention of it. You see, you see, he must have told himself, they all know, you're a man with a great black mark on you, you're not fooling a solitary soul. And so he made a heroic effort to be the Simon Lamoreaux of old, such as that was.

We never did go back to the rental house on Cape Ann. That summer Mitzi arranged for us to ride the train to see her family along the Chesapeake Bay. I think I led you to believe that she'd severed ties with the St. Pierres when she ran away to nursing school, but in fact she'd kept in touch with her brothers and their wives. She'd just never established the habit of going home, or having them come north. The Lamoreaux household was held to be a remote outpost. Mitzi encouraged this, I'm sure—she could avoid having to make excuses for Simon's, well, his whole demeanor. Maybe, too, she wished to shield him from their judgment.

Simon rode impassively, observing the mudflats, the nether parts of cities shimmering in their brown air. Now and then, Mitzi touched his arm and slipped him a morsel of information: it was Vincent's oldest boy who was the staffer for Senator Mathias, and so on, not so much at once that Simon would feel besieged. I read my book. I strolled about, eavesdropping, bumming the occasional smoke. Since we seldom ate out, there were few public displays of grace-saying, but in the dining car it was unavoidable, and I needn't tell you Simon made no effort to be unobtrusive. If the rails were noisy then you raised your voice. But Simon's graces had undergone a slow transformation. No longer were they reflexive offerings of thanks. A chill had come over his rhetoric, a reluctance. Even a blush of sarcasm, which, believe me, was not his native tongue. "And we model our patience on Your own," he said in closing. "Which is without measure." People stared. I stared back until they flinched.

Surely, Mitzi thought a change of venue would be therapeutic, but the trip was also a chance for her to watch him. How would he behave away from home? We stepped off the train into the kind of Maryland heat that gloms onto you like shrink-wrap. Simon insisted on toting our bags himself. He sat up front with my uncle Vincent, hands upon knees. There were stops at the fish market and the liquor store, where Vincent had his memory refreshed concerning the Lamoreauxs' status as nondrinkers. He was eight years Mitzi's senior, a banker and a gentleman, ruddy-cheeked from boating, still boyish through the gut. My aunt Phyllis was his second wife, mid-thirties, chesty, a harmless flirt.

Mitzi's other brothers and spouses and some of the grown children were coming to Vincent's that evening for a grill-out. We were given a chance to "freshen up." Simon toweled off his head and changed his shirt. It was either business suits or barn clothes for Simon. Even with Mitzi's counsel, he never managed to look casual, sporty. Later, the group began to assemble. The slightest wheeze of temperate air rose from the water. There Mitzi was with her eye on Simon, there I was with my eye on them both, and taking in, as well, the whole ambiance chez St. Pierre, which seemed gracious and effortless, but at the same time brutally foreign to me, an indictment of my narrow life.

Simon shook hands. He made the requisite small talk, holding a tumbler of V-8 equipped with a bushy stalk of celery. He was the tallest man there, and the oldest, fifty-seven that summer. No one mentioned my sister, directly or indirectly, no one insinuated that there was anything to be gotten over. This was simply a long-overdue social call. We produced the occasional squall of laughter. Dinner was served, the grilled fish and the crabs, the cold salads and the corn bread and the rest. Scattered across the stone terrace, balancing the black-glazed crockery plates on our knees, we ate, Mitzi beside her brother Andy and his wife, within monitoring distance of Simon, who was nodding at Leon St. Pierre, the youngest of Mitzi's brothers, to all appearances paying close attention. They were discussing the long bond. I felt a hand on my neck. The honey-haired Phyllis, bothered by my sitting apart. A shame there weren't kids my age, she said. Had I gotten enough to eat? More iced tea? There were pies coming, Boston cream, peach. I said I was fine. She diverted me into a short recital of my summer activities, and when I looked up, Simon was gone. There was his plate on the stone wall, attracting a yellow jacket. Mitzi looked up at virtually the same instant. She stood, scanned the lawn where it sloped toward the estuary, the fingers of one hand crooked at her breast. She took a few steps, but then Simon strode through the sliding screen door and it was plain he had merely been to the john. Was it possible Simon would pull this visit off? That there'd be no incident, that he'd take this opportunity to rejoin the human family?

Let me tell you this: There was no incident. Saturday, Simon endured a breezy boat ride. Sunday morning, he endured a trip into town to Christ Church. The St. Pierres were of Huguenot stock, and how they'd wound up Episcopalian I have no clue, but we accompanied a multigenerational assortment of St. Pierres to the ten o'clock service. The church was all stone blocks and shafts of watery light, the central pulpit resting atop a kneeling, sword-planted Sir Galahad with rose-marble bangs. Simon honored the rites of Episcopalians, all but communion and the recitation of creed, standing, raising his voice in song, enduring the sermon's bland irrelevancies, Mitzi continuing to take stock of him, as I continued, as clandestinely as possible, to study them both. In retrospect, there's the issue of how Mitzi could watch Simon so fixedly and yet do nothing to halt his slide. Given her training, her low threshold for deception. A big topic, I grant you. But understand how dicey it was reading Simon, how he could give the impression, as he did that week in Maryland, of bearing up. A different day you'd swear he was a walking case of clinical depression, in dire need of medicating. Simon being Simon, it was never simple. Mitzi knew damn good and well he'd accept no counsel, no drug. Imagine the dim view Simon had of "mental health professionals." And, in matters of "the spirit," hadn't she always deferred to him? In hindsight, I see how his struggle had come to intimidate, even revulse her. It made her own sadness cheap and profane. Was he unaware of this side effect? How can he not have known? What did he say to her? Whatever it was wasn't enough. In any case, the service finally ended. We filed outside into the wavery heat, already wilting, groping for dark glasses, all but Simon, who walked down the steps straight-backed and squinting, pausing in the middle of the street to glare at the church from the outside, the handsome masonry, the luxuriant ivy, the configuration of up-reaching spires, as if to say: "So is this what You like then, all this here, this pomp?" It's so tempting, remembering, to picture Simon punctuating the moment with raised fists. But no, the rage was all internal. We took our seats in my uncle Vincent's Lincoln, the air-conditioning was cranked up, we drove away to the pleasures of Sunday afternoon, and there was no incident.

Then came my much-anticipated senior year at C.H.S. I pawed through college catalogs in the guidance office, made my choice, applied nowhere else. It was at home I expected the battle. Why so far away, Julia? The Midwest? Don't you think, under the circumstances— But none came, not from my mother, not from Simon, for whom it would be further evidence of my desire to keep my distance. Arrangements were made. I couldn't believe this was all it would take to effect my release. I waited for the shoe to drop, for them to sit me down and explain why the Michigan plan wasn't feasible after all. Yet the school year slowly evaporated ... it was mud season, then high summer, and again I was working at Ingersoll's, and no such disclosure came. Simon mentioned driving me to Ann Arbor. I thanked him and said that really wasn't necessary. I was taking so little with me, I could fly. Did it matter where we said our good-byes? Simon said no, of course not. He said part of him still couldn't accept that it was time for me to leave home. He'd miss my companionship. He smiled then, impersonating an ordinary father. I quit work soon afterward. Those last few days of August I stayed home in the evening. Simon and I walked up the Post Road together, standing off in the crackly grass if a car came. There was nothing apoca-

lyptic in his talk—he went so far as to say he dearly regretted not having seen Carly off to college, sounding only, I
thought, wistful and bucked up. He'd been telling me about
the other boarders in the rooming house where he'd lived
when he was away at school, just a little freelance reminiscing, no moral to the story. On our last walk up the drive, he
said, "You've been an anchor for me, Julia." That was all, no
big theatrics. I found myself thinking of one of those coffee
cans filled with concrete tossed over the gunwale of a row-
boat—I thought of it settling to the lake bottom and the
boat tugging against it.

But you know where this leads, don't you, Miles? To the
white barn with the cupola? To the knot that was not a
bowline?

I was in class in Angell Hall when I was summoned to the
telephone. It wasn't Mitzi but her friend Jessica Shasky. Bless
her heart, Jessica just laid the facts on me minus any great
prologue, as if I'd been waiting for the call. She listed off what
I was to do, explained that there'd be a ticket for me at
Metro. I asked could I talk with Mitzi. She said it would be
best if I waited until I got home. She said she'd pick me up at
the airport herself. "How's she doing?" I asked. "How's she
handling—" "You want the truth?" Mrs. Shasky said. "She's
furious." "At my father," I said. She said, "At him, at his blessed
church, at herself." She started hacking and covered the
mouthpiece and when she came back she said, "Julia, listen to
me carefully, you'll survive this, do you understand?" I said,
thank you, yes, I knew I would. Outside, it was a mild October day, hazy. I walked to a coffee house, down one of those
side streets off State. There was a church across the way, all
roof slates and pigeons. Do you remember it? People say: "I
was numb." Well, I was not numb. I was very much not numb.
All the same, I wasn't flying off the handle, I was keeping it
together pretty admirably, I thought. I drank three or four
cups of coffee and watched the birds on the spine of the

church roof, and I thought, lucidly enough, This is who I am now. This person. It wasn't even noon yet. A boy had been eyeing me, a guy, twenty-one, twenty-two. Less shaggy than the prevailing style, not bad-looking, vaguely Eastern European. Would it be okay if he joined me? It's a free country, I said, words to that effect. He unburdened himself of a satchel and lowered himself to the other chair. "Karl," he said. I nodded. Karl laced his fingers together on the tabletop and they were attractive, tapered fingers, I have to say. "You were looking pensive," he said. There was the slightest "*f*" sound where the "*v*" belonged, and it undercut the whole pick-up line thing. "Do you have a car?" I asked him. He did. It turned out to be not much of a car, a wayward old Citroën, but it ran, after a fashion. I said, "I have to be at the airport in seven hours, can you help me with that?" He didn't hesitate. "And occupy me until then?" I asked. He said, "Apsolutely." I can't say I'm overly proud of my judgment, but as it happened, Karl was not an asshole. He walked me to his apartment, via the Law Quad, we got the Citroën and drove to the Arb and killed a couple of the hours hiking up and down the hills, Karl expounding on his schemes and aspirations, then went back to the apartment, smoked his last chip of hash, and I slept with him. What can I tell you? It was what I wanted. Was it my first time? No, I'd seen to that already, senior year, not very satisfactorily, but never mind. Anyway, Karl didn't seem to find my scrawniness too severe a drawback. We drifted. I woke later, sticky, my heart hammering. "Jesus," I said, "it's five-thirty, how can it be five-thirty already?" Karl stirred, placed a cool hand on my belly. He said, "Skip the airplane, no?" I said, "I can't skip the airplane, Karl, my father hanged himself." He looked me in the eye, ready for this to be some American expression you didn't take literally. I couldn't help him there. Karl who'd been, really, an attentive lover. "This was when?" he said. I said, "Yesterday." So now he'd been let in on the nature of our afternoon together. He began to distance himself, to find me not so tantalizing. I was hopping on one leg, trying to yank my jeans up, going, "Shit, shit," and Karl—this is the part I've never forgotten—Karl just fought off his moment of disgust, and said, "I'll get you to the plane, Chulya." I said, "I haven't even been back to the fucking dorm yet." He said, "No, I'll get you to the plane." And he did, bless him, talking nonstop, distracting me, the Citroën blowing blue smoke. Later, aloft, I had the lingering physical sensation of his having been inside me, and wished he were again, though I knew I wouldn't want to see him when I got back. The night after Simon's service I came down with a howling bladder infection, no doubt attributable to this escapade, and had to trouble Mitzi for Gantrisin, which took some little while to work, and in the meantime I was in agony, not to mention nauseated from the pills and whacked from the whole dreadful day, but all that was still forty-eight hours in the future. I punched off the reading light, tipped my face toward the jet of air, and shut my eyes. I'd done none of the errands Jessica Shasky had advised, informing the registrar and so on, but, sweet Jesus, I hadn't missed the flight.

I need to tell you one more thing about what Simon did. He called the police. Remember this was the 1970s. No cordless for Simon, no cell phone, no voice mail. It was a Wednesday. Simon had dressed and eaten his Shredded Wheat and, to all appearances, driven off to work. Mitzi had set out for the American Legion in Willimantic where they were doing a blood draw. At some point during the next two hours, Simon returned home. A little past eleven-thirty, he placed his call to the authorities, saying he'd like to report a death. This afforded him a limited window of opportunity to get to the barn and up the extension ladder. I assume the rope was already in place. The last thing he would've wanted was to be caught in the act, so he had perhaps ten or fifteen minutes if the patrol was at all efficient. The timing of the call was itself critical, because he'd want "the mess" cleaned up before Mitzi's return. So he climbed into the cupola, rested momentarily on that interior ledge where the two of us had sat, then wiggled the ladder aside and listened to it tumble horrifically to the loft floor. He was wearing his suit pants, but had removed his jacket and tie. He'd shaved that morning, applied witch hazel. Just below the opening to the cupola ran a crossbeam, and I imagine he lowered himself onto it because departing from the upper ledge would've left too great a margin for error. So there he was, balanced on this timber in the dusty light. Maybe he stalled a moment, reassessing, or giving his Messiah a parting shot—maybe this parting shot was simply a dose of the Messiah's own medicine, a moment of stony indifference. I refuse to speculate further on that, Miles, I'm just going to leave that alone, if you don't mind. But when he dropped, he dropped straight, having measured out enough slack to insure that his neck would snap. On his desk in the side room lay a manila envelope, containing seven sheets of legal tablet, on which he'd spelled out the state of the Lamoreaux family finances, etc. Mitzi and I would not be without resources. He listed policy numbers, the location of keys, and so on. Very thorough, very succinct. Other than this one document, however, nothing.

No further valedictory.

In the short time I'd been in Ann Arbor, Simon had written me half a dozen letters. Typed, using the back sides of outdated Travelers memos. Waste not, want not. Mitzi's, of which there were two, came handwritten in her peckish script. I found the reports of life on Old Post Road vaguely irrelevant to my new state. No, it was more than that: I felt them—the letters themselves—exerting a sly gravitational pull I was at pains to resist. I plucked them from my box, awarded them a single reading, let them languish in my bag with other ephemera, used them as bookmarks. I wasn't homesick, not Miss Julia. How could I know these same sheets of paper would be virtually my only evidence to reconstruct the period between my leaving and Simon's plunge?

It was November now. I'd been gone from Ann Arbor a scant two weeks. I was beginning to think I should just stay home—possibly commute to the University of Hartford winter quarter. "Don't be foolish," Mitzi said. She was adamant about getting me back on the plane. She didn't need me disrupting my life on her account. It was true, she was full of rancor toward Simon, and how could this acid fail to splatter me as well? She heard herself taking this tone, knew it was unfair, yet couldn't stop herself. "Don't you dare blame me," I might've fired back. "You were the wife." I held off. Remorse would kick in later, or if not remorse, her sense of duty. She'd wave her hand through the air, wandlike, dismissing the ill will, the furies, the imponderables. She'd pull me into a hug, which required my bending down. She'd say, "Oh, Julia, sweetheart." I hugged her back, but it had been a long time since we'd had much physical contact. She'd put on a cool fierce front for the Messiahs the day of the service, hadn't cried a drop, but several times since, in front of me or Mrs. Shasky she had, in frustration and exhaustion, I thought. She'd taken to stuffing a Kleenex up the sleeve of her sweater. By the time I left, Jessica Shasky had convinced me it was for the best, my return to academia, that Mitzi needed time alone, and that she, Jessica, would watch out for her. I let myself be seduced by this reasoning. The two of them drove me to Bradley Field and saw me off, and then I was back at Detroit. No Karl this time. I took a shuttle. It was slamming down rain and then the rain went to sleet and our long Indian summer was done.

I implied above that when Mrs. Shasky telephoned, her news came as less than a complete shock. But it isn't true that I'd expected this of Simon, foreseen it. If Mitzi had missed it, I'd missed it, too. I only meant I believed Mrs. Shasky right away. I underwent no spasm of denial. And when (with difficulty, because Mitzi refused to discuss them), I learned the details, they all seemed very Simonlike. Back in Ann Arbor, I felt a gaping need to look through his letters again. One saving grace was that my roommate had begun to ingratiate herself around a sorority house, so I was granted frequent spells of privacy during this time. Simon had been particular about setting the moment for me: "It's Sunday night about eight and I'm typing this at your sister's desk." Like that. He told me there'd been a frost and the windowsills downstairs were crowded with Mitzi's unripened tomatoes. He told me he'd been to meeting that morning and Mrs. Verlag had asked how I was adjusting to college life and he'd said I'd become very independent and he wasn't worried about me in the slightest. He wrote well, Simon, not as stiffly as you'd imagine. No pontificating. But if I thought I'd turn up a foreshadowing of his intent, a coded warning, there I was frustrated. I found the letters suffused with sadness. As I said, his argument with the Redeemer had gone underground. It had become so much a part of him, I'd read right past it the first time. What I saw now was a man turning to the mundane lay of things for solace, and finding none. Or too little. I realized I'd never really come to grips with his love for my sister. That it was unequivocal, undulled by time. That he couldn't help himself. Nor were further pleas directed at me—to not desert him, and so on. I could tell you I believed he'd absolved me, freed me from our strange confederacy, but the truth, of course, is that he'd just given up asking.

Let's call this enough, okay? I've been at it three days, off and on. I'm shot. And one other thing: much as I wouldn't mind hearing from you, I'm going to be gone a while. Business and not-business. Through Christmas week more than likely. Not generally my best season, let's leave it at that. But afterward?

Au revoir, Miles.

Fanning sat where he was, mute. He massaged his eyes with the heels of his hands, then ran the scroll bar back to the top of the message. *Had a very fair sleep last night.* He was shot himself, certainly in no shape to read it through again, this torrent of story. Yet he did, and much later found himself once again at her *Au revoir.*

And to you, Fanning thought.

10

Seduced by their smell, Fanning bought a paper cone of toasted almonds and rode the escalator, at large among Christmas shoppers. Berets and head wraps, camel-hair coats with swaying camel-hair belts, crinkly rain-gear iridescent as moth wings. Nobody he knew, nobody he'd seen before, or would see again. He strolled with no clear purpose, eyes softly roaming. He'd UPS'd the box to his mother three days ago, the smoked salmon she liked, the jams, a new recording of "Transfigured Night" and so on, marking it *Don't open until the 25th. This means you.* Pure folly: she'd be into it in the time it took to locate a sharp knife. He wandered through a Williams-Sonoma, accepted a Dixie cup of mulled cider, admired the copper-bottomed cooking pans, racks of glassware the blue of old Milk of Magnesia bottles. He came out empty-handed. SunBreak was low-key as to gift-giving, but every December Fanning took a night to write out notes of thanks, one by one—what bounty there was he shared as bonuses, and called that good. Despite the vagaries of what sold and what didn't, the company had done if not spectacu-

larly, then not shabbily, a little better each quarter than the
year before. Several award nominations. He poked along, in
and out of a store with games, towers of stacked boxes, CD-
ROM ware, basketfuls of mechanical gizmos and puzzles and
tin wind-up toys. He passed the open doorways of Victoria's
Secret and The Limited and a shop offering overpriced choco-
lates. His back to a railing, he loitered in a crossdraft of holiday music, not the usual dross—this was medieval, recorders
and timbrels and hand claps. He was lulled, carried away.
Today had been a rare bright day in the city. On foot, earlier,
he stopped on Pine above the Market and turned back toward
the water, found himself stupefied by the volume of sun-
shine, half-giddy. Now, overhead, the skylights were graying,
dimming, and with them the day's palpable air of reprieve.

He'd bought nothing for Kyra, the first time in seven
years. Disorienting, but in the spirit of their agreement.
Whenever they ended this separation, he'd ask if there was-
n't something she'd like. She'd insist she was fine, he didn't
need to buy her things—anyway, it could wait until her
birthday, etc. But one Saturday they'd be out together and
some article would catch their eye and he'd get it for her, and
that little resolution would come, as would others he couldn't
guess at now. Assuming they did end it, assuming they recon-
ciled—but that hardly seemed like the right word. It wasn't
as if they'd been at each other's throats. He took the down
escalator, thought of her driving to Tillamook, hoped the
roads stayed dry. No black ice, no fleet of wreckers. She'd
have told everyone at home about their arrangement, but
how she couched it, how bad he'd come off, he couldn't guess.
*Miles has gotten so self-absorbed, so withdrawn, I have to have
more . . . I can't . . .* or maybe she'd simply told them, *Miles
and I are seeing where we go from here, mid-course correction,*
using a tone that said she wished to keep her own counsel. It
was good to have a place where you were adored, where your
side would be taken without question—he didn't begrudge

her that. Still, it unnerved him, the thought of the whole
Cannaday clan souring on him at once, being leery of him.
Except for the Christmas Fanning and his new bride joined
his mother in Fort Myers, and the one they'd holed up on
Weymouth Street after the accident, Fanning dopey with
painkiller, they'd driven to Oregon and shared themselves
around, sleeping in the guest cottage at her folks', or at
Jimmy and Starla's, or Todd and Margie's. Sprawling boister-
ous meals, bundled-up strolls through the orchards at night.
Aunt Kyra and Uncle Miles. He had to admit he hated thinking of her back in that world without him.

Outside again, Fanning walked with his hands jammed
in his pockets, his hair ruffling in the wind. A transitional
hour. Lights had come on, streetlights, headlamps of taxis
and double-jointed buses, but the gloaming spilled from the
alleys, pooled beneath awnings and parked cars and in the
lee of cement barricades. Head down, eyes narrowed against
the particulate, he waited at a crooked intersection under
the Monorail, then set across amid the surge, his fellow citi-
zens lugging multiple shopping bags by their twine grips.
He was ambushed there, out in the open, by the thought of
Simon Lamoreaux buying no gift for his oldest girl that first
year, a frugal, God-fearing man moved to generosity, and no
one to lavish it upon. Fanning was bumped from behind,
had the heel of his shoe stepped on, squashed. He caught his
balance and reached the sidewalk, feeling clammy and
chilled where his skin was exposed. He knelt, righted the
back of the shoe with his finger. When he began to walk
again, across the upper reaches of Belltown to where he'd
parked, Simon Lamoreaux seemed to be at his side, match-
ing him stride for stride, Simon bereft, haranguing and
lamenting in that craggy fearsome tenor Fanning remembered clearly for the first time in decades.

*   *   *

Then it was the twenty-second, the Monday before Christmas, and Fanning was consumed by last-minute details for SunBreak's annual Winter Solstice concert, to be recorded live tonight and released next September. Gillespie and Burns, Sylvia Rivard, the Bloom Island Quartet, eight acts in all. Aaron and Martina and a few others, including a piano tuner, had been at the hall since before lunch. Sound check was at three. Fanning perched in the front row of the balcony with a yellow pad. The stage had a simple layout: oriental rug, shell of white reflectors, red poinsettias on short staggered columns at either side of the arch. Strictly speaking, the Solstice had not been Fanning's brainchild. Strictly speaking, it had sprung from Gloria de Santos, who'd pestered Fanning until he succumbed. "Doesn't have to be carols and all like that. Just music for a winter night. Even pagans celebrate, no?" Gloria was decidedly nonpagan herself—she'd been raised in the winterless clamor of San Antonio, a faithful Catholic, as he'd told Julia, but somehow her argument worked on him. Anyway, the show was tradition now, and Fanning had come to like it, his chance to stride across the stage in good duds, swallowing his own little dose of stage fright so he could introduce his artists. Fanning watched the machinations below, jotted notes with his felt-tip, tried to enjoy himself.

In years past, Kyra'd drop by about now, joining him at the railing, rubbing his pant leg and offering some direct observation that had eluded him entirely. Later, they'd spiff up and arrive at the hall as a couple. Fanning would get that jolt he sometimes got, seeing Kyra as others did—leggy and self-assured, on the arm of her lover. Tonight, Fanning showered at the Hospitality Suite, removed his tux from drydock, rolled packing tape around hand and wrist, sticky side out, and patted the outfit down for stray hairs and specks of God knows what. His neck ached where it met the skull, almost a searing. He hadn't eaten since a few bites of sub sandwich around one-thirty, but there was no time now, he'd have to forage at the trays backstage. He killed the lights and headed out, then came to a halt in the corridor, convinced he'd forgotten something vital—he tapped his pockets for wallet and keys, went so far as to unlock the door again and stand within the room trying to isolate what had set off this nagging, finally having to give up and drive across town to the hall. Not officially a sellout, but a nice house nonetheless. He put on his game face and worked the lobby, shook hands, ran into people he hadn't seen in months. If they asked about Kyra, he told them she'd already left for Oregon, elaborating no further. Give her our love, they said. Fanning said he would indeed.

Backstage, he grabbed a few slices of kiwi and apple and summer sausage, drank off a plastic cup of red wine, hoping none of it found its way to his shirt front, and at twelve minutes past eight was out at the microphone telling the assembled what sublime stuff awaited them, brought out Sylvia Rivard, gave her a squeeze, and finally retreated to the wings. As she played, his eyes passed along the faces visible from this acute angle, and they wore various music-listening expressions, subdued half-smiles mainly, but here in mid-row was a tall, knobby-headed older gent, unaffiliated with the parties on either side, from the look of it. His gaze struck Fanning as too absorbed, too involved, plus the way he was canted forward, lips and teeth parted as if he might issue a spatter of wild commentary, and even the brows, standing out, oblique, brushy, reminded him of Simon Lamoreaux, and when Sylvia finished and Fanning reemerged to say a few words about the next act, he stared into the middle distance, then up toward the depths of the balcony, the spots in his eyes—anywhere save those first rows, stage right. But finally he couldn't help it, and found himself speaking straight at the man, as if they knew all about each other, were old kinsmen or enemies. When Fanning was finished, he saw the man tilt his head so the woman at his left could speak into his ear before the quartet began, and Fanning thought, *Not alone after all, hard of hearing, nothing more mysterious than that.* When Fanning picked him out again, a harmlessness had settled over the man, a beatitude, but the disquiet remained with Fanning, sourceless now, free-ranging.

After the show, Fanning walked Gloria to her car. He thanked her for everything, bent and kissed her powdered cheek, said, "My best to your husband."

"Poor Felix," she said.

"He's lucky to have you," Fanning said. "Your daughters are coming home?"

"Tomorrow night, all three."

"I'm happy for you," Fanning said, shutting her door, and he was. He watched until her taillights blurred into the north-bound traffic, then went in and helped with the teardown, wound mike and monitor cords, tied them off and tossed them in the trunk. Later, people headed out for drinks. Fanning always picked up the tab for this after-party, and did so tonight, but bowed out early himself, not half-past twelve. He stood and looked his way around the long table. "You know what, that was fine work," he said. "I'm blessed, swear to God. But I need to get along." He smiled, took in the farewells, the *Merry Christmas*es, gathered briefcase and coat, and began threading his way toward the parking lot. Only then did he realize that Aaron had followed him outside in his shirtsleeves.

"You seemed kind of distracted tonight," Aaron said.

Anyone else and Fanning would have shrugged this off. "It showed onstage?" he said.

"Maybe a little. Because I know you."

Fanning shook his head.

"I just wondered if you were okay, Miles."

"Peopled-out for one night, I guess."

Aaron said, "This situation with Kyra, can't be easy."

Fanning agreed, not easy. He'd mentioned Julia Lamoreaux to no one. If this had been another sort of moment, if he'd been less tired, less superstitious, believing Julia belonged to a secret life of his, a life he wasn't sure he was ready to acknowledge, he might've tested the short version on Aaron. He almost did anyway, but instead touched his friend on the shoulder, told him to go inside before he froze to death.

Not since that leaden Friday in November had he been back to his house. He inched down the treacherous incline of Twenty-first, rolled along Weymouth, and stopped outside 2448. The walkway was lighted, low fixtures submerged in the unkempt ground cover and fallen husklike camellia leaves. A wan glow hovered in the upstairs windows. He sat thinking, *She's already left, I'm sure of it,* but it took some minutes to talk himself out of the car. The air smelled like snow, a smell out of childhood, a smell like iron pipe. He doubted it would come, snow—more likely to be a slushy rain, clumping on the windshields.

He let himself in. That sense of intruding, of snooping, so potent last time, had dissipated. Christmas cards lay on the front table, some unopened. No sign of decoration anywhere. The heat was down, the icebox stripped to bottles of soy sauce and kosher dills and diet colas. She'd had the cleaning service before she left—his tracks would show in the vacuumed rug, but he couldn't seem to generate any worry about that. He went to the computer room and looked for the square enveloped marked *Miles* waiting against its glass bowl.

Gone.

He made a cursory check of her desk drawers, and among the books, but couldn't turn it up. Whatever had been written there, she'd changed her mind about letting him see it.

He sank to the sectional in the big room, and after a few

minutes picked up the remote. He'd purposely not brought a
TV to the Hospitality Suite—in all these weeks, he'd watched
no news, nor indulged his late-night habit of fiddling his way
through the dial, the way he now was. Tree frogs, the skinny
young Sinatra, hockey highlights. When the charm had worn
off, stupid with fatigue, he climbed the spiral stairs, freed his
body of clothes, peeled back the bedcovers, and toppled in.
Compared to the humorless futon, it was like falling into
meringue.

But, thank God, no bad dreams, no *wraith out of Dickens*.

Three nights he stayed home. If the phone rang, he let the
voice mail absorb the messages. When it rang just after ten on
the twenty-fourth, he was at the back window, watching the
drizzle on the floodlit paving stones . . . he guessed it was
Kyra, and steeled himself not to pick up, then thought,
wrong, Sully, home from the late service on the East Coast. So
Fanning stretched his legs out on the stairs and talked to his
oldest friend. How was Pascale? How were the girls? Fine,
everyone fine. Pascale has Danielle reading the Babar books
in French. *Je suis Babar, roi des éléphants.* But what's with
you? Sully asked. Last time I called, Kyra was quite vague
about why you weren't on hand, and when's Kyra ever vague?
So I thought, okay, don't push, but what's the deal?

Fanning reclined his head against the plaster, felt the little
chill on his bald spot, and told his friend what the deal was.
But it's not *permanent?* Sully said. Fanning said no, no, Kyra
just had this idea that they'd . . . then suddenly he couldn't
bear talking about it. He found himself saying, "You remember that day at the Civic Center?" The subject of Carly Lamoreaux had not been raised between them in many years, but
of course Sully knew what day he meant.

"I remember almost nothing between then and graduation," Fanning began. "Besides being interrogated, plus a few
random . . . I must've had finals and all the rest. How did I
seem?"

"There but not there is the closest I can describe it."

"But what did I think had *happened?*" Fanning said. "Did I think she'd been dragged away and murdered? Or was it pure denial? Why wasn't I frantic?"

"When were you ever frantic, Miles?"

"I was that bloodless?"

"I think you believed it would be resolved in a few days. I mean, I certainly thought so, we all did."

"You did."

"At first, sure."

"But then the time started to pile up."

"Yes."

"What's so strange about this," Fanning said, "you were always making me out to be uptight, or too cautious—"

"It was just your way, Miles. No one held it against you particularly, you know that."

"But when something actually happened, it barely seemed to register." Fanning got to his feet and carried the phone toward the glass doors where he'd stood earlier. "I came up to Wells to see you, later in the summer," he said. "You were with that Sandy Costello."

"*Sandy Costello,*" Sully said. "Lord, what a spitfire."

Fanning gazed at his terrace, at the water collecting in the seat of a lawn chair no one had brought in. "I want to know if we talked about Carly," he said.

"I'm sure we must have."

"You don't remember it."

"Not specifically."

"I'd love to know what I thought," Fanning said. "It's like I went, *Well, so much for Carly. On to the next thing.*"

"I think you're being awfully hard on yourself, Miles."

Fanning didn't answer.

"What brought all this up?" Sully said.

"Oh, that Kodály piece came on the radio. *Psalmus Hungaricus?*" This was only a partial evasion. In fact, starting his

car in the SunBreak lot a week earlier, Fanning *had* come
upon the Kodály in progress—he knew it instantly, that wave-
like crashing and ebbing by the full chorus that had so
aroused and shaken him as an eighteen-year-old. He sat listening, eyes shut, thinking I bet they haven't trotted this
puppy out in years. Why in God's name now? But as to telling
Sully about Julia . . . he could have launched right into it,
beginning with *julamo*, with *Are you the Miles Fanning
who*— He could've recited the whole bloody thing—Sully
would've eaten it up. He'd have peppered Fanning with questions, dispensed words of wisdom. But for the second time,
Fanning held back, letting their conversation veer off down
other alleys.

In the morning he drove to the studio and worked a couple of
hours in seclusion, called his mother in Fort Myers, then
made for the ferry dock in Edmonds, waited in a lighter-than-
average queue, watching the *Yakima* come and rock back-
washing against the cluster of pilings and the city-bound cars
spew off it. Then he was aboard himself, walking to the stairs
in a stiff diesel-scented wind. On the backseats of other cars,
he saw the shine of foil-wrapped boxes, loops of ribbon.

Up on the main deck, Fanning shuffled through a sparse
line at the snack bar, getting coffee. "Triple time on Christmas?" he asked the cashier.

"In my dreams," she said.

A black woman of about forty, low-slung, rather handsome, with wide glossy cheeks. She gave Fanning his change,
and said, "The other girl got her a couple kids. You know how
it is."

Fanning offered a smile. "You're a saint," he said.

"I'm something," she answered, showing off a row of
pearly teeth.

Fanning sat on the port side and stared out. The water was

black, foam-specked, with more chop than he'd imagined— he felt the boat sway in the cross-current, saw his coffee slide up and down the walls of the cup. The Sound was as barren of ship traffic as he'd ever seen it. He'd thought, on his way here, he might drive as far as Port Angeles, drop in on Ryugi and his paramour, but lingering at the window he knew he wouldn't. He'd only ridden the ferry for something to do. At Kingston he'd get in the other line and ride back. After a while he went to the bow and joined six or seven other hearty, underdressed souls clutching the railing, watching land approach.

11

AND THEN, WITH barely a day's warning, Julia Lamoreaux was back.

Fanning stepped into the lobby of the Queensbury. But for the tiny white Christmas lights, not yet re-stowed, it looked much as he remembered, an oasis of inactivity. No one awaited him. He strolled to the gas fire and stood. Through an arch, he heard the ting of the elevator and turned. An older couple in his-and-hers London Fogs, who crossed from carpet to terrazzo, and vanished with a whoosh into the revolving door. Fanning consulted his watch: on time, give or take. He waited. When the elevator sounded again he again lifted his face, but the car was vacant. Outside the hotel, it was a night more like the end of March, drizzle, a not-frigid wind off the Sound bringing smells where recently there had been none. A week ago it had snowed five inches, crippled the city.

El Niño.

Fanning went to the desk and asked if by any chance he had a message, a Mr. Fanning? He was handed a sheet of memo tablet: *Running late*, it said. *Why don't you just come up? 612. J.* He looked about the lobby sharply to see if he was

being watched, but who'd be watching him? He slipped the
notepaper into the pocket of his topcoat, made his way to the
elevators, put his finger to the button. Then he was standing
in the oblique lighting of the sixth-floor hallway, athwart the
fisheye in Julia's door. He hesitated, then tapped with his
knuckle.

She was some time in answering.

Draped in a drooping chenille bathrobe, magenta, she
stood aside for him to enter, head slightly bowed, the bangs
falling forward. If Fanning had been expecting a snappy
remark at the sight of him, he was mistaken. He passed into
the lit part of the room, holding his coat. The curtains were
drawn and the bed, though made, had an unquiet look.

Julia motioned him to one of the padded chairs. Fanning
sat. She cinched her belt and settled into the chair opposite,
flapping the hem of the robe over her knees as an after-
thought. On her feet, cotton crew socks, baggy. She ran her
fingers down her face, staring glassily in his direction. This
was more or less how he'd pictured her condition at the end of
that marathon e-mail, which was what, three weeks ago?

"We could skip tonight," he said.

No, she said, she was okay, just . . . she'd gotten in
midafternoon but had sort of *folded* and then, abruptly, it was
half-past seven.

Fanning nodded.

She seemed a good ways from going anywhere. He looked
about, discreetly. There was a cloth-sided case that likely held a
laptop. A leather duffle, zippered compartments flopped open.
Two small puddles of clothes leading to the bathroom.

"Here again on business?" he asked.

"That's right," she said, giving Fanning the makings of a
smile.

"You survived the holidays," he offered.

"And yourself."

"Well, I did," he said. It occurred to him to describe how

Simon had barged into his consciousness that late afternoon in December, but he thought better of it. Not yet.

He said, "If you'd like more time—"

"You antsy?"

Fanning said no, not antsy.

There followed an awkward moment, two people silently eyeing each other, except, for some reason, it wasn't terribly awkward.

"Coffee then," he said.

She said, "Would you run in an IV?" She made a face: ancient caffeine humor. She inclined her head toward the bathroom. "An electric pot, in there," she said.

Fanning took this to mean it was his job. He got up. She'd barely taken possession of the room, but even so, it felt strangely intimate to be at her sink, running the water, looking down at her toiletries, the canvas case with its crimson stays, the few tubes, the floss. The bathroom was old, retrofitted, but with the original flooring, a grid of chipped porcelain tiles, black diamonds on white. Someone had added a wall-mounted hair dryer, and a telephone that reached to the toilet. The coffee came in gauzy packets. He dropped one in the brown plastic basket and touched the switch. What was he doing here? Hard to say. No, it wasn't, not that hard.

She hadn't moved, but appeared more lifelike through the eyes. He watched her drink. "You're tracking better," he said.

"Looks can deceive."

Fanning got the carafe and dosed her again. He said, "We could order up."

She hunched her shoulders. "Think?"

"How bad can it be?"

"Jesus, don't say that."

In any case, they ate room service, a sprawling seafood Louis for Fanning, a small bloody steak for Julia Lamoreaux.

He watched the branching veins in the back of her hand as she cut the meat and lifted it to her mouth, the fork turned over, European-fashion. Her fingers were bare, dusky, the nails unglossed. The bulky cuffs of the robe were turned halfway up her forearm.

She glanced up sharply as if he'd spoken. "You want a bite of this?" she asked.

"You have it."

"Sure?"

Fanning nodded, not wishing to say she looked like she couldn't spare any. He watched the knot of muscle in her jaw.

He laid his napkin aside and stood and fixed more coffee. Returning, passing by her shoulder, he said, "It's a shame, though."

"What is?"

"I wanted to take you out for squid. Had my heart set on it. There's this wonderful little Italian dive."

Julia squeezed him into focus. "Oh, sweet," she said.

"Another time."

"Another time, yeah."

Fanning was about done fussing with his salad. He sat back. It was only now he realized that the room's air was conspicuously smoke-free. He waited until her eyes returned to his. "Cold turkey?" he asked.

She made a momentary show of not knowing what he was talking about.

Fanning put two fingers to his own lips.

She looked away.

"How long?" he asked.

"Few days."

"How many?"

She said, "Would you like it in minutes?"

What possessed you? No, he didn't ask that. She'd get around to telling him, or not. He watched her push the last wedge of steak around in its juice and tuck it in her mouth.

She had this certain way of chewing, zealous yet austere. After a moment, Fanning said, "Patch?"

Julia shook her head. No patch, no Zyban.

"Brave girl," he said.

She gave him a look: Let's not go there, all right?

Fanning gave her a look back.

In a minute, he slid away from the table and stood and Julia stared up at him. "Here's what I'm going to do," he said. "I'm going downstairs. You can shower and see how you are, and if you're up to an expedition I'll drive you down to the studio." He reached for his coat, giving her no time to object. "Let's say I'll hang around until nine-thirty. If I don't see you I'll assume crashing won out."

She stared down at her left wrist, which was bare.

"It's almost nine," Fanning said.

Julia nodded.

"You don't have any cigarettes with you," he said.

"Nope."

He turned away and went to the door and let himself out.

Fanning stuck his head in the lounge. No basketball on tonight. Two of the little tables were occupied and one man in shirtsleeves sat round-shouldered at the bar, thumbing a paper. Fanning had no desire to join in. He'd had a goblet of red wine with the meal, and that seemed to be all he wanted just now. He walked outside and stood under the canopy and watched the cars pass. The rain had picked up, seemed to come at an angle. After a while, the doorman approached and asked if he needed anything. Fanning said he was only getting air. The man returned to his post, and Fanning looked across the street at the plywood barricade and vacant window sockets where a building was being gutted. It was too soon to check his watch but he did anyway. He went back inside and milled about. It got to be nine-thirty, then a little after, then quarter to. Well, so, he thought. He pictured her face down on the bedspread, the lights still blazing. He ran his fingers along a chairback. When he turned, finally, she was at the border of the carpet, watching him without expression, her hands plunged into the pockets of her raincoat.

Fanning's impulse was to tease her, about the extensive repair work this must've taken, but just before he'd looked up and caught sight of her, the prospect of driving back alone had washed over him like an icy silt, and so, in relief, he said nothing. Julia didn't say anything either. They crossed the lobby and went one at a time through the revolving door and out into the blowing rain, Fanning pointing up the street as they walked quickly, heads down, the water glazing his eyeglasses. In the middle of the next block, he felt her take his sleeve. "It's just up ahead there," he half-shouted. "Under that blue neon?" And then he was unlocking the door for her and they sat in Fanning's car shaking the water from their hair. He raced the engine and the windows began to defog.

Julia squinted over at him. "There's a guy in San Francisco," she said, still catching her breath, "name of Al Nino. He kept getting all these phone calls, I mean like a hundred and fifty, people blaming him for the weather. Finally had to unlist his number."

Fanning smiled.

"You think I'm making this up?"

He watched her hunt through her coat pockets for a Blistex, watched her squeeze some out and knead it into her lips with one finger.

Fanning pulled into traffic. This time of night, it was a scant ten minutes to SunBreak. He went a few blocks south, cornered onto Union, but he was overcome with the desire to stretch this part out, the in-transit time. Abruptly, he doubled back and drove her around by the Space Needle, which was virtually impossible to see from so close underneath, and with the rain battering the car windows.

"You've been up there countless times, I suppose," Julia said.

Fanning said, actually, he *could* count them. In all his years here, he'd been up the Needle a total of once.

Julia accepted this without comment.

After a moment, Fanning said, "To be perfectly honest, I thought the thing was going to shake apart. I lasted about eight minutes."

"Huh," she said. "How about flying?"

Fanning said flying was all right. If you were in business you had to fly.

She went, "Big bridges?"

"I wouldn't be the one up there painting them," he said.

He maneuvered his way down to First and drove her toward the Market, pointing out more things she couldn't see. She wasn't the most relaxed of passengers. Her leg shot out, her hand kept going to the overhead grip as he made ready to turn. He said nothing. When was the last time he'd had company in this car? Undoubtedly it was Kyra, a week or two, possibly three, before the start of their experiment, but he couldn't dredge up the specific occasion. A run to Safeway? Or the night they'd eaten at Saleh Al Lago, when Kyra had reached across the linen cloth and snapped her fingers in his face as if to bring him out of hypnosis—Fanning had almost batted the hand away, but said only, his voice under control, "Please don't ever do that again." But no, they'd taken separate cars that evening, both coming from work. Then, unavoidably, he remembered the night of the glazed streets, remembered hanging upside down in Kyra's Accord, his head swelling with blood, his arms flopping against the soft fabric of the roof. And the boy, the boy in the delivery van.

They passed the Art Museum with its giant hammering man, they passed Lombardi's. Fanning pulled inside the chain-link behind SunBreak and shut off the motor. Both sat back, the seats sighing in tandem. Fanning held up a wad of keys, and fished out the pair that operated the rear entry.

"You okay?" he asked.

Julia said yeah sure, peachy.

Fanning elected to believe her. They went toward the cowled light in a low-angled dash, two escapees. Fanning unlocked the steel door and shouldered it open and let Julia inside. He slapped the flat of his hand to the freight elevator switch and swung back the grate and they rose two flights at a stately pace, accompanied by an electric floor polisher and a bale of cotton rags, the old cables chittering overhead. Fanning located the third key and they were in SunBreak's back corridor.

Fanning went ahead, firing up the lights.

"There's a somewhat more elegant way in here," he said, walking her toward the front, past the studio doors, past Aaron's office and the conference room, through Gloria de Santos's territory out to the reception area, where the Sun-Break logo was imprinted on a panel of white Lucite. The outer wall was naked brick and in the space between the windows hung blowups of half a dozen of Ryugi's jacket covers. Julia passed along them, nodding, nodding.

It wasn't as chilly as Fanning had feared—someone must've been working until minutes ago. He removed his coat, gave it a couple of brisk shakes, and held out his hand for Julia's.

She stood weighing the request.

"Hang on to it if you want," he said.

"No, here, I'm sorry," she said, and stripped off the raincoat. Beneath, she wore a plain black turtleneck and jeans, no adornment except for a small silver buckle where the waist was cinched.

Fanning gave her the tour. In the main studio he explained how it was sometimes preferable, acoustically, to isolate each player—he showed her the booths with their foam-baffled walls—but often they recorded live here in the big room. He gave her the hundred-words-or-less version of analog versus digital. He told her about the massive bootlegging of American CDs in spots like Hong Kong and Bulgaria—not that SunBreak's artists were much of a target for piracy. He mentioned the grand irony of his starting a company like SunBreak in Seattle at the same moment in history that the city was putting itself on the map as world epicenter of "grunge." He talked a little about the art of recording, the layering of sound on sound—he played her the tape of a work-in-progress, *The Iron Dog Suite*, separating out the tracks so she could hear each alone, then stacking them back up. He watched her reflection in the window to the control room but it was unreadable.

"Had enough?" he asked.

She came back from wherever she'd gone.

Fanning said he didn't want to bore her.

"I'm not bored," she said.

Fanning nodded and let the tape run.

Julia sank onto the piano bench and leaned her elbows back onto the closed keyboard cover. "How'd you do all this?" she asked.

Fanning said he wondered it himself.

But she required more of an answer than that.

Fanning let his hands fall against his legs. "My father left me a little money," he said. "I'd been around the edges of the business for some time, reviewing, some magazine work, profiles, and so on, I had various connections. But I was basically nowhere, not *engaged*. This was the summer of 1984. I had long talks with my friend Sully and his wife. They'd been married only a few months, and had both just landed conservatory jobs and were all pumped up, and managed to infect me with this flying-leap mentality, so I sank my father's money into some gear, hired Aaron and Gloria. At first we worked out of a shop up in Ballard where they used to rebuild speedboat engines."

He slid a folding chair beside the bench and sat.

"And you stayed afloat," Julia said.

"But I hate to think of the luck it took. I made some supremely boneheaded moves. When I'd been writing I listened to everything, a great raft of stuff, and thought I knew what I liked, and why, but when it came to signing people, *betting* on them, that was treacherous. We'd get into the thick of some project, and between takes Aaron, who has a brilliant ear, but also an almost Old World sort of tact, Aaron would make his suggestions, and I knew just by the way his mouth drew back that he'd already heard what I'd later hear for myself, that the work was ordinary, that whatever I'd been seduced by initially had gone into the ether. Or we'd get someone I was dead sure about and the sessions would go beautifully and there was that wonderful relief when you know your instinct wasn't wrong, but we wouldn't be able to get the recording distributed correctly, or it would get distributed but go unnoticed, and though we'd had a good rapport with the artist, and these hopes, next time she'd sign elsewhere."

Partway through this last speech, the Iron Dog played itself out. Fanning climbed to his feet again. "Let me put on one more," he said. "Mind?"

He left her and went to the archive and reached for Billy Caughlan's first SunBreak recording, which wasn't where it belonged, so he stepped down the hall to his office and pulled a copy of the CD reissue from his desk drawer, and came back by way of the control room, pausing to look at Julia through the glass. She was bent forward now, elbows on knees, thumbnails tapping at her teeth. He could follow the knobs of her spine up the stretched black cotton. He picked the Caughlan disc from its case and put it in the machine and eased up the mains in the outer room and watched her a few moments more.

"Sometimes things work out otherwise," he said, rejoining her. He told her about his trip to Vancouver, spring of '86. He'd gone to hear a three-day festival of young composers, some of the pieces being too manifestly in the contemporary classical vein for SunBreak, and some too skittish or lobotomized for Fanning's taste, but he introduced himself around, and, in fact, they almost did sign a Taiwanese girl who wrote for electric violin (a couple of years later, her stuff began appearing on Nonesuch and he regretted the indecision on both sides), but it was the second night when he found himself in a club listening to a solo pianist, a kid who looked like his day job might be wheeling bodies through the morgue. Bristles of red-blond hair, a bony gaze, a jumpy way of riding the bench. The playing was all improv'd, Fanning suspected, and only he and a handful of others paid it any mind. When Fanning went to him at the break he saw something else, a *presence*, and realized the man was older than he'd first thought, perhaps nearing thirty. Fanning asked if he'd recorded. The piano player said he'd self-produced two cassettes but had none with him that night. Do you come to Seattle? Fanning asked. The man said sure, he'd grown up in Everett. Fanning gave him his card and said would you please call me. They studied each other. You could do better than this, Fanning said, we both know that. So that was when he and Billy Caughlan first met, an important night. For a moment, Fanning considered telling Julia about Billy and Kyra, but he let it lie.

He stopped talking and followed Billy's playing, which he should be mortally sick of by now, but by no means was. He didn't ask Julia's opinion, and apart from meeting his eyes and giving an abbreviated smile, she didn't tender it. He watched her stand and roam the studio, arms folded at her waist yet the fingers still jittering on either sleeve.

Fanning motioned to her. "We don't have to stay," he said.

Julia looked at him as if, through a fault of her own, he'd badly misjudged her.

Fanning said it was all right.

She said, "I never sit and listen to music. I don't know if I ever did. Not that much. In the car I listen, but I need to be in the right frame of mine. I get . . . restless."

"You have news on most of the time," he said.

She nodded.

"You're drawn to what you're drawn to."

"Yes."

He looked at her.

"But this isn't so bad," she said, teasing again now.

"No," he said. "It's not bad."

"What was the name again?"

"Caughlan. He's had a few tunes on movie sound-tracks."

"Like what?"

Fanning named the one with Susan Sarandon.

"Didn't see it," she said.

"Don't go to the movies much either?"

"I go to movies," she said. "Now and again."

Billy Caughlan was slowboating through a long bluesy number. When it was over Fanning stood and went into the control room and ejected the disc.

Julia wandered in behind him. "Thank you," she said. "I liked that."

Fanning said, "I'm glad."

"And what about the Hospitality Suite?" she asked.

He said, "That's not ordinarily part of the tour."

Fanning unlocked the door to his lodgings. "Hold on," he said, crossing into the dark space. He snapped on the tasseled floor lamp and the reading light adjacent to the futon. "The fluorescent's lethal," he said.

Julia squinted up at the depressing infrastructure overhead, then scanned the box-lined shelving, the tower of books
by Fanning's chair, the stationary bike, the meager kitchen
facilities, the computer table where tiny gymnasts tumbled
across the screen in endless configurations.

Fanning knelt and cranked the radiator valve. He listened,
heard nothing but a far-off pinging. The rain beat on the
stone sill inches from his face. He checked to see if he'd
opened the valve all the way and listened again. It wasn't a
degree above fifty-five in here. He sat back on his haunches.
Then a series of shudders down in the pipes, like the work of
a crazed man with a ball-peen hammer, and the chambers
began suddenly to fill. Fanning rose, his knees cracking. He
saw Julia leaning back against the linoleum-topped counter
by the sink, the coils of his hot plate just losing their glow.
Smoke twirled up from the cigarette in her mouth.

"Don't you say a word," she said.

"I wasn't going to," Fanning lied.

She drew on it, her eyelids faltering. "There is a God," she
said.

Fanning watched. No use getting in the way of this. When
she'd worked the cigarette down to the filter, she wet the
remains under the faucet and looked around, holding it like a
dead bug. He pointed. She deposited it in the shopping bag he
used for trash.

"Someone left a pack in the studio," she said. "In the
event you were wondering."

"I'll have to speak to them about that."

She shook her head ruefully. "That's it," she said. "Just
that one."

Fanning asked if she wanted anything to drink. He listed
off what there was.

She said whatever he was having.

Fanning put scotch in two juice glasses, ran in a minute
amount of water.

Julia was already slunk down on the sofa. Fanning took a seat on the shambling hassock of his reading chair. He raised his glass to her and she lifted her own and drank and let it rest in her hand atop the sofa cushion.

She asked, "How much more of this exile?"

"A little while," he said. "Few weeks."

He watched her drink.

"And how will things be then?"

"Between Kyra and me?" Fanning bent and put his weight on his forearms. "Like they were, I suspect, only . . . altered."

She stared at him: *Don't you hold out on me.*

"We'll be warier," he went on. Why had he said this? He'd not been thinking it—maybe it was only that wariness was such a speciality of Julia's.

"Won't you be sorry to give all this up?" she said, flicking her free hand at Fanning's domain.

He said, "I admit there's a certain appeal."

"Short commute."

Fanning smiled softly.

She extended her glass and he took it and stood and made two more drinks. He held the bottle up and thought it was good for one more apiece, barely. Some host. Returning, he saw that Julia had tipped her head back, and was reclining her cheek on the sofa bristles. Her earrings were pewter, some rudimentary design, the same pair she'd worn that night in November. The one he could see lay inert against the hollow below her ear. He thought maybe her eyes had closed, but no. He reached over from behind and suspended the scotch above her breastbone and she took it.

"It's strange to have you here," he said, continuing around to the hassock. "But—"

But what?

He looked at her. "But not bad."

"There's a vote of confidence."

"You know what I meant," he said. He asked how long before she flew home.

She said Friday.

"Friday," Fanning said. "Evening?"

"Seven o'clock in the A.M.," she said. "I have a lunch meeting. Obligatory."

Fanning nodded.

Up through the ceiling he could hear the rain flogging an expanse of sheet metal. He set his drink on the throw rug and stood and held out his right hand.

Julia took it by the wrist and let herself be pulled upright.

Fanning kissed her.

Though he'd seen her medicating her lips earlier, they were dry now, motionless on his, and yet, he thought, exquisitely alert.

"What's this about, Miles?" she asked.

Fanning said nothing. He studied the disposition of her face, he feathered the wine-colored bangs. Then he kissed her again, his hand going to the small of her back.

Now he felt her fingers against his shirt front, but perhaps she'd only raised them in order to keep their chests apart. Gradually, he relaxed his arms and let her back away.

She stood blinking at him.

"Julia?"

"I'm not——"

Fanning girded himself for the rest of it. She had that look he remembered from the first night at the Queensbury, closed-off, self-lacerating.

"I don't want you kissing me," she said. "I'm not in the market."

Fanning let out a breath he'd kept too long. "All right," he said, "no kissing." But he was at a total loss. He looked off at the streaming windows, which were no help. He said, "I'll drive you back if you want."

Julia's mouth made a sideways hitch. She sat again, tucking one leg beneath her. "I wasn't saying that," she said.

Here would be the time to explain himself, or to make light of the moment. He could already hear the words—they sounded paltry and feckless. *I just thought*— He held his tongue.

Finally he said, "Would you like me to scare you up another smoke?"

"No thank you," she said. "I quit."

Fanning said he'd heard that rumor.

After a minute, Julia said, less a portion of the rancor, "Miles, I didn't come here for any kind of physical . . . thing."

Fanning said right, he understood, he got it.

Eventually, of course, he did drive her back to the hotel and offer her a chaste good night at curbside. He watched her disappear into the building, and sat a moment before driving off. It occurred to him she might very well not be there should he call in the morning.

He lay on the futon in his boxers—it was too damn hot in the apartment now, even with the window open to chopstick height. He got up and took a lukewarm shower, then tried reading for a time.

He thought: *I didn't say the first goddamn thing about her e-mail, why* was *that? Just this glib, rambling*— *And all that about the studio, techno-bullshit when she couldn't have given a rat's ass. Just grandstanding, just being a goddamn show-off*—

He slept a while, was awake again, sorting through rags of dream.

Then the phone rang. Ten to four.

She said, "I'm sorry, Miles, could you come over here?"

"This minute?"

She said if he possibly could.

Fanning knew better than to ask. He yanked his shirt off the chair back and stuck an arm in the sleeve, then withdrew it and took a fresh shirt from the iron bar. He questioned his face in the shaving mirror, and what he saw was both routine and starkly appalling. He ran a dollop of toothpaste onto his finger and sucked it off, then spat.

He went out the back way, stood under the overhang looking at the night. The rain had tapered off, just a few random drops coming now, and he heard the faint white noise of wet tires on the freeway.

For the third time that night, Fanning drove to the Queensbury. It didn't matter what she wanted, he realized, he would give it. He rode the elevator again, walked the sixth-floor hall where already newspapers lay at the doors, though not the door of 612, which was wedged open with a stub of pencil.

The only light was the desk lamp with its green glass shade turned against the wall. Julia was sitting up in bed, wearing what appeared to be a threadbare camisole.

Fanning came and stood nearby, his arms dangling.

She asked him to sit, please, and he sank to the edge of the mattress.

"Sleepless in Seattle?" he asked.

"Aren't you hilarious."

"All that coffee I fed you."

She said not to worry about it.

He told her the rain had finally quit.

Yes, she'd been to the window and seen. She moved her left hand so it lay adjacent to his.

Fanning touched the ends of her fingers.

She said, "I'm all fucked up, Miles."

He said it was okay.

"You know, I'm just really and truly—"

Fanning lifted her off the pillows until the plane of her face met his chest. He felt her lungs fill and empty.

She said something then, but it was lost against his shirt.

When he didn't respond, she pulled back and stared at him. "I did want that," she said. "The physical thing."

Fanning nodded.

He let his hands move down her arms. The skin was cool, goosebumped. He lowered his head and kissed her shoulder bone, then the gully beneath the ear, where, earlier, the ear-ring had lain. Her hair smelled of hotel shampoo, and was still damp, but she had another smell, like burnt almonds, he thought.

"What would you like me to do?" he said.

"That."

Fanning stroked her arms, then her back, his fingers spread, bumping up and down the ribs.

She kissed him on the side of his face, small persistent kisses, avoiding his mouth. Then, all at once, she withdrew and thumped back against the mounded pillows and looked at him, assessed him.

"I'm getting this right?" she said. "You want me?"

Fanning said he did.

"Tell me."

"I want you."

"Say my name."

Fanning said, "I want you, Julia."

"The whole thing."

"Julia Isabel Lamoreaux."

She bunched her mouth and looked off. "How *can* you?" she said.

Fanning ran his fingers along the ridge her leg made in the blanket, looking at her.

He peeled back the bottom of the camisole, baring her stomach, kissed it. The muscles jumped, her hands descended onto his head, locking it in place, but, gradually, the tension left them. Fanning proceeded.

"You're all . . . dressed," she said.

So Fanning removed his clothes and slung them on the

chair where, hours earlier, Julia had sat annihilating her steak. Then he lay full-length on the bedsheet, her backside grazing his flanks. She'd kept the camisole on. It was only now he appreciated how little padding she had on the bone.

She said, "You need to understand something, okay? I haven't done this in a long time."

How long? he asked, lips at her ear.

"It's embarrassing to say."

"It'll come right back."

"No, I was never good at it."

Fanning went *Shhh.*

Julia switched around so he could see her. She said, "I'm not horseshitting, Miles."

Fanning held her.

Julia said, "I couldn't ever—"

"Let go of yourself."

"Yes, maybe. And, you know, objectively, it wasn't possible to see myself as all that *fetching.*"

"It's not objective," Fanning said.

She said nothing to this.

But after a moment she jerked away and climbed out of bed. She went to the wall switch and put on the overhead light, which rained down an unmerciful wattage. She was uncovered below the waist. Now she hiked up the camisole and yanked it off and held it balled in her fist. She glared in his direction, inviting the same from him.

She said, "Tell me you've seen a grown woman with less tit."

It was true, she was uncommonly flat-chested. But her skin was smooth and unblemished, the same dusty olive Carly's had been. She gave off shadows. "It's just a different look," he said. "Think of marathon runners."

"It's been a marathon, all right."

"Come back to bed," he said.

Julia stared at him where he lay, then pivoted and went

gracelessly into the bathroom. Fanning heard water running. After a moment, he got up and killed the ceiling light and sank to the edge of the bed. Minutes passed, ten or more. Fanning waited, hands drooping from his knees. He dared himself to think of a stranger night than this. Finally he stood at the bathroom door and spoke her name. He wrapped his fingers around the doorknob, took them away, called again, listened, grabbed the handle and turned, certain it would be locked. Then what? What would he do then? But the door gave. Julia was up on the tile counter, her back to the cool mirror, her fist at her mouth. Fanning reached over and cranked off the water. The last of it swirled and escaped down the drain.

He made no move to touch her.

"Two naked pilgrims," he said.

Despite herself, she smiled, her eyes half-mast. She said, "Two buck-naked pilgrims."

"At five in the morning."

"Is it five?"

"Why not?"

She put her hand on his chest hair, snared it between her fingers and tugged a moment, then let her forehead tip against him.

"Let's at least sleep a little," Fanning said.

She said, "Oh, sleep."

She wrapped her legs around his thighs and he slid her off the counter. They staggered two steps backward then Fanning eased her to the floor and they went to the bed. He made sense of the disheveled bedclothes and held them open for her and she rolled in. Fanning detoured to the desk lamp and flicked it off, then joined her.

He lay on his back and she lay against him with both hands gripping his upper arm as if it were a tow rope. He waited to hear what she'd say now—this was, after all, Julia Lamoreaux. He felt her shoulders rise as she sucked in a sharp draft of air. He waited, but it reemerged in a long raspy out-breath, smoke-tainted, and she was profoundly asleep. Fanning rubbed her neck with the fingers of his free hand. *Julia,* he thought, *such a gusher of words when we're long-distance, so very few when I'm close enough to touch you.*

When he detected the first gray in the sky, he went to the tiled bathroom and used the phone, leaving a message Gloria would hear when she arrived. Reschedule the nine-thirty, tell Aaron he'd catch up with him later, etc. He offered no excuse. Gloria would take umbrage, she'd march down and see what was what in the Hospitality Suite and receive no illumination, but Fanning wasn't worrying about that now. He emptied his bladder, rinsed his unshaven face. Back in the other room, he bent and checked on Julia, who had the sheet clutched to her collarbone, two-fisted, but was otherwise dead to the world. He reached for his glasses and pulled back the layers of window curtain and stared out at this particular Thursday morning. Raw as he ought to feel from the night past, he found himself engulfed in a localized euphoria. All he saw interested him. Lights still burning, wet asphalt, wet awnings, the charcoal-bottomed cloud bank over the Olympics. He thought of how his forty-two-year-old buttocks must look from the vantage point of the bed. Helplessly, he smiled.

He eased the sheet hem out of Julia's grip, skimmed his hand back and forth across her chest until the skin tightened and her eyelids finally parted and she regarded him, wobbly at first.

"Boy, I was way down there," she said.

Fanning leaned upon one elbow, still wearing the ecstatic's grin. "Too much sleep you lose your edge," he said gently.

She stared at him, blinking. She let her hand stray onto his stomach, then down to where, now, he was hard as a cudgel. She said, "But I gotta—"

Fanning said do whatever you have to do, I'm not going anywhere. While she was in the bathroom he touched himself, gave himself a fierce yank or two, just more or less amazed at this whole business. He studied the line of light beneath the bathroom door, saw it blotted by shadow as she moved about. He swept away the covers, swung his legs to the floor, waited, tried not to think, *Please, not this again* . . . but now the door, and she was crossing the rug, gangly, flatfooted, yet with an odd slinkiness, a sidelong, narrowed-eyed look aimed at no one but himself, her sternum glistening with some smear of lotion or scent, and Fanning found himself undone by this humble gesture, this concession. He sprang from the mattress and took hold of her and their limbs tangled.

Julia said, "What I said before, I'm . . . just be careful, huh? You're not really big or anything, are you?"

Thus Fanning exercised a wicked caution entering her. He moved by the millimeter, braced on locked arms, monitoring the set of her jaw, the roll of her eyes beneath the veined lids. When he could go no further, he let his weight settle on her and rocked minutely against her pubic bone as if this were the last dance in a darkened gymnasium.

Her hand came up and slid down the side of his face. "That's enough being careful," she said.

Restored to clothing, they sat side by side on tall stools at a Starbucks, blowing on their coffees, studying passersby outside the glass. Keeping their hands to themselves. Fanning cast a discreet glance at Julia's Danish, on which lay darkly toasted almonds. He smiled, remembering her skin's smell in the night.

"And you're going back tomorrow," he said.

Julia nodded, still gazing out.

"First thing."

"Uh-huh."

They drank indolently, dawdling. Fanning refilled the cups.

Almost ten o'clock now.

They made a pretense of walking the streets a few minutes, noticing things for each other's benefit. An easy wind blew between the buildings. By twenty-five after they were clicking across the hotel lobby with a feigned nonchalance, by twenty-five to they had the plastic card swinging from the door handle, and once more were thrashing among the bedsheets. Fanning had to admit it had occurred to him earlier that Julia might possess some hopeless aversion to sex, some dysfunction he couldn't begin to unravel, but now she came and came and came. The cords in her neck were strung like wire cables.

"Oh, no more, no more," she said. "Have a fucking heart. I'm *finished.*"

But, actually, there was a little more yet. Then they gave each other the gift of unconsciousness.

Fanning scissor-kicked up through gradations of blue water, breaking into spangled sunlight. He swept his hand through the sheets. Cool, vacant. He opened his eyes. Julia was in the fuchsia robe again, slouched at the table, bare feet splayed on the chair opposite. She was smoking. Fanning watched patiently. She'd broken off the filter this time, he noticed. She exhaled reluctantly, stubbed out the last three-quarters of an inch and sat white-knuckling the chair's arms as if she might suddenly be catapulted into space. She swiveled abruptly and fired a look toward the bed. Fanning raised his fingers in a salute. She came and sat by him. She said, "That earlier ciga-rette, that was the next-to-last one."

Fanning said he'd guessed as much. He ran his hands up inside the sleeves of the robe. "You're lost in there," he said.

She looked him in the eye, allowing the insides of her forearms to be stroked. "And don't try to find me, either," she said.

Fanning drew her down and kissed her.

"I taste lousy," she said.

Fanning said he could barely tolerate it.

"I'm not ready for this," Julia said. "Physically. I'm sore."

"I don't want you to be sore."

She lowered her head against his chest, and they rested and neither spoke.

"I wasn't ready myself," Fanning said then. "I had no idea about this."

Julia wriggled forward and lifted up, letting the halves of the robe part. She brought a nipple to his lips. She said, "Just for a minute, okay? Just with your teeth a little."

"You're going to get into trouble," Fanning said.

She told him hush.

Fanning used his teeth a little. Through her breast he felt the curvature of rib bones and the gaps between the bones, and when he shifted to the other side he felt her heartbeat, a hard slow thudding.

"*Stop now,*" she said, and rolled onto her back and flattened the nipples with her own fingertips as if to deaden the sensation, the way you'd squeeze a fresh burn.

Fanning's breath caught, watching her.

He bent and kissed the backs of her hands, one then the other. Slowly, she let them fall away.

This time, no sleeping. Fanning planted his feet on the floor and contemplated the act of standing. He looked back at Julia.

"You hungry?" he asked. "You must be."

She made a gesture with her head.

"That yes or no?"

"I can't move," she said. "They're going to have to wheel me out of here on a hand truck."

Fanning smiled and looked away.

After a while he went into the bathroom and took a gargantuan leak, then ran the shower, soaped up, and stood grasping the shower pipe, letting the water beat on his forehead and run down.

He came out wearing a towel. Julia lay in the same position, but he knew at once her mood had turned. He located his things and dressed, taking his time, giving her as much solitude as he could. Finally, he sat on the bed and tried to engage her eyes.

"Let's go eat," he said.

"I don't think so."

He knew if he pushed she'd be gone. "Look at me," he said quietly.

She said, "Miles—"

"No," Fanning said, "I can't go yet. We can eat and then I'll drop you off and you can be by yourself tonight. That's my best offer."

And how reluctantly he made it. The single most erotic day of his life. Blindsidingly so. He expected the spell to wear off, wouldn't it have to? But it was on him hard now. He couldn't bear to be apart from her.

"Goddamn it," she said.

"I know."

She was weeping.

He blotted her cheek with the corner of the sheet, then with his thumb. "Come on," he said, "throw some clothes on and let's eat something."

So Fanning coaxed her into leaving the room with him, and they went in his car to a restaurant—as it happened, a little Italian place. No squid on the menu, though. Fanning had

never had a bad meal here, nor anything but the most cordial
discourse with the waiters, who were, by and large, middle-
aged Italian men of great solicitude.

He discussed the food with her, he talked in a relaxed
way about the recording projects awaiting him. He made no
direct reference to these past hours. He didn't even know
how to think of them yet himself—the gaudy pounding
physicality, the low comedy, or what veins of meaning they
held beyond that, twisting back as they did to a seventeen-
year-old girl, presumed dead. His instinct was to rehash it,
detail by detail, but he'd lose her in a heartbeat. She was
already beginning to retreat, and it would be the retreat into
work. The black case holding the laptop would be unzipped
before he'd set foot in the Hospitality Suite again. There'd
be no e-mail enlivening his screen for a time, no phone
sounding at the odd hour. He understood this with a razor-
like clarity. He hoped she wouldn't be in for a fresh bout of
insomnia, but that was out of his hands. He hoped to God it
would be temporary, this backing away, hoped that when he
saw her again, whenever it was, he'd not find her more
deeply shellacked.

Later, in the car, she declined his offer to be walked into
the Queensbury.

Fanning nodded. He picked up her hand and ran it finger
by finger across his lips. "Safe travel," he said, letting go.

"Yes, thank you." She reached down for her purse, turned
to the door, but stopped and swiveled on the seat, stretched up
and kissed him on the mouth, on his cheeks, on the mouth
again, and then she was gone.

It was early enough that someone might be working in
one of the studios, so Fanning made his entrance with a certain stealth, then undressed again in the sanctity of his room.
He reclined the futon to its sleep position and lay in what
passed for darkness, unable to get comfortable. The futon

seemed an exercise in asceticism, chaff-filled, a penitent's bed, but Fanning felt like no penitent. He could ring her room, of course, he could still do that, but he rolled onto his side after a while, flopped the pillow over in search of a spot not yet fogged by his breath, and, against the odds, slept.

12

NOT TWO WEEKS later, Kyra called the Hospitality Suite. Just shy of the four months. Fanning packed and went home.

It was his home, after all. Weymouth Street.

A night neither drenched in hoopla, nor freighted with declarations. Kyra had made a nice supper, medallions of beef, costly out-of-season asparagus. They sat opposite, conversing, slowly eating. Kyra watched him and he her. She said, "It's like you've been on safari."

"You have no idea," Fanning replied, half-smiling.

She said how strange, not to be beside him at the Solstice concert. "It was good?"

"Everyone missed you," Fanning said.

The talk would start, the debriefing, yet not this night. Kyra had cropped off the great braid—her hair was in a tousled, chin-length cut with white-gold highlights. Fanning asked if she'd ribboned off the ends of the braid and saved it in a box. She gave him a curious smile, as if remembering a story from the far reaches of girlhood.

"But you don't mind this," she said.

"You'd look lovely in a crewcut," Fanning answered.

He rose and carried away their plates. Kyra followed him to the kitchen and brought back dessert, a pale lemon chiffon bordered by mocha-filled pastries. They ate and gossiped and let the food settle, then left the dessert dishes where they lay and went upstairs, Fanning and his wife.

As Fanning watched from the bed, Kyra stepped from the bathroom in a ribbed tank top and silky drawers. She dispensed with these and slid atop him, lit by the streetlight slanting through the louvers. "It's been forever," she said. "I didn't think I'd miss this so much." She put her mouth to his. Fanning ran his hands up and down her flanks. Fourteen days had elapsed since he'd last glimpsed Julia Lamoreaux, nor had a word passed between them. *That* talk would start again, too, but these next minutes Fanning gave in to his wife's immediacy. He maneuvered her so that the weight of her breast tumbled into his wide open palm. He hefted it, let it tumble again, feeling no less than traitorous.

When they rested it was all of ten-thirty. Beginning to chill, Fanning drew up the quilt.

Kyra said, "I can't believe you wouldn't want to know what was in my card. And don't go, *What card?*"

"You were testing me," he said.

"Of course I was."

"I decided leaving it alone was the right answer."

"There wasn't a right answer."

He asked what she'd written.

"Nope. You're never going to know."

"Just tell me."

She realigned her body alongside his, facing out.

Fanning idled his hand on her stomach. "Okay, I'll never know then."

She put him off a few moments longer, then said, "It wasn't that complicated, Miles. I said, *If you've come because you miss me, or us, if you think this is a lousy plan then just move back*

now. We can straighten things out another way. Words to that
effect. I was feeling like I'd railroaded you."

"And how did you know I'd been here?"

No answer to this.

Fanning took it to mean she just knew.

They showered together in the morning. Kyra left for work
first, as was their old pattern, then Fanning drove to the studio. No one mentioned his living arrangements. All the same,
people seemed to have gotten the word—there might as well
have been a reader board posted in the anteroom: BOSS
RETURNS HOME. He asked not to be disturbed and shut himself
in his office and fired up some liner-note copy he'd been
laboring over. Gloria found reason to barge in not ten minutes
later. Fanning barked at her, then immediately begged for-
giveness.

"You want to be left alone, I leave you alone," she said.
Banged the door on her way out.

"I hadn't lived by myself since before Billy," Kyra said. She
was on the corduroy sectional, cross-legged, wearing a long
white shirt and possibly the same black tights he'd seen strag-
gled out on the bedroom floor that day. "I thought the solitude would be useful. I suppose it was in some ways—I
tended to things, in *myself,* and, you know, took care of little
projects. Brought work home. But some nights I did
absolutely nothing, went straight from my office clothes to
my pj's. Total sloth." She seemed to be smiling, but the new
haircut made her face harder to read. "Actually," she said,
"I'm not that fond of solitude."

"You never were," Fanning said. "You're happier out in
the middle of things."

"I am, that's true." She looked at Fanning. "But what about you?" she said. "You haven't said anything. You worked the entire time, didn't you? You spent about two minutes thinking about us."

Fanning refused this bait. "I have to admit it's been hectic down there," he said. "We wrapped up *The Iron Dog Suite*."

"Do I know that one?"

"I guess you wouldn't. But it's excellent work. There's nothing much to compare it to. Heavy on the percussion. I can bring a tape home if you want."

Kyra leaned forward and lay her hand on the cushion, palm up, so Fanning would place his on it. He did. "Four months was too long," she said.

Fanning nodded.

"Let's not try that stunt again."

"No."

He waited for her to say, "Do you mean that, Miles? Will you *please* convince me?" But in his absence she'd apparently reached her own decision: to take him as he was, not to demand what wasn't in his nature to supply. And it had come with a price, had cost her some of her native optimism. Fanning found himself stricken by an affection for her, a fresh admiration. She slid over and kneaded the back of his skull where his neck aches always began. He let his head tip forward, let himself be ministered to. All the same, he knew what he felt was too small, lacked weight, ballast— without knowing quite when, he'd become a counterfeit husband. He feared that this wisdom was tattooed across his face, that despite her new approach to him, he'd look up and she'd recoil . . . *What is it? For Christ's sake, Miles? Don't do this to me.* But she squeezed his hand then slipped hers away, said she needed to finish up in the kitchen and left him on the couch. Fanning watched her go.

*   *   *

On the fourth night they made love again. It was pouring out-side, the needle-clogged gutters sending splashes of water onto the slats of the balcony. So commonplace a sound when he lived here, but he'd forgotten—he stopped what he was doing, raised his head to listen. Kyra said, "What is it, Miles?" letting her nails skate slowly down his back. "Just the rain," he said. He could barely see her—it was darker tonight, the blinds cranked all the way shut. When he began again, he found he'd wilted a little—he adjusted his angle, moved with a greater urgency, but this failed to help. The one thing willpower is powerless over. Kyra rocked against him another minute or two, then quit.

"Did you already—?"

"No," Fanning said. "But here, let me just—"

Kyra rose onto one elbow and Fanning nearly slithered out of her. "Four days and you're already sick of me," she said.

Fanning reached through the dim light and found the side of her face. "Don't say that," he said. "Okay?" He brushed his knuckles across her cheek, smoothed back her hair. "Maybe we're just rushing things. Isn't that possible?"

He felt the muscles in her thighs contract, keeping him in place. "You want to try again?" she said.

"If you do," he said.

"It's not me that has the problem."

Fanning held her, listening to the rain, feeling her exhala-tions on his skin. He started again, small movements, small movements at first, and then after a minute he was better, he was okay again.

Toward morning he woke. Kyra was still in her monolithic night sleep. He had a picture in his mind, not so much a dream as an image crystallized out of the murk of returning consciousness: Carly on a sorrel horse, bareback, with Julia behind, arms locked about Carly's waist, cheek flat against the hollow between her shoulder blades. Not in a paddock, but along some grassy-centered lane bordered by sumac and wild grape, both girls in flannel shirts and jeans, red tennis shoes for Julia, laces dangling. Nothing he'd ever seen in life—he'd never even watched Carly ride. He'd toured the stables with her once, but there'd not been time for anything more that day. And the thought of Julia up on some horse—

But it hung on all day as Fanning worked, this picture. Late afternoon, the rain reduced to mist, he threw on his coat and climbed to the roof above the studio and stood looking off at the mouth of the Duwamish, the orange cranes swinging their loads of freight in the container yards, the traffic thickening on the expressway south. The more he thought about it, the more the grassy lane seemed to be the one that had skirted the hedgerow behind his parents' house. The horse was walking, unhurried, *clomp, clomp,* Carly with a light grip on its mane, its shadow and the shadow of the girls briefly darkening patches of the hedgerow's underbrush as it went along.

Not that night, which passed uneventfully, a fair replica of old evenings around home, but the next, Fanning said he had something to tell Kyra. They were in the kitchen, the butcher block between them, the supper cleanup almost finished. She turned a sharp, immediate gaze on him.

The timing was bad, Fanning said, couldn't be poorer, but he needed to go out of town on business.

"When's this?"

"Monday."

Kyra frowned outright. "You just got here, Miles. Where to?"

Boston, Fanning explained, not saying that only this afternoon had he grabbed up the phone and made the reservations, without even informing Gloria.

"You never go to Boston."

Fanning agreed, it had been a while.

"Can't it *wait*?"

"If it could wait I wouldn't be going," he said, not meaning to sound so argumentative. "It won't be that long. Only a few days."

Kyra studied him, tucking the short hair behind one ear. "I could get time off," she said. "I've put in God's own amount of extra hours."

Fanning said it wasn't that kind of trip, he was booked up solid, he just didn't think it would work out terribly well.

Kyra seemed equal parts sadness and defiance. "Okay," she said. "I get the picture, Miles."

Fanning might've tried to put her at ease, might've insisted there was no picture to get, and so on, but he couldn't do it. Instead he said he was sorry, which was true enough— sorry for having become so abject a liar, sorry for all that would follow, but he was acting on behalf of an instinct that refused to be put off.

Sunday night, Fanning went upstairs to pack. A couple of minutes later, Kyra came into the bedroom, kicked off her moccasins, cocked her head to take out an earring, but the instant it became clear Fanning meant to reach his bag from the storage rack, she left and stayed gone until he'd clicked the latches on the suitcase and slid it out of sight, only then returning. She took off her clothes in front of him with no great care, as if her nakedness weren't a concern of his any longer, finally saying into the mirror, "Why didn't you just stay away? Why'd you even bother—?" then crossing to the bathroom, leaving the door open as she brushed her teeth and ran a washcloth around her face, only disappearing from Fanning's view as she sat to use the toilet, and then she was flapping the covers back on her side of the bed, getting in, saying, "You could've opened the card, Miles. I can't believe you just took one look at it and strolled off. What a perfect example—"

Fanning stood looking down at her, his remorse compromised by the wish that he could head to Sea-Tac this very minute and not have to wait until morning. Would you forget the card? he said, he wasn't discussing the goddamned card anymore. When he got back they'd talk, they'd talk when he got back.

13

FROM 37,000 FEET, Fanning could view both shores of Lake Erie. They were snow-laden, and on the lake trailed the short white wakes of commercial haulers working late on a February afternoon. In one sweep, he saw the home ground of both sides of his family—his father's, east of Cleveland in those square townships laid out when it was a frontier called the Western Reserve, and almost directly across the water, farm country as well, the town of Port Dover, Ontario, where his mother had been born, daughter of a schoolteacher who emigrated to Genesse County, Michigan. But for generations, the Austins had farmed in Port Dover or Simcoe or York, having fled Pennsylvania in the 1790s, Empire Loyalists. Or such was the story, what Fanning knew of it.

In the aftermath of his father's death had come a frenzy of wading through file cabinets and cartons of woefully outdated tax returns and elastic-sheathed folders. It was the only time Fanning ever saw his dignified Canadian mother lose control, those weeks before the absolute fact of her widowhood set its hook, when she was wanton in shedding things, banishing them from her sight before their worth was established, which cast Fanning in the unlikely role of preserver, conservator. For the most part, he found papers that *could* be trashed, documents that had outlived any conceivable interest to anyone. "Your father was an incorrigible pack rat," his mother said. "You should know this about him, Miles, and let me tell you another truth: A person can't keep everything, do you understand? You simply can't hold on to every single thing. You have to make *room*. That's the nature of life, like it or not." So Fanning skimmed papers like a maniac, salvaging this and that, no longer holding anything up for her verdict, because this never varied: "No, for pity's sake, pitch it." What about his father's LPs? "Take them if you want," she said. "I'll never listen to all that. I don't even know if the turntable works anymore." So Fanning boxed them, had them shipped to Seattle. Then, beginning not many months later, and continuing to this day, Fanning would be called at work: What had become of such and such, some critical piece of evidence the tax man needed pronto, or all the clippings from his parents' *wedding*, pasted into a scrapbook with a bluish cover, white script, certainly that wouldn't have been thrown out, and on and on, consternation and disbelief in her voice. Fanning had come to recognize its sound instantly. He'd learned to say, "No, I'm sure it'll turn up, it's probably in the attic—" not reminding her of how she'd been. And sometimes things did resurface, but, for the most part, they did not.

In one clasp envelope Fanning had found his great-grandfather Fanning's discharge papers from the Civil War (Fanning had been named in the man's honor, though no one ever called the original Miles "Miles"—it was M.P. or simply Boss. He'd invented a device to keep the journal boxes of railroad cars from overheating, founded a company to manufacture it, made a respectable bundle, spent it down, and was left behind by the times). But in this same packet were five sheets of stapled onionskin paper, the carbon of a speech, hand-corrected in pencil, that M.P. had delivered to a school class in East

Cleveland on 29 May 1905, Decoration Day oratory on the topic of the War Between the States. This Fanning had saved and read and photocopied for himself, and could not help but think of now, as the plane made its way east in the diminishing light. The opening was a great wad of patriotic bombast, not uncommon for its day, Fanning imagined, Teddy Roosevelt's America. He forgave it and read on. Three times, M.P. had run off, underaged, to fight for the Union, and was twice sent home. He talked of his father rising at family prayer and saying the men who bought and sold human beings must not be allowed to murder John Brown at Harper's Ferry, and of his own grandfather helping convey runaway slaves to boats so they might cross the dangerous lake water to the sanctuary of Ontario, and of being taken by his father to Painesville, Ohio, February 1861, to watch Abraham Lincoln pass in a train car on the way to his swearing in as President. Then the depictions of battle, notably Missionary Ridge and Chickamauga, M.P.'s salute to comrades taken by minié ball or sepsis in makeshift field hospitals, then another flourish of rhetorical finery in the closing. Yet, Fanning thought he heard the man himself here, transcending the boilerplate, still virulently antislavery after the passage of forty years, and truly sad in his heart on this mainly ceremonial occasion, surrounded by bored schoolchildren.

Fanning stared out the nicked plastic of the plane window. Niagara Falls came and went, bronzed, striated by shadow. He lowered the shade and tilted his head back, still hazily imagining his forebears, those few he knew by name, and the others, pair by pair, gone like landmarks on the ground below him. Yet again, he asked himself what he thought he was doing, plunging into a trip like this, replayed the last disheartening exchanges with Kyra, tried to goad his doubts off center stage. He'd had the option of flying directly to Hartford, but it would've meant a switch in Chicago or Detroit or Kennedy, or else a commuter flight down from Boston, and so he had chosen the nonstop to Logan, believing he'd rather drive the remaining distance, even if it made a hellish long day, believing he'd rather immerse himself in the place at a speed he could control. When he checked the window again, there were stars, and he felt in the plane's tilt, the first intimations of descent.

Short of midnight, Fanning took a room along the highway. In the morning he stepped outside to broken clouds and wafts of air that later in the day would be well above freezing. He unfolded a road map against the steering wheel of the rental car, studied it perhaps longer than necessary. Hartford itself he had no desire to see: the Civic Center, the streets and alleyways in its proximity. He backed the car around and headed in the direction of Clarion. The day following a day on the plane was never fun—he'd have a neck ache that needed medicating, plus a cohort of obscure muscles that had seized up overnight, the arches of his feet, for instance. But, in fact, he'd slept well, without preamble or interruption, and nothing hurt, even the neck—it produced its customary ground-glass sound as he checked the traffic over his shoulder, but that was all. He stopped for coffee to go and drove on. He'd lived in the West long enough that the gentle roll of the terrain always struck him when he returned, the profligacy of the hardwoods, even now, as bare-limbed as if it were their inverted root systems he saw. And the hedgerows, and the stone walls along the secondary roads, swarmed over with leafless poison ivy vines. He made a turn that shunted him away from the downtown of Clarion—he had no desire to see that either, except possibly Julia's old high school with its "deco touches," but for all he knew it had been given over to the wrecking ball by now. He crossed into New Albany, where he'd been just once, to the best of his recollection.

Carly had directed him to the church building that day.

He had no clue where it was now, nor did he feel like stopping to ask. He drove, hoping it would present itself. Snow had drifted into the gullies and against the windward side of barns and sheds, but it was old snow, and there'd been a serious thaw recently. Along the roadside were hunks of muddy sod wedged up by snowplows, and in the south-facing fields patches of furrowed ground. Fanning tried the bottom end of the radio dial, located a Chopin étude, one of the less showy, more contemplative ones—it prefigured Erik Satie's "Gymnopédies," he thought—but he found it too forlorn this morning and after a minute he switched it off. He saw subdivisions carved from hayfields, yet not so many. The countryside seemed less built-up, less worked-over than he might've imagined. He turned the car at random, looking, expectant. He passed a filling station, then an antique dealer's, where he could've gotten directions. He came to an unmarked T in the road and sat twisting his hands on the top of the wheel, staring into a growth of scrub pine. To his left, the road rose and curved. He took that way, and there, immediately, was the church.

The snow piles edging the parking lot were shrinking back in the sun. The gravel had a soggy, unstable look. The church was white-painted and black-shuttered. Behind it lay the burying ground bordered by the spear-pointed pickets Julia had described. Fanning saw no footprints in the vestiges of snow. None coming back anyway, he thought, revisiting a joke of his father's. Fanning's was the only vehicle in the lot, and scarcely any passed on the road, one bread truck barreling along. He'd intended nothing more complex than five or ten minutes of touching base here, getting his bearings, but found himself climbing out and walking toward the grave markers. Kernels of corn snow collected along the tops of his shoes, wetting his socks. He worked the gate. Here were names he recalled from Julia's recitation: Eich, Gutschenritter. The earlier stones were slate, which accepted a finer engraving tool, the more recent ones granite. Nothing in the way of ostentation, names and dates solely. A light wind riffled the few spruce trees within the boundaries of the iron fence, and enough sunlight fell to leave stubs of shadow that would darken a moment then go pale. By and large, the names were German, as he'd been led to expect, but there was a Smith-Peterson and a Saltonstall, and some were without doubt French-Canadian, including the stone where he squatted now, which read Claude S. Lamoreaux, and its mate to the right, Henriette Lamoreaux. The grandparents, surely. Henriette had been in residence here nearly forty years longer than her husband. Childbirth or influenza, Fanning thought, staring off, resting his hand on the stone.

He was not a frequenter of boneyards, a browser, a tracer of inscriptions. Excluding the day of the service, asquirm on a folding chair, woozy, sweating uncontrollably in the greenish light cast by the temporary canopy, he'd been only once to the vast Florida necropolis that housed his own father's remains, and on that occasion he'd lingered no more than five minutes regarding the raised copper-toned lettering on the nameplate lying flush with the cropped St. Augustine grass. The open lawns were sun-blanched, and under the pines the ground quivered with vague shadows, but overall it was a somber, dispiriting spot, and Fanning was left with the clear understanding that his father wasn't there. If people wanted to perk up the gravesites with cut flowers or plastic pinwheels, if they wanted to talk down at the earth as if a loved one were paying rapt attention, that was their business. Fanning never went back. Nor was the day rendered a whit more transcendent by the discovery, moments later, that he'd locked his keys in the car, which necessitated a series of phone calls back at the facility's office, a two-hour wait for a representative of the rental car firm, and Fanning's having to again stand adjacent to his father's plot, this time making small talk while the proper master key was located.

Fanning bent and fingered the snow from his shoes. He'd given no particular thought to Simon's whereabouts. Given her anger, Mitzi could've done just about anything with him. The stones nearest Claude and Henriette were contemporaries of theirs, non-Lamoreauxs. Fanning meandered toward the backmost railing, scanning, stepping where the snow was thinnest. Only then, just as he thought: *No, enough of this horsing around*, and was about to backtrack, did he find himself at the block of mica-flecked rock belonging to Julia's father. It sat low to the ground, beveled where it bore the name. After a time, Fanning thought to wonder about Mitzi herself. This far corner was lightly populated, allowing room enough either side of Simon for a companion, but Fanning, kneeling now, clearing the snow with his hands, then sweeping in broad strokes with both arms, on the off chance a marker lay flush to the ground as his father's did, ascertained that Mitzi had left other instructions.

He stood again, catching his breath, brushing off his sleeves, sadness on Simon's behalf beginning to well up unbidden, and he might have stood there longer, letting it have its way with him, but a car veered off the road and churned up the rutted incline and parked noisily in the lot alongside his. A smallish station wagon, mud-spattered.

Fanning watched the occupant get out. A man, on the short side, hatless, wearing a lightweight parka. Fanning took a last look at the silver water collected in the letters of *Simon Claude Lamoreaux*, then began to make his way back across the snow. By now the man had spotted him—he waited at the corner of the building, one hand shielding his eyes.

"Thawing," Fanning said, drawing close.

The man agreed that it was.

Fanning introduced himself.

"Marvin Biggs," the man said.

They shook hands and went around toward the front steps, and it was now Fanning saw what he'd failed to notice when he'd arrived, sure that providence had delivered him to the proper doorstep. The sign read not THE MESSIAH CHURCH, but THE HOLY GOSPEL FELLOWSHIP, MARVIN BIGGS, PASTOR. Fanning had been readying himself to explain what he'd been doing out back, but this new information halted him in his tracks. He wondered, momentarily, if the church had simply altered its name, but this was all wrong—just looking at Biggs, you knew he was cut off a wholly different bolt.

Fanning toed the softened earth. He said, "I have a friend who used to come here."

"One of the Messiahs."

Fanning nodded.

Biggs said, "We bought the building in '88. I guess that would make it ten years this coming fall. They'd pretty much petered out by then."

Fanning shook his head again.

"You hate to see a congregation come to that," Biggs said, but before Fanning could summon any appreciation for Biggs's ecumenicism, he went on, "They were an odd bunch, I'll tell you that straight out. Not what I'd think of as true Christians, to be perfectly frank. Rudderless. Not steered by the Word."

"Well, there's different ways, I suppose," Fanning offered.

Biggs looked him in the eye and said with a gleeful ferocity, "We at the Fellowship believe in the One Way, Mr. Fanning." But he was smiling, apparently glad for the company. He sorted through his keys for the one to the building's main door, asked Fanning if he cared to have a peek inside.

Fanning thought of the benches and straight-backed chairs arrayed in their circle, and of the small raised area on which a speaker might stand, and of the whitewashed walls unblemished by representations. He thought of Simon suddenly springing from his seat at the Christmas service, next to which, regrettably, an extra chair had been left, his fleeing the room in long, board-creaking strides, seeking air.

"Guess I'll pass," Fanning said. "I'm sure you've livened it up a bit."

Biggs smiled. "Oh, you could say that," he said. "Oh yes. It's a good deal brighter. Not to mention the baseboard heating."

Fanning said, "You didn't happen to know the Lamoreauxs?"

Biggs said afraid not.

Fanning rooted his hands in his trouser pockets. "You wouldn't know what became of any of the Messiahs?" he asked.

"Can't say I do," Biggs answered. "There weren't but a few of those people left, and that was, well, some time ago now."

Fanning nodded. But after a moment he asked, "Would there have been any names on the deed?"

Biggs said, to be honest, his church had gotten the building for back taxes.

"I didn't think churches paid tax," Fanning said.

Biggs said actually he'd streamlined the story just a bit—the property had first fallen into the hands of private owners, a young couple, and it was they who'd defaulted. He didn't think any of the Messiah names would be involved—besides which the deed currently resided in a safety deposit box over in Clarion.

Fanning said, "Well, no need to trouble with that, then." He stuck out his hand again and Biggs shook it.

"You found who it was you were looking for out there," Biggs said.

Fanning said yes, thank you, he had.

"Feel free to come see us any time," Biggs said.

Fanning thanked the man.

Crossing the gravel lot, he debated going back and asking Biggs for directions to Clarion, but didn't want to, and then remembered being in his father's car with Carly, hearing her as he'd let his foot off the brake at the bottom of the hill: "No, *left,*" poking him, "don't you have any sense of *direction?*" And though she was teasing, they still barely knew each other, hadn't yet kissed—Fanning had felt a quick rush of embarrassment or keen disappointment in himself, all out of proportion with the moment, but the car had a bench seat, and Carly scooted over and rode only inches to his right, as if they'd already logged hours and hours of road time together, and when she fed him the rest of the directions, it was with a fond matter-of-factness that put him at ease. If there was a moment he'd begun to love her, you might as well say it was then, though why he'd not remembered it until now was baffling. In any case, faced with the same choice, he again turned left, gunned the engine and drove. The blacktop was sandy, nearly dry, undulating with the terrain. He remembered none of the other turns, and for all he knew was getting royally lost, but inside of fifteen minutes he found himself at a stop sign abutting a more substantial thoroughfare, and as he waited for the traffic to clear, he squinted across at a vestigial road marker, a thin spire of pebbly concrete on which was bolted an enameled plate that read, vertically, Old Post Road.

His mind's eye was fixed on the barn with its eight-sided cupola. Then he pictured himself in the midday dusk of the house's wraparound porch, explaining, and asking permission to have a quick look at the premises, wondering if he'd be taken for a man with ordinary sentimental motives, or a more complex, possibly sinister agenda. He was lost in such rumination, when, sailing by a pair of newer, sherbet-colored Cape Cods, he was suddenly upon, then past, the Lamoreauxs' old driveway. It was tarred now, and the giant maples along the road were disorientingly absent, even the stumps. He braked and yanked the car to the shoulder and stared. Without question, it was the right place. Where those new houses had gone

up there'd been an acre or so of weedy grass, too rocky for
Simon's mowing tractor, giving way to a stand of popple Fanning could remember leafing out that spring. The plum trees
along the side of the Lamoreaux house were missing, too,
replaced by neatly spaced evergreens and a split-rail fence—
in fact, now that he looked, the whole property had been gone
over by professional landscapers. You had to expect change,
only fools didn't—Fanning found himself chagrined to have
been so caught by surprise. But that was minor, that was small
spuds. Here was the true shock: no barn. You could see where
the ground still rose, an incline broad enough for a double
team of thick-legged horses to drag up hay wagon or sledge,
but the cellar hole had been filled and there on the plateau
stood a two-car garage, equipped with an upstairs, loft doors,
and so on, a decent-sized structure. Even so, it looked puny in
the space vacated by Simon Lamoreaux's barn.

Fanning made a U-turn, drove up to the house, braked by
the junipers. He climbed the porch steps and put his finger to
the bell and waited, but understood at once that the speech
he'd rehearsed would not be required. Everyone worked
these days, no one was left home making egg custards or ginger snaps on a Tuesday afternoon. He didn't bother peering
into the front room. He stepped off into the side yard and
studied the upstairs window he knew to have been Carly's,
not caring that he left tracks, then circled around and identi-
fied Julia's room, and thought of her with her elbows parked
on the sill, looking out, a hot night, the attic fan drawing the
air past her damp skin. He took the liberty of sitting on the
back steps a while, studying the barn's absence with a
renewed sense of disbelief, finally hauling himself up and
walking toward it. At least, the retaining wall was still
there—near-round cobbles compliments of the last ice age,
stacked five high, blotched by lichen the color of dried tan-
gerine rind. He saw Julia mashing out her smoke on one of
these very rocks as Simon talked, as Simon continued his

seduction of her, which was not, of course, a seduction of the body. He saw her bare heels dug in.

Fanning looked off. Before him lay an expanse of uncorrupted hayfield, then a skyline serrated by pinetops. How much of this land had once belonged to Simon he didn't know, but it couldn't matter less now, who'd owned what. A high gauze of cloud had come with the early afternoon, and though the day had yet to cool, those shafts of sun were gone. Would he have entered the barn, found an angle from which to view the open space beneath the cupola? It hadn't been a conscious part of his intention, but maybe he would have, maybe the temptation would've been too potent to ignore. Out on the Post Road a vehicle slowed, catching Fanning's ear. He straightened, prepared to be caught trespassing. But it was nothing—a truck downshifting, gears lugging. Nonetheless, Fanning removed his hand from the wall and retraced his steps to the rented Ford and got in. What an undertaking to make a barn disappear—think of the timbers, twelve-by-twelves at least, all those struts and the dense floor planks with their raised knots and forged, square-headed spikes. Think of the stalls, and the manure chutes and the twin lofts, the ten thousand roof shakes. Nothing you'd enter into lightly, a demolition like that. The funny thing was, Fanning thought, lingering out in plain view now, the engine idling, the funny thing was he didn't *need* to walk around inside it, gawking. He could see the barn's interior with a freakish clarity—he wrote this off to the zeal of Julia's storytelling, but knew that wasn't the whole of it. He'd been all through the barn with Carly—and not on that first weekend, either, because a new comfort had existed between them, and, outside, clumps of snow weighted the tree limbs, but the sky was cloudless, fathomless, which meant it was the drive he'd made to Clarion during Christmas week, when he hand-delivered the bracelet in its square white box from Rice's Jewelers in Fitchburg. So he'd actually seen with his own eyes the tool-

heavy room where Simon and his remaining daughter had
cut the fresh panes for the cupola, and now he remembered
Carly hoisting herself onto the work bench and swinging her
legs as she told him about the draft horses that had wintered
here years and years past—though Fanning lived in the country himself he couldn't have been more ignorant on the subject of livestock. He listened generously, in love with her
mouth, its guileless display of knowledge. They both wore
heavy jackets and Carly had on headgear he guessed you'd
call a tam. It was just cold enough for her breath to show. She
told him about the thoroughbreds she currycombed after
their exercise in the summers, her routine at the stable, the
discrepancy in temperament from one horse to the next, even
those sharing a dam and sire. And so on, Carly talking and
Fanning drinking it up, relaxed enough with her physically to
stroke the knees of her jeans, and finally she'd thrown her
arms around his neck and said, "Help me down, Miles," and
wrapped her legs around his hips, and he stepped back, letting her slide down. They'd walked then to the barn's main
concourse, where an oblong of sunlight fell on the knobby
oil-spotted floorboards. Carly stepped into it suddenly and
they kissed, Fanning bending over, for she was no more than
five-four, the coats bulking between them, but a fine long kiss
nonetheless. And then what? Eventually, they'd have had to
abandon the barn and rejoin the Lamoreauxs. Was he invited
for supper before the drive home? He had no memory of it, no
memory of the Lamoreaux house spruced up for the holidays,
of Julia slinking around in the background. How had he
treated this new knowledge—that he loved, was himself
loved? Because even if he was only just beginning to know, he
knew. By that night, there was a difference, a recognition. But
had he driven up toward Worcester and home with the radio
thumping, slapping his free hand on the wheel or punching
the buttons, impatient for a better song, or had it made him
want to shut the damn radio off so he could think, so he could

relive her lips on his lips, his mouth on the line of her jawbone and the warm skin where it disappeared into her turtleneck, and run through the sequence of words she'd spoken at
the car window before he'd had to break away? Or had he
treated it with less care than it deserved? Not exercising the
cool sexual disdain of some boys—Fanning wasn't like that.
But maybe he'd merely pocketed this new fact and headed
north, letting his mind roam.

He drove again.

Except for coffee, he'd put nothing in his stomach since a
raisin bagel at the motel, and half of that he'd left behind on
the Styrofoam plate. He was legitimately hungry now, hungry in a gnawing almost menacing way, but was of no mind to
do anything about it. Nor could he say what he expected of
this driving around Clarion and its neighboring towns. The
sun had just now sunk into a shelf of clouds that looked as
though it might reach to the Great Lakes. In minutes, the
light was sallow and Fanning drove toward Hartford, until he
began to see signs for the larger motel chains, and abruptly
pulled in and took a room. He shut its door behind him, hung
up his coat, and stared at the expanse of bed, frozen, almost
panicked with indecision, then lay down, shoes on, and
though it was only ten past five in the afternoon, he slept.
When he woke it was after seven. In his sleep he'd twisted the
bedspread up around himself. He had that thought he sometimes allowed himself, that had been known to provide a certain sly comfort: *No one on earth knows where I am.* But he
found it sour and disturbing now, and forcibly he unwound
himself from the bedcovers and stood and turned on more
lights and knew that for God's sake he had to eat something
before the jitters set in. So Fanning ate in the dining room
attached to his motel, alone in an overpadded booth, first
drinking a glass of scotch, then a second, unhurried, with his

slab of prime rib, an end piece nobody but he seemed to trea-
sure. He cut the meat, lathered it with a horseradish having
the spunk of smelling salts, and gradually found his wits
restored.

Back in the room, he pulled out a legal tablet and made a
list of surnames he recollected from the Messiah graveyard,
trying to remember if Julia had mentioned others, but could
add no more. He wasn't quite sure what he was after—someone else's memory of Simon, or Carly, or Julia, that might
lead him . . . he couldn't say where. Maybe it was the looking
itself that mattered most. He lifted out the city phone directory on the slim hope that its territory included Clarion or
New Albany, but from the map it appeared to stop just short.
Fanning consulted his tablet, picked Gutschenritter, which he
took to be the most obscure of the names. He spoke with
directory assistance. But there was no Gutschenritter in Clarion or New Albany or any of the small towns adjacent. He
thought to try the Greater Hartford book now, and down
below a slew of Gutierrezes, amazingly, there were three such
names, and before his resolve failed, he dialed the first, D., got
the voice mail of a woman he judged to be in her twenties,
and left a bare-bones message. He turned to the next: Helmut. Helmut was likewise unavailable, but had no answering
machine. The phone rang and rang, and Fanning finally let
the receiver settle back into its cradle, wrote *N/A* after the
man's name. He tried the third, William F. William F.'s
teenaged son answered as if he'd been camped waiting for
another call, but sounded like a decent sort, a talker by nature.
The father ran a muffler shop, which was where he was now,
and wouldn't be home before ten-thirty at the earliest, but he,
the son, could assure Fanning that the whole family went to
Emanuel Lutheran on Capitol Avenue . . . well, the father not
every single Sunday, but pretty often, and beyond that, as far
as he knew, they'd never even been to Clarion or whatever
that other town was.

"If you don't mind my asking," Fanning said, "do you know if your family's related to any other Gutschenritters in this part of the state?"

"My dad's got a brother up in Taunton, Mass.," the boy said. "That's it. He had a sister but something happened to her before I was born. Some kind of serious illness."

Fanning thanked the boy and rang off.

He dialed the out-of-town operator again and started in on the Eichs, betting he'd have more like a dozen to deal with, but in fact there were no Eichs at all. Nearest thing was an Eichorn in Scantic.

He looked at the other names on his tablet, set his pen down, and for a number of minutes did nothing whatsoever.

It had snowed in the night. Fanning stood at the window, staring down two flights at the black rectangles in the parking lot left by the early risers, but runnels of water were beginning to course down windshields, and the cloud cover he'd taken as unimpeachable was already thinning, showing scraps of bare sky. He finished buttoning his shirt, omitted the necktie, and packed up. By ten o'clock he was in Clarion again, seated in a roadside diner, tearing hunks off an immense cinnamon roll, licking the gooey sugar from his fingers without shame. He drank his coffee and thought about the day and exempted himself from the perils of expectation. Finally he was at the till, wallet out. The waitress said had she been a betting woman she'd have put money on his not being up to it, cleaning his plate.

Fanning smiled. She had maybe a couple of years on Fanning, hair permed into auburn ringlets tight to the skull, and her accent was the same one Julia turned on him when she so chose. Fanning said it kind of surprised him, too. He pushed a dollar back across the counter. "You didn't know a family name of Lamoreaux?" he asked. "Out on the Post Road?"

"Doesn't ring bells."

Fanning nodded. They were virtually alone in the place and he might've freshened her memory a little, referred to Carly as that girl who went missing in Hartford, way back, you must remember that . . . but he refrained.

"There's a mess of LaBontys," the waitress said. "But you don't even *want* to know that crew."

Fanning said never mind, it was just a shot. He thanked her the way he'd thanked Biggs the day before, then was driving again, sugar-buzzed, his lower abdomen beginning to cramp, but for all that, his spirits had been leavened overnight. He found himself recognizing turns in the road, a parked yellow road grader, certain lines of sight. He passed the antique dealer's whose fold-out signboard had caught his eye yesterday. FINE OLD THINGS, it said. OPEN. On impulse, he stopped. There was a foot brush by the door and he attempted to remove the mud from his walking shoes. Lost cause. He made no pretense of looking about the shop, but went directly to where the owner sat in a spring-backed wooden office chair. A man of sixty-eight or so, wearing half-lenses, reading what proved to be *Oranges* by John McPhee.

Straightaway, Fanning was asked if he wanted coffee.

Fanning explained about his recent stop at the diner.

"You put away a whole one of those, did you?" the man said. "You have my admiration and condolences."

Fanning asked if it would be correct to assume that the man had lived in this bailiwick some little while.

The man said it would.

Fanning rested his forearms atop a chest-high, gadget-stuffed display case. He asked if the man recalled the Messiah Church. "I was by there yesterday," he said. "Noticed it had changed hands."

"You were an attendee?"

Fanning said no, not himself.

The man shook his head as if they were in the early stages of negotiation over the price of a fine old thing.

Fanning picked at the corners of his mouth for any residue of icing. "It was the Lamoreauxs I was interested in," he said at last.

The man nodded.

Fanning said, "I knew the daughters."

The springs of the man's chair made a sudden, ravenlike complaint and he stood, motioning for Fanning to follow him through a doorway into the building's back room, which had the aspect of a giant shed, tall-ceilinged, heated by two wall-mounted gas heaters, currently silent.

"That hall tree," he said to Fanning, pointing.

Fanning studied the piece. It was a dusty walnut, with the remains of some gold leaf scrolling and half a dozen ivory knobs.

"I never could get what it deserved and now it's been here so damned long I'd hate to let it go. But there was a cedar chest and a pair of nicely turned bed frames and six maple chairs with caned bottoms, a trestle table, various odds and ends. A clutch of old tools. Those items all went, one by one they did. Out the door."

A few beats slow, Fanning understood what he was looking at.

"The other daughter didn't want anything," the proprietor said. "She lived——" He made a hand motion meaning out, away.

"The San Francisco area," Fanning said.

"That would be about right, yes," the man said.

Fanning stared. "This was in that kind of foyer," he said, and the man said it was indeed. He touched Fanning's elbow and maneuvered them out front again, where there was heat and he could take a load off.

"You knew Simon," Fanning said.

"I'll go you one better," the man said. "I knew Claude

Lamoreaux. My father owned the dairy Claude worked at all those years. I remember him from when I was a boy. Simon was a wagonful of chimpanzees next to Claude. I'd watch Claude unloading the bottle racks after his route, and you could see his back was killing him, but not so much as an aspirin passed those lips. I seem to recall he'd lost his wife fairly early on. It'll turn a man dour, but Claude was dour from the womb would be my guess. He'd've come out saying: *Well, here's a tough stretch of road ahead.*"

Fanning smiled. "A Messiah," he said.

"That he was. But they weren't all that way, not to that extreme, and if you ask me, which you're not, I'll take them over this new lot any day of the week. They looked into their hearts, which isn't so bad a thing, and they tended to their own affairs. Judge not lest ye be judged."

Fanning watched the man sling the dregs from the bottom of his mug and stand to refill it. Maybe he'd take a little himself, after all, Fanning said.

The man nodded and wiped dust from a second mug with his shirttail and asked if Fanning wanted it plain or specialty of the house, which turned out to involve a bottle of Christian Brothers in the deep drawer of the rolltop desk.

Fanning said the latter, thank you. He took the cup and let the brandy fumes sear their way into his sinuses before he sipped. He said, "Here I thought it was some old solvent I'd been smelling."

Now the shop owner smiled, sitting back. "Solves what it solves," he said.

After a minute, Fanning asked how well the man had known Mrs. Lamoreaux.

"I'll tell you what," he said, "there's people who found Simon a disquieting man, just too curious a specimen to feel easeful around, but he was no great puzzle to me. The wife was another story. For all the good manners and the cheery, self-assured way she went at things . . . now understand I'm talking about the time before their trouble, but even then I had the idea I didn't know her, not more than the top sixteenth of an inch. She seemed unsettled to me, someone who had to constantly talk herself into believing she'd made the right choices. After Simon died, she lived in that place alone, gave it a good, I suppose, four years, but then she'd had enough. Came on her like a shift in the weather, I presume, and once she drove away that day I never laid eyes on her again. The pieces were on consignment and I'd send her a check in the mail, up to Boston."

Cambridge, Fanning thought. "You knew she passed away last summer," he said.

"I didn't," the man said. "I'm sorry to hear it."

After a minute, he told Fanning that once, when he was a younger man, Mitzi had drawn the blood from his arm. Down in the old high school gym. He couldn't even feel the needle prick, he said, and then confessed he never much cared for watching the blood come out and fill the bag.

Fanning said he was the same way.

After a moment he asked if Mitzi was the one who'd had the barn pulled down.

The man snorted. Perhaps he'd been waiting for Fanning to get around to this. "Not an unreasonable conclusion," he said. "Not in the slightest. But in point of fact it was the Baldings, who if you're interested bought the place off the Palmiters, who was who Mrs. Lamoreaux sold to. My impression is Mrs. Balding wanted an ordinary garage with electric door openers and the like."

"She must've wanted it a whole lot," Fanning said.

The two men stared at each other.

"You may have guessed I don't begrudge a person what he decides he needs to do," Fanning's host said. "Nowadays it's all grief counselors and get on with your life, but some things aren't gotten over, I'm sorry to report, not for some people."

Fanning nodded. Then he said he'd tried to contact some

of the Messiahs the other night, explained his abysmal lack of success. He repeated what Marvin Biggs had told him, the petering out.

"That part's true enough," the man said. He tore off the top sheet of a receipt pad and dug up a pen and wrote. When he was done he creased the paper and handed it to Fanning. "Here's who you'll want to see, but I'd give her a jingle first. Number's there."

Fanning drained his cup and set it down.

"Call from here if you want," he said. "Tell her I told you to." Fanning's first impulse was to refuse and go looking for the privacy of a pay phone, but the man grabbed his cordless from its housing and laid it on the glass case, saying Fanning would have to excuse him, he had a matter of some urgency to see to just now.

The name belonged to Mrs. Emily Schmidt and Fanning naturally assumed delicate bargaining would be in the offing, but in fact Mrs. Schmidt answered on the second ring, and interrupted him midway through his opening salvo to give him directions to the house, which proved to be less than a mile away. She said she had nothing on the docket beyond making herself a corned beef sandwich and she could as easily make two, so why didn't he just come now, if he was coming?

What could Fanning say to that?

She was perhaps the same vintage as the antique dealer, a good-sized woman, clad in corduroy trousers and checked shirt, not a woman who'd turned many heads, Fanning imagined, but she seemed robust and clear-eyed and Fanning understood he'd not need to pick through what she said for layers of motive. The Schmidt house stood at the end of a short, oak-lined lane: red brick, as modest and no-nonsense a place as he'd expected from the voice on the phone, except that a sunroom had been affixed to the south wall, actually more of a true greenhouse with caulked glass panes, Fanning saw, now that she led him down into it, into its rich humid stink of peat pots and split-leaf rhododendrons, stringy air ferns and tiers of plants he couldn't begin to name, some in early bloom. Mrs. Schmidt pointed to an old wicker settee and Fanning gratefully sat. There were the corned beef sandwiches, as promised. Dark rye, grilled, with unslivered dills. Two tumblers of root beer. She said this was the only material thing she'd ever pined for, this hothouse, and her kids had had it built for her after her husband died. She motioned for Fanning to eat. Fanning took a huge bite of sandwich and thought how there wasn't one thing about this day that had gone as he'd foreseen.

"They're awful greasy," she said, "but once in a while I can't resist. I could make myself another right this minute."

Fanning watched her go at her mouth with a cloth napkin. He went at his own, then wiped his fingers and sat back, wondering how to begin to ask what he had to ask.

But Mrs. Schmidt started in with no prompting on his part. "It's not that we couldn't see it coming," she told him. "What I considered the older generation, the old mainstays, they just pooped out one by one and wound up out back, and then it was our turn, but, Lord, I don't know, families moved—Mr. Koenig took a job with the Sanitation Department over in Providence. There was a divorce and only the wife came to meeting afterward and then she stopped. Gracie Verlag. But the real blow was the next generation, the kids, they didn't fill in the holes, so to speak. We were never a big flock to begin with, you must realize. Start with my own five if you want to. There's not one I'd trade for anything on this earth, but two left the state when they got the chance, and the ones who stayed wanted nothing further to do with the Messiah Church." She looked at Fanning directly. "There just comes a time," she said. "People's ideas change."

Fanning nodded.

She said, "Now there was some effort made at recruit-
ment, but this wasn't like joining the Rotarians. You had to
have the constitution for it. Somebody's coworker might show
up a few Sundays, but they wouldn't last. A few other strays
wandered in and some of these, if you want my honest opinion, I didn't think much of. I didn't believe they had the best
of intentions. I didn't know what they wanted from us, to be
frank. In any case, we had to close up shop. Not a happy occasion. You may have seen what's in there now."

Fanning said he had, yes.

Mrs. Schmidt shook her head.

"I suppose it doesn't matter so much," she said. "I practice
out here. I come and I sit where it's warm and green and put
my feet up and have my conversations with the Savior. A congregation of one. I sometimes cower to think what those old
Messiah men would make of me, but, you know, the point
was never to be miserable. We were not about mortification of
the flesh, Mr. Fanning. It's His sun and these here are His
growing things, and I suppose if you want to get right down
to it, it's His corned beef, too."

Fanning smiled. Before the smile fled his mouth he asked if
Mrs. Schmidt had any specific memory of Carly Lamoreaux.

"She'd be your interest here."

Fanning said it was complicated.

Mrs. Schmidt took this at face value. "Well, she was the
age of my oldest girl, Iris," she said. "I won't say they were
fast friends, but Carolyn would spend time here. One summer
they were out with butterfly nets every morning. They didn't
see so much of each other after Carolyn started going to that
other school. And then, of course, that sad business."

"Yes," Fanning said.

"I suppose they wondered if you had something to do
with it."

"Just at the start," Fanning said. "Just briefly."

"Still, to be sus*pect*ed," Mrs. Schmidt said.

Fanning nodded.

Mrs. Schmidt offered to refill Fanning's glass, but he said he was fine.

"She would've been the kind to keep the church going," Mrs. Schmidt said. "I always thought so."

Fanning said, "Her sister says it was mostly about pleasing Simon."

"The sister."

"Julia."

"Yes, I worried about that one," Mrs. Schmidt said. "People were all the time comparing her to the older girl. But Julia seemed . . . it's hard to put your finger on."

Fanning said he knew.

Mrs. Schmidt said, "Carolyn was one of those genuine spirits that happen along. I suppose I said the same sorts of thing to Iris, *Why can't you be more like your friend?* But Iris was my oldest and I didn't know then that they're each the way they are. I suppose it was me who drove a little wedge between them with talk like that. Iris turned out fine, she's a perfectly good mother herself, but back then she could be kind of, oh, a bumbler. The right words didn't pop into her mouth always, though I knew she meant well. Carolyn's gaze was always so adult, and she never had skin trouble the way Iris did."

Mrs. Schmidt looked about at her greenery. "Well, I was just one of the mothers," she said after a moment. "I don't suppose I knew all that much about her when you come down to it, just impressions. She must have had her mysteries."

"If I can ask," Fanning said, "how did people take Simon's——"

"His leap of faithlessness? There was something of a schism over that."

Fanning said he'd noticed the marker stone.

"Oh, we'd never have refused burial, not in a million years."

"Julia says he couldn't tolerate God's silence."

"Yes, I suspect that's right," Mrs. Schmidt said. "But you see there was discussion—I hope you appreciate this side of the Messiah mind, the hunger for good-hearted argument after the nonspeaking of prayer. Look at what Job had been put through—could Simon possibly believe he was more deserving of special treatment? Some said this 'God's silence' business was just a label Simon had given his suffering, and show me man, woman, or child who escapes suffering, and there was talk about the effects on the survivors, of course, and some of this was of a scathing nature. But the opposite view was taken, too, there was sympathy. Some of us simply couldn't find it in our hearts to blame him, and I suppose that was my judgment as well. Maybe *schism*'s not the right word—we were more a convention of crows. But let me tell you, there was something central about Simon. I know what you must have thought of him at the time—" And here Mrs. Schmidt allowed herself a smile, a spasm of unguarded pleasure. "Imagine approaching Simon Lamoreaux on the subject of dating his priceless daughter. Imagine the fortitude you needed, Mr. Fanning. But what I wanted to say, Simon had a queerly high-pitched speaking voice for a man so long in the beam, almost like a great heron you'd think sometimes, but he was as eloquent and as well-reasoned and passionate a man as belonged to our community, and watching his slow demise was torturous, being subjected to his own silence, as we finally were, which was as stony a thing as you'd want to run up against, believe me. So you could say, and not be grossly off the mark, that the day that girl failed to come home was the day the Messiah Church began its own coming asunder."

Fanning listened to the trickle of water inside the greenhouse, issuing from rubber hoses unseen behind him.

"I don't suppose you knew Julia so well," he said finally.

"She was my boy David's age—I'm sure they had a class together, I couldn't tell you what. Government, maybe. But they weren't friends especially, no. I only saw her at meeting. There was a general feeling she was trouble in the making, and I can't say I didn't share it. All the same, the craving for taking the opposite position, that was bred into her bones, that made her more the Messiah type than her sister ever was, for all Carolyn's sweetness, forgive me for saying so."

Mrs. Schmidt stood and collected their plates and Fanning began to stand, believing the interview to be over, but she motioned for him to stay put, and left with her arms full and Fanning mulled over what she'd said, and then she was back, handing him an oatmeal raisin cookie the size of a griddle cake.

"You've got to help me eat these," she said. "I can't seem to shake the baking habit." Fanning accepted the cookie and broke off a corner and put it in his mouth.

"But what I remember about the younger girl is the way she sat with Simon after it was just the two of them. Week after week."

"She feels she abandoned him in the end," Fanning said.

Mrs. Schmidt said, "But how could it be any other way? She's not still taking herself to task about that?"

"I think it's safe to say."

"You've stayed in touch, then?"

At the word "touch" Fanning detoured into the memory of his lips progressing down the centerline of Julia's shallow belly, and he simply said they'd met again recently, and it was only now, in Mrs. Schmidt's benign presence, in this close air, that Fanning was visited by the withering thought that he'd betrayed Carly—it was irrational, of course he knew that, it was beyond hope of addressing. Regardless, a tremor sped through him, a moment's sick panic. When he looked up, it felt as though minutes had elapsed. If so, Mrs. Schmidt seemed unfazed. Stretches of undisturbed quiet would be the norm here, Fanning imagined.

"Those Messiah days," she said, not with a sigh, because

Mrs. Schmidt wasn't the sort to issue sighs, but with a single muscular exhalation, "you can't picture things any different, you have your husband and children, all those meals to make, all those trips in the car, then that part of your life's finished, it's as gone as twists of steam off the pond." She slapped her hands down on her pants legs, and smiled. "You'll have to pardon my dime-store philosophizing, Mr. Fanning."

Fanning didn't know what to say now, and so he said he supposed he ought to be going, she'd been more than generous, he'd taken up enough of her time. Yet he didn't budge. Half the cookie still rested in his palm.

"I did think the wife drew back from him," Mrs. Schmidt said then. "You kind of wished they'd've pulled in tandem. Not that I'm casting blame. But you get the feeling if she'd just spoken to him a certain way, with a tenderness, I suppose is what I mean, but maybe she expected the same from him, where was the acknowledgment of *her* loss. I don't know, honestly. They were strong-willed, the both of them."

Fanning said, "Julia said Mitzi had stopped going to meeting even before this."

"Yes, that's right."

"As you said, it's not for everyone."

Now an odd look distracted Mrs. Schmidt, her broad calm features darkened—Fanning took it to be annoyance, as if he'd spoken out of turn.

"It wasn't that so much," she said.

"No?"

"Oh, that part's true enough, but I mean to say there was more to it."

Fanning waited.

"It was one of the newer members, a Mr. Byrnne—he'd been . . . well, *pestering* her." An orange cat emerged from under one of the long tables and rubbed about Mrs. Schmidt's legs, tail in the air, before bounding up into the house. "Oh, yes, this Mr. Byrnne, I suppose you could say he was a handsome man. Not to my taste, but he had a great thatch of sandy hair, wetted down with hair oil, not an especially tall fellow, but trim yet, on the wiry side. He was more Mrs. Lamoreaux's own age and he'd come from the same general neck of the woods as she had, the Tidewater area, I believe, you could hear it in his pronunciation, the way you heard it in Mrs. Lamoreaux's, only more so. I don't have a clue as to how he'd found us—I'm sure he wasn't one of those someone had coerced. But after several weeks of being among us and shaking hands with the men afterward and not saying much, he stood one Sunday and thanked us for accepting him, and gave a bit of a speech about the missteps in his life, as if we expected him to come clean before us. He'd failed at his marriage, he said, which he regretted, and he'd been naive in business matters, trusted the wrong sorts and run up debt, and so on—I don't recall the half of it. Anyway, he came to meeting faithfully for a while, and we either took to him or not. There were those who saw him as a man rebuilding his life, and of course that's a very attractive idea to some people, but I can't say I cared much for him myself. It wasn't so strong a feeling as revulsion, don't get me wrong—he just seemed to try too hard, or to miss the gist of who we were. I felt, underneath it all, he was an angry, a disappointed man. I suppose I saw these reservations as a shortfall of charity on my part. But I'd noticed how he'd chat up the younger women during the social period, and how he would sour if he was rebuffed. Rather soon, though, he began to confine himself to Mrs. Lamoreaux. Simon was oblivious—he'd be elaborating on some point with one of the men—but I could see that this Mr. Byrnne . . . I wish I could call up his first name for you, but I'm afraid it's gone . . . in any event, it was plain to me he had a thing for Mrs. Lamoreaux. He thought he was being discreet, I suppose, but it showed plain as day, to me it did. Now Mrs. Lamoreaux must've been flattered, at first, some fraction of her. Even so, she was in no position to be accepting the advances of another man, and right under Simon's nose. Can you imagine? Here we all were standing about eating crumble cake, drinking cider. So she must've spoken to him, discouraged him, and he seemed to have gotten the message because although he kept attending he gave Mrs. Lamoreaux a wider berth, and I said to myself, that's that, then."

Fanning adjusted his limbs and the settee made a friendly comment in return.

Mrs. Schmidt went on, "Now you might get the idea we were thick as thieves, we Messiah women, but it wasn't that way especially—there were friendships that spilled into our everyday lives, but you have to understand, some of the families came as far as thirty miles every Sunday. What I'm leading up to, Mr. Fanning, is that Mrs. Lamoreaux and I weren't terribly close. So I was somewhat taken aback when she telephoned me the middle of one week and confided that this Mr. Byrnne had called her at her home—he'd managed to catch her on an afternoon when she wasn't working, or maybe he'd made it his business to know when she worked and when she didn't. He'd made no real overture in this phone call, but it was followed by a second call, and a third. She said she wouldn't be telling me this except she knew I knew he was smitten with her. Now, this surprised me, I have to admit—my face must've betrayed me, she must've looked up and seen me watching. And, she said, she was calling because she'd always considered me to be so level-headed and knowledgeable. I had to laugh at that, I mean inwardly. What expertise had I ever had with men, besides Elmer and my own boys? And besides, I'd always taken her to be the one with the savvy in that area. But I thanked her for her trust. I said she had to refuse to talk to Mr. Byrnne if he called again, and, if that didn't produce results, to tell Simon. I could see Simon rising to his full height at meeting and announcing that a troubling situation had arisen in our midst. You couldn't imagine a man like Mr. Byrnne prevailing against Simon Lamoreaux, despite the difference in their ages, and Mr. Byrnne's, well, his good looks. As I say, Mrs. Lamoreaux might have found his interest in her reassuring in the beginning, maybe she'd been the kind who had men sniffing around constantly when she was younger, but I can't believe she was truly *tempted.* I think she'd genuinely had enough of this Mr. Byrnne. But she would've cringed at the idea of informing Simon. So she agreed to just stop taking his calls, and I reminded myself to ask her how it had gone when I saw her at meeting that week, but only Simon and the girls appeared, nor was she in evidence the following week. Mr. Byrnne continued to come, looking peevish, I thought, and though I didn't see it, I imagine he must've asked the girls about their mother. She'd have primed them with some cover story, which she must have used on Simon at first, something of a physical nature, something mundane like cramps, that first week. "Tell them I'm indisposed," she'd have said. But in Simon's case she must have eventually provided a theological rationale, once it became clear that she intended never to rejoin the other three on Sunday mornings. Simon would've listened with great care, and I'm sure he debated her mightily, but of course he wasn't the sort to drag her there bodily. So that was that. I never talked to her about it again. I assumed the situation had been resolved. And my guess is she didn't confide in another soul about it."

14

THAT EVENING Fanning located a hotel in Hartford that offered e-mail services, and addressed a message to *julamo@netrisys.net.*

Where's Mitzi buried? it said.

The better part of three weeks had gone by since their day in bed.

He checked back at midnight. Nothing. He was billeted on the hotel's top floor, the "concierge level." It was not among Fanning's favorite things to view the ground from ten stories up, nonetheless he stared out at the night, the city's shine and where it gave way to the darkness of undeveloped countryside. He drew the curtains, had a single scotch and slept until 3:45, lay thinking, then achieved one more REM cycle before dawn.

He made a semblance of dressing and went to the floor's breakfast lounge. The coffee cups were small, overly dainty in Fanning's opinion, but he filled one and gingerly toted it to the workstations.

One new message in his in box: *You're using a different account. Are we on the road?*

He examined the send-time, added the three hours and saw it was only minutes old. He pictured her in the magenta robe, barefoot, slumping at the keyboard, 5:32 A.M. Be online, he thought.

He typed: *You didn't answer my question.*

Addie Bundren, she replied.

Fanning typed: *?*

Nothing now. Fanning finally went and forked himself up a pair of sausages and a slice of underripe melon, refilled his little cup and then another.

Don't you read books? she'd written. *All this poor woman wants is to be buried with her own people. You wouldn't think that would be too much to ask for, except the river's flooding and the husband's a world-class cheapskate, not to get into the supporting cast of miscreant sons and other hapless busybodies...*

Fanning wrote: *You took her back to Maryland.*

In a thing like a cocktail shaker, Julia answered. *In my carry-on luggage. Why the sudden interest?*

Give me your phone number, he typed. *You're not home, are you? Give me the number where you are.*

More delay. Fanning took calm slow breaths and waited.

Then: *I don't want to talk, Miles, I want to type. Come back tonight.*

You won't stiff me? Fanning asked.

Julia: *Isn't that your speciality?*

Fanning: *I'm not kidding.*

Julia: *Oh ye of little faith.*

Fanning showered, made himself presentable, and used up the day dropping by local record stores. He shook hands and talked the talk and the hours dissolved. Each time he climbed from the car he was struck by the mildness of the air—maybe, here in lower New England, this would be one of those rare years when the melt came early and people were spared the soul-clobbering dumps of March snow. Making his rounds, he assiduously avoided the heart of downtown, those blocks surrounding the Civic Center. Midafternoon, he returned to his hotel room, exhausted, lay with his shoes off and eyes closed, but in a half hour he was up again, unrested and stir-crazy. Far too early to even think about checking the in box. He took the elevator down, telling himself he was a sack of shit to come this distance and not go look at the whole of it, nor, immobilized behind the wheel of the rented Ford, could he seem to write this errand off as a sentimental and meritless gesture. The day had an hour of bona fide light left in its repertoire. Fanning pictured himself knotted in late-afternoon gridlock—lost, drained of will. But not even the gods of traffic would intervene. He glided straight to the Civic Center as if on rails. He made himself study the building's facade, the banks of doors, made the car slowly trace the route along the pitted sidewalks, and though the neighborhood was rougher to the eye, it was not unrecognizable, and the final reprieve Fanning had dangled before himself, that the whole shebang had gone up in a paroxysm of urban renewal, this too was denied him.

He bumped the car into the alley, and, amazingly, recollected the exposed patch of nineteenth-century cobblestones at its mouth. A slimmer space than he recalled, this alley. He'd been on foot then, and it hadn't been so late an hour, or time of year. He flipped on the headlights. A watch-capped man came hugging the side wall—a gloveless palm shot up across his eyes, his head dodged as if slipping a punch, and he went past. Fanning studied the rear view until it was empty, then a minute longer. He edged the car forward, drawing even with the recessed area to his left. Always, in his mind, he'd called it "the alcove." Odd choice of word, he thought now. One slender building, mid-block, ending, for reasons unknown, thirty feet short of the alleyway, creating an opening, a gap. There was room enough on the brick wall of the

adjacent building for tall windows in the two upper floors—
they had wide stone sills, on which had been clay pots with
geraniums in bloom. Fanning left the lights splaying ahead,
got out and took a few steps and stood listening, checked the
alley mouth again, then cast his gaze into the alcove but could
barely see for the build-up of shadow. He got into the car,
slammed the door, sat panting, then jockeyed it back and
forth, a foot or two at a time until the headlights shone
straight into that bastard space. He got out a second time.
Wooden pallets standing on end, a tangle of what looked to be
ripped-out electrical conduit, the cold remains of a fire. Stub
ends of pallet boards, blackened nails, blackened curls of bottle glass. The bench had been anchored in concrete footings.
He ran his shoe along the side wall, felt where one of the
square wooden legs had been sawed off. He cast a look up at
the slot of sky—it was a faint rose, marked by a dissipating
contrail. Fanning walked to his car, got in, and punched the
door locks. He drove out the alley's far end, the tailpipe touching down at the dip, giving a quick abrasive *gritch*.

He lay, head propped, and watched CNN a few minutes but
couldn't face the stridency of the national news, allegations
about the President and a young staffer. He shut it off and
dozed. When he woke, it had gotten to be eight-thirty. He was
hungry again, wanted not a drink but more coffee. Shaving
impatiently with the worn-out disposable he found in his
Dopp kit, he realized he couldn't abide the hotel's tony dining
room, but had to get outside again, into the air, had to drive,
so then he was out Farmington Avenue, stopping at an old-
time diner called the Oasis, wolfing down a hot beef and
gravy, drinking coffee he would dearly regret later, taking
more with him, slipping it into the car's holder, driving again
with no motive but the shredding of time and the need to
move through space, which he did with a mindless concentra-

tion to the details of handling the car, reading the illumi-
nated signs, and when the tank was down past a quarter he
refilled and stayed on the major arterials to keep his bearings,
another forty-seven miles appearing on the trip odometer, the
agitation at last subsiding enough that he could think about
locating his hotel again, and when he realized this he eased
off the gas and drew out the return, and when he finally shut
off the engine in the parking compound and stepped into the
cold air, his abiding thought was that he'd barely recognized
himself this entire day.

Still scarcely nine o'clock in the West. It was possible she
wouldn't get around to sitting at the machine until much
later, and he'd have longer to wait yet, or that she'd stiff him
anyway. Regardless, he logged on.

One new message in his in box:

Date: 21 February 1998 20:59 (PST)
From: julamo@netrisys.net
To:mfan@hotmail.com
Subject:The subject
  MF:
  You want me to talk about the sex but I don't want to,
not now, not first thing.You're going to have to take that as
a given.
  I went up the coast for a few days. Maybe you guessed.
But somehow the "safe house" lacked its usual charm, so
I've been working since. No surprise, huh? It's the one thing.
Always there, always more of it.Am I right, Miles?
  First let me say it's not like I obsessed about you for
years, it's not like I dreamed of having you tracked by blood-
hounds. You were just this name, this "Miles Fanning" I'd
seen tastefully emblazoned on Carly's notebooks, heard
yelled up the stairs: Tell your sister Miles Fanning's on the

telephone. A somewhat offbeat name stuck like a burr in my memory, belonging to a gawky boy in a black station wagon who hadn't inspired any great upswelling of interest in me, to be frank, until late that winter when I observed the subversive effect he was having on Miss Carolyn, most especially that morning in May when we exchanged looks in the bathroom mirror and she seemed ready to take me fully into her confidence.

I'd think about her later, when I was in my mid-twenties, I'd go over things again and again, being, I thought, ardently rational. I'd pull everything out and examine it. Imagine a naturalist, or let's say a naturalist's apprentice. Imagine me reporting back with my earnest findings. There it would come yet again, the slow shake of the master's head: "I'm sorry, no. Please go back and use your eyes this time, Julia." Can you hear the voice? Infinitely patient and fatherly, but also, well, not infinitely patient, a bit smug, too, betraying perhaps a loss of faith in his choice of student. Back I'd go to use my eyes for the umpteenth time. I'd think, Christ Almighty, there's nothing else to see here but what I'm seeing. And please understand, the subject on the specimen tray wasn't just how my sister could disappear between Points A and B when they lay, let's be generous and say three whole blocks apart, but the entire goddamned chain reaction that ensued.

Still with me, Miles?

Then I'd think: Maybe it's much simpler, maybe I've been making it too hard. So I'd concentrate on "what's staring me in the face," and sometimes I'd feel like I was right there, right on the fucking cusp—in the next ten seconds I'd see the double helix for the first time. And sometimes, in this keyed-up state, I'd think: Of course, there was the boyfriend. There was this Miles Fanning. Had he not, one day, said, "Meet me at the bench next week," there would be no riddle. No rope trick for Simon. No "this Julia" as opposed to . . . well, another Julia, the "correct" one, the one who was supposed to be. You know what I'm saying? The "Meet me at the bench" was certainly simple enough, the one homely fact hidden in plain sight. But now the great naturalist had become a kind of Zen master. He'd say: "Wrong answer, facile not the same as simple." He'd say: "You'd deny your sister love?" He'd say: "You want causes? You might as well include the boat that carried your great-great-grandfather not running aground in the Gulf of Saint Lawrence."

Then what, Miles? What to do then? Time to pack away the evidence again. And wasn't it looking kind of dingy anyway? Kind of overhandled?

So there I was, a youngish woman with a college degree, an employable commodity if you were willing to overlook certain qualities (not everyone was, as it turned out). But, as you know, I found my way to the writing of technical manuals and product documents et al., and where the next person might've found this a major yawnfest, I took to it with a rabid heart: Be utterly clear, use the fewest words, explain things in order. Let's be grandiose and call it an exercise in purification: binderfuls of hopeless engineering sludge filtrated down to the simplicity of tap water. Every day, a mission, every two weeks a check. Then after I went with Lomax I could work at home on occasion, which had its upside. There was a general belief afloat that I was gifted at this clarity business. I acquired a certain renown, to which I replied with my usual, um, good cheer.

What a rich joke, when you think about it.

In any case, that's where I wound up my twenties, and though no one would mistake me for a "hopeful" person, I could plainly recall the act of remaking myself in high school, that single eruption of moxie, and, more recently, coming upon what you might term a "calling," so I'll admit I did have a certain hope with regard to my thirties. I'll own up to that. I thought there was an even chance they'd be different, that next allotment of years. Not more of same. I mean, away from work. In what's referred to as one's private life. But, contrary to what I said above, Miles, the thing was, the evidence never really went back into the drawer. It was always lying about.

Naively, I'd thought it might lose its potency over time, or I'd get distracted by a relationship, or life's little fiesta. What can I tell you that you haven't seen with your own eyes? It didn't, I didn't. Can I put this to you in the most succinct way? Use my "gift"? Terrible things happen to people, the grossest, vilest things—weights no next of kin should have to shoulder. But they go on, some people do, some don't curdle. One humble example: the Korean woman downstairs had her husband and two sons taken away and shot and left in a sewage trench and later the third son was burned to cinders in an oil fire, and nothing but gentle words from her. I find these little bags of tomatoes on my doorstep, jelly jars filled with blossoms. I refuse to see myself as the victim here, Miles, please be a hundred percent clear about that. I don't give two shits about "victimhood" or "blame." On the other hand, what's the deal? Why am I like this? Why can't I give it up?

As you'll have surmised, I was a Net junkie from the first instant. One night I was screwing around with people-finding search engines when it occurred to me to type the words "Miles Fanning." Spontaneous act. And there were the Miles Fannings and the M. Fannings of America arrayed before me. Telephone numbers, e-mail addresses, and believe it or not, it took only three tries to find the right one. Sheer luck, I suppose. But I had to make contact. Once I knew you were alive, parked at a keyboard somewhere, not making the effort was no longer an option.

You might ask what I thought would be gained. Did I think I could just divest myself of this story and be done with it? The grand purgation? I've never thought it worked that way—I always thought the great unburdening was a lie. Anyway, I didn't think, I just acted. But I was real sure you were going to hear the parts you'd escaped knowing. Once I got rolling, I realized it was entirely possible I'd end up feeling crappier for the effort, but by then talking with you had acquired its own, well, trajectory.

The two surviving participants.

I had a pretty good idea the impression I was making that first night in Seattle, but you know what I thought: Screw it, here's a guy who just moved on. Who says you get to just move on? Admittedly, it was different for you. Maybe you and Carly weren't fated to be soulmates for all time, I'll grant you that. Even so, most young men would've come seriously unglued under such conditions. Tell me I'm wrong. But here you were. Unmarked, unscathed. And so devoid of curiosity. That's what struck me on the airplane home. He's all bricked up, this Fanning. All block and mortar. So I had to call you—and here my resources were tested, acquiring the unlisted number of Mr. Fanning's Hospitality Suite. But that first phone call had nothing to do with apologizing for being a bitch.

But you'd rather talk about the later part, wouldn't you?

Okay, let's assume you listened to me out of loyalty to Carly, a conscience thing, or to see if I was truly a crazy woman, or because I'm just so goddamned fascinating you couldn't help yourself, take your pick, but that, regardless, we forged some little connection, in spite of the fact I believed your role would be finito the minute the story ended, or when you'd given me some satisfactory reaction to what I'd made you sit through . . .

Let's even admit that, upon reflection, I enjoyed what we did (and did and did). You need to hear that, don't you? That I liked it, that you got to me. Well, here it is in print. For the record. You're still getting to me, Miles. But where does that put us? You know what I'm saying? You went back, didn't you? Abandoned the Hospitality Suite for home and hearth? What am I supposed to do with that nugget of info? Where do I stash it?

Tell you one thing, I'm absolutely not messing up your marriage. Believe it or not I have limits. And something else is eating at me, you might as well know. The possibility that I engineered this whole fiasco out of anger at Carly . . . for leaving me in the lurch, for cutting out on me so goddamn early. Very imaginative move, screwing her boyfriend. Childish thoughts. I know, I know. Nonetheless.

Kind of jammed up here, aren't we?

It just stopped, as if she'd hit Send by accident. Fanning knew better. He clicked it offscreen—it was like refolding the pages of a letter, replacing them in their envelope before letting yourself read them for a second time. He stood to unkink his shoulders. The computer room was all darkened windows, an aerie with a lone occupant. He watched the wing lights of a private plane slant by, in-bound, let his forehead touch the cool of the glass.

When he sat again, another message was waiting.

The phone number.

Fanning discovered he had no pen, the printer no paper.

So then he was scooting down the muffled corridor to his room whispering the sequence of digits over and over, snatching up the phone and punching them out.

And damn if he didn't get her voice mail.

He said nothing, recradled the receiver. He went around the corner to take a leak, cut it short and dashed back and dialed again before the numbers fled.

"Ah, it's you," she said, less testy-sounding than she'd seemed in type.

Fanning said it pleased him to hear her voice.

"Yours is okay, too."

Fanning said she'd never guess where he was.

"I don't feel like guessing games," Julia said, but not unkindly.

Eyes shut, ankles crossed, taking his sweet time, Fanning began recounting his last couple of days. Marvin Biggs, The Holy Gospel Fellowship, clearing snow crystals from the grass either side of Simon's stone. FINE OLD THINGS, the hall tree with its yellowed ivory knobs, and so on, telling about his stop at the house on the Post Road, telling her the great maples had come down, and how, picturing the stumps being yanked from their sockets he'd been reminded, sickeningly, of wisdom teeth. Finally, he mentioned the barn, downplaying it, then asked if she remembered the Schmidts.

"The Schmidts," Julia said without pause, "Elmer and Emily. Five or six kids, one Carly's age. Elmer always looked like he'd just come in from the great out-of-doors. Red-cheeked, his head giving off steam, that's how I thought of him. He was the one they asked if they needed some obscure tool, or if someone's battery had to be jumped. Mrs. Schmidt I kind of liked, I don't know why. She was . . . when she stood to speak you never knew what it was going to be. Nobody could've looked more normal, but she surprised you."

Fanning said he'd liked her, too. He described the hot-house, the congregation of one.

"What's this *about*, Miles? Going there."

"It's like a chain of things," he said. "I kept doing what seemed to come next."

On some level, of course, the entire trip was as indefensible as it was compulsory.

Like hers to Seattle.

He said, "You remember a Mr. Byrnne?"

"Should I?"

"He went to the church. Part of a year at least." Fanning reconstructed him from the few details Mrs. Schmidt had provided.

"Well, as I said, new people blew through every so often. But I might remember someone like that, kind of a pretty boy? Drove some big car, big and green. There *was* somebody like that, I could almost swear."

Fanning repeated what Mrs. Schmidt had said about Mr. Byrnne's fascination with Julia's mother.

Julia didn't respond at once. "I have zero memory of that," she said finally. "It seems truly, I don't know—"

"You think she made it up?"

"Mrs. Schmidt? No, there's no way. Not her."

"Apparently it was the reason Mitzi stopped going to meeting. So he'd get the message loud and clear."

"No kidding? She said that? I always assumed it was like I told you, Mitzi had finally taken as much of the Messiah Church as she could stomach."

"Maybe they're both true."

"But making a play for Mitzi. And at meeting? What could've been going through his head?"

"People get these attractions," Fanning said. "Not necessarily based in the head."

"Thanks for that insight, Miles. But what do you *think*? Did anything come of it? I'm serious."

"Mrs. Schmidt felt sure Mitzi put him off. That it was entirely one-sided."

What reason did Fanning have to doubt Mrs. Schmidt? None at all. He sat and stared, letting the silence ride. There seemed, for the time being, nothing more to say on the subject of Mr. Byrnne and Mitzi Lamoreaux, odd as it was.

"Julia," Fanning said finally, "what you wrote about stealing Carly's boyfriend."

"Forget it," she said. "Psych 101."

"No, because I had the same . . . when Mrs. Schmidt was going on about Carly, that hit me, too, that I'd betrayed her, and then I had the same reaction, that it was a worry I'd never get a grip on. I had this moment of . . . almost nausea."

"It's just everything," Julia said. "Welcome to the club."

"I really don't believe she'd begrudge us——"

"Don't, okay?"

"What?"

"Speak for her."

Fanning clammed up.

"Look, I'm sorry," Julia said. "People go So and So would've wanted—— It gives me the creeps, that talk. It's not you, Miles. But you did betray her. You just walked off, without so much as——"

Fanning swung his feet to the floor. He paced as far as the curly cord would let him.

He said, "Aren't there things you've done that make no sense, looking back?"

"Besides sleeping with you?"

"Okay, besides that. But I thought you were in favor of it."

"I said I was, just don't make me keep yakking about it."

"You brought it up," Fanning pointed out.

Julia said nothing.

"It's true, I carried on in a way that's hard to explain now," Fanning said. "Maybe I was block and mortar as you so kindly put it. It's also true that I loved your sister—she knew it, she believed it. I have no way of reconciling these facts, except to say it was how I reacted, a boy's reaction, one boy's."

Fanning reached back and switched off the bedside light glaring in his eyes. "I don't have anything else to tell you," he said, "except how grateful I am you searched me out, no matter what your motive was——I mean, Julia, grateful doesn't touch it. What if you hadn't? I can hardly face that. But, listen, about your sister . . . being out here I keep remembering specific days, and not just thinking of her as this *event*, this one ugly thing that happened. Plus I keep wondering how she'd have turned out."

"Like your wife with shorter legs," Julia said.

Fanning didn't argue. He didn't fire back any smart

remark, any rebuke. She'd said this before. It'd disturbed him that first night at the hotel, and it did again. Julia's sizing him up, knowing the woman he married would be a permutation of Carly Lamoreaux, that Julia could toss this off without having laid eyes on Kyra, when he was blind to it himself. Then he thought of Kyra's telling him, during the break before Billy Caughlan laid down the definitive take of "Caughlan's Condition," that she was too all-American for Billy. Fanning had read this as a spark of self-mockery, late-night flirtation, nothing more. But he hadn't yet known how literal Kyra was. For all her qualities—the blatant beauty, the effortless way she navigated the physical world—Kyra lacked something Billy simply *had to have:* a shadowy side, a misdirection, a complexity of spirit that wouldn't pale beside his grapple with the keyboard. And now, Fanning realized icily, he'd reached the same point himself. He couldn't say with any clarity, any floor of self-trust, if what he'd felt for Kyra had ever been love, if it had ever grown beyond desire and pleasure, beyond the habit of being loved by her.

"Hey, you didn't nod off on me?"

"I'm here," Fanning said.

They talked, another hour, closer to ninety minutes, Julia saying she couldn't believe he'd flown out there, Fanning telling her it was a question of seeing things for himself, Julia rushing on, "But you'd only been home, what, a few days?" asking how he'd sold the trip, how his wife had taken this news, then before he could respond, saying, "No, don't answer, I don't want to know." And this was how it went, Julia vacillating, Julia relaxing into her ordinary banter then stiffening, as if speaking to herself, doling out instructions, saying again what she'd said about not defiling his marriage, not being able to stand having that guilt on her head, Fanning trying to break in and say, "Kyra and I are—" but not knowing how to say it yet, the fact of his marriage's demise only becoming truly real to him in these moments, and when it became obvious this call would have to end, both of them worn raw, repeating themselves, Fanning was overcome by the same reluctance that had seized him at the hotel in Seattle, the gut-fear that if he let her go now it could prove irreversible, and they underwent an elaborate exchange of "good nights," interrupted by last-minute thoughts, additions, corrections, Fanning finally saying aloud, "No, don't go yet," Julia answering, "I know, I know, but goddamn it, Miles—" and there were more minutes of this, until at last Fanning was curled on the bed, the connection broken.

Sometime before dawn Fanning went through the motions of going to sleep, submerging himself under the thin hotel blankets, but when he woke, not even an hour had elapsed. He lay clutching his knees, beginning to shake, fine tremors buzzing his teeth, larger contractions taking over the broad muscles of his stomach. There was nothing to do when he got like this but run a bath, and thank God he wasn't still back at the Hospitality Suite with its makeshift stall shower and meager pissing-down drizzle of warmish water. He ran the tub hot and got in when it was only four inches deep, splashing his chest and scrunching low. The tub filled and the shakes began to abate. He reached out his left foot and let in more hot, let it come at a steady echoing trickle. He lay back with a washcloth obscuring his face. He fell into a half-doze and woke thinking: *It wasn't Sophia Buzzati.*

Because that night Sophia had been located, questioned, and though she was a notorious rule-flaunter, a gaudy loudmouthed Italian girl, loose-gaited and irresistible, this day she'd done nothing more sinister than walk out of rehearsal, stroll the mile and a half to her house, bored to death with choir, and had lain on her bed most of the afternoon talking to a boy from Holy Cross over the telephone. That was fact,

that was known. It had to be another girl—Fanning recalled
no names beyond Sophia's, so he simply pictured a less-likely
candidate: lank-haired, a girl with one of those long-chinned
New England faces, but a girl with her own mysteries, as Mrs.
Schmidt had ventured of Carly. And let's say, Fanning
thought, that while Moorcroft waited their turn to file onto
the risers, this girl had said to Carly, "Could I talk to you?"
Carly would've understood she meant not here, but somewhere private, so Carly had nodded, then squinted across the
patchwork of faces and picked out her boyfriend, who happened to be gazing at the stage, so the two girls had gone outside, unnoticed, around the corner of the Civic Center. What a
relief to be in the air, what a sweet day, even if it was hazy
and a bus came by with its fumes, because in less than an
hour she and Miles would have their time, and she tried not
to "live ahead" as they called it at meeting, but it was hard in
practice, and even in this warmth, goosebumps flared across
her shoulder blades, making her suddenly arch her spine as if
she'd accidentally backed into something pointed. So she
turned to this girl, who wasn't, strictly speaking, a close
friend, and saw instantly what the trouble was. So Carly said
the girl's name, maybe it was Anna, and Anna said, "What
am I supposed to *do?*" Though they were outside and no one
could overhear them, the girl couldn't stay in one spot, so they
began walking along the side of the building then down a
side street. Carly said, "But I'm not the one you should be asking—" and the girl, this Anna, said but Carly was *in* with
those girls, girls who had information, you had to go to New
York, that's all she knew. There was no mention of the circumstances, no boy's name given. Carly wouldn't pry, but
expected Anna to say, "It was only *one time,*" some plaintive
remark about luck, or being lied to, but you could see in her
lips it was all self-loathing and fear now, and she was saying,
"I don't have hardly any money of my own that I can get at.
I'm just totally—" In the collective memory of Moorcroft

girls was the member of the '69 class who'd gone to someone here in the city, someone "reputable," and had come within minutes of bleeding to death, alone in her parents' house in Avon on a Friday night, thinking it would stop on its own, they'd said there'd be bleeding, a story that could easily have lapsed into outright tragedy—it was bad enough everyone in the world found out, bad enough she'd never bear children. So that hovered in the air, unsaid. Carly would try to settle Anna down, have her take three deep breaths so they could talk it out sensibly, she'd say, "There's no chance you're wrong?" The girl answered with a massively doomed look. By now they'd gotten as far as Market Street, and without sneaking a check of her wristwatch in front of Anna, she knew they'd have to start back soon. But Anna was saying how *stupid, stupid,* she was, how she screwed up everything she touched. Naturally Carly couldn't let that line of thinking go on—she didn't try to hug the girl, or stroke the lifeless hair, but took the girl's large, moist hands firmly in her own and made her make eye contact, and said, "This will come out okay, I know you don't believe me but it will." And then Carly said she'd find out what the girl needed to know, and only then did the girl begin to relax, the tension in her grip easing. "You've got to promise," Anna said, and Carly gave her promise, and the girl said, "But the money—" and Carly said that too would get figured out, things were just ganging up on her right now. In the background, Carly was thinking not just of the time, but of the plastic wheel of pills (the seal still unblemished by thumbnail, though soon, possibly tonight, which was right for her cycle, she might take the first one), how could she not be thinking of that as Anna started thanking her, saying how people simply didn't like her the way they liked Carly, etc., and now Carly did have to say, "We have to get back, Anna," because it was nearing lunch break and they'd walked a good distance on the opposite side of the building from where she was to meet Miles. But the girl said, "You go, I'm just—" and they may have briefly tusseled over this, or Carly may have said, "Okay, but do go back, and you have to try not to *worry*, okay? I'll see you afterward," and set off alone, only then examining the time—it was six or seven minutes to twelve, not bad, but she picked up her pace, thinking of Miles, the chambray skirt brushing her bare legs.

So down this street on who knows what errand—because no matter how you configured the story there had to be an element of randomness, of malignant chance, you couldn't make it work if you imagined it as strictly premeditated— came Mr. Byrnne in his green Bonneville, a car, though several model years out of date, like no other found parked beside the Messiah Church, it went without saying. And so he would've slowed to a low cruise at the sight of Mitzi's oldest girl striding along, and when he was sure it was in fact her, called out. Said, "Hey, what do you know?" And what reason would Carly have had for not getting in, for not sliding onto the warm vinyl?

"Oh, do me a favor," she said, asking him to drive her to the alley mouth—the thought of beating Miles there was suddenly delicious. The talk with Anna might have clanged in her ear like a cautionary tale, but it had the opposite effect, made her squirrelly with wanting, so she pictured herself already on the bench, lounging, as if she'd been there for hours, and this way, too, she wouldn't be sweaty from this fast-walking. God, it was perfect.

Then, pulling out into traffic again, this Mr. Byrnne said, "That's funny, I was going to ask *you* a favor."

Before Carly could ask what it was, Mr. Byrnne said, "That mother of yours is something, isn't she. But man—" He reached across and touched Carly, just above the elbow, making sure he had her attention. "She's a tough one."

Carly said Mitzi could be, you know, kind of high-strung, kind of opinionated.

"She's been playing hooky from church," Mr. Byrnne said. "Hasn't she?"

Carly said she was sure it was only temporary. Then she said, "Here, go down this street, it's over in that—"

Mr. Byrnne seemed for a moment as if he didn't want to turn. He gave her a funny look, but slowed the car then and said, "Okay, down this street."

And now Carly said, "So what was the favor?"

"The favor," Mr. Byrnne said. "What I wanted," he said, and they came now to a stop sign and he braked and looked both ways, studying the flow of vehicles as Carly looked at him, at the T-shirt showing through his dress shirt, at the heavy red-stoned ring on his right hand. "What I wanted, what I'd like you to do is just give her a message for me, that's all. Nothing too hard."

The car still hadn't budged. Carly swiveled around to see if anyone had come up behind them yet, but no one had.

Would it be here, Fanning wondered—the first glint of not-right feeling, here when the Bonneville was actually at a full stop?

Or maybe Carly said, playing along because in a minute there'd be Miles, because she was recklessly happy, maybe she said, "What's your message?"

And he said, his foot finally pressing the accelerator, "I just wanted you to ask her why she's been ducking me. Can you do that much?"

He'd swung into the outside lane and Carly said, "You've got to make a right up at the next—" but he went past it. She said, "Take the next one then, I've really got to get where I'm going."

Mr. Byrnne said, "But you haven't said if you'll help me."

Maybe, the mood she was in, Carly hadn't been paying strict attention to the content of what Mr. Byrnne had been talking about from the start, so it was only at this point she thought: He wants my mother in *that* way. *Mitzi.* It struck her simultaneously as ridiculous and impossible, pathetic.

So she said, "I really don't think that's something I can do."

By now he'd driven two blocks past the alley and was still in the left lane. But he was smiling, and she remembered how he'd smiled at meeting once he was done spilling out the story about his miscalculations in life, a smile of abundant gratitude, of release—this wasn't the same smile now, but neither was it gross and sarcastic, more just teasing, jesting, when he said, "You can't? Not even that much?"

And here Fanning thought if it had been Julia, Julia at a comparable age, not Carly, among whose trove of gifts wasn't the gift of saying other than what she meant, the bullshitter's gift, if it had been Julia she might've said, "Sure, I can tell her, but I know what she'll say."

So Mr. Byrnne would need to ask, "Yeah? What's that?"

Julia would've said . . . but, no, Fanning thought, it's not that she would've *lied,* inventing a remark of Mitzi's favorable to Mr. Byrnne, that, for instance, something in his little swagger appealed to her, etc. If anything, Julia was a compulsive truth-teller. It was the way she'd have delivered it: "Mitzi'll say: *Oh, him, he can't hold a candle to Simon Lamoreaux,*" looking across at Mr. Byrnne, Julia wearing an expression he wouldn't quite know how to interpret. And she might've gone on, "Yeah, Mitzi'll say: *That Mr. Byrnne isn't nearly somber enough for me—you know how somber I like my men, somber and out-of-style.*"

How could he possibly have countered this? That he could be somber as a stone post, that he could be as out-of-style as the best of them? But Fanning had the idea that sooner or later the car would've come to a stop again, and Julia would've emerged from it—whether in one untelegraphed move, separating herself from this creepy man and running, or with a trace of repartee lingering between them, some aura of mock-conspiracy, he couldn't say.

But Carly's guilelessness. *Jesus Christ*, Fanning thought.

He stripped off the washcloth and stared down the length of his naked torso and listened to the water guttering out the overflow.

How much of this was he up to?

Carly's earnest statement that she was now legitimately late?

Mr. Byrnne's dropping of pretense as he adjusted the car's speed, aiming for the freeway on-ramp, his saying, "Just settle down, *Carolyn*, we're going to have a little talk, you and I. Understand? We're going to drive and we're gong to talk and to be honest, I don't give a goddamn where you need to be right now." And maybe something in Carly's increasing discomfiture didn't sit well with Mr. Byrnne, eliciting a backhand across her face, too sudden to even flinch from, the ring catching the corner of her mouth.

Because Fanning believed—would forever believe—that Mr. Byrnne had improvised as he went along, that the very furthest thing from his mind as he woke to that new day was how it would end, that something had gone wrong once they were in the car, beginning with the damage that fucking ring had done—some kid's college ring he'd found under the bed of a hotel once.

Behind closed eyes, Fanning thought: All right, you've hit a girl, possibly blood has been drawn, a token amount, but it's nothing you couldn't explain away. *I don't know what came over me*— This would be a part of the story Mr. Byrnne had omitted at meeting—the way women could rile him suddenly, could give him this hideous boxed-in sensation, like having his arms bound to his sides, his mouth taped shut. But the point was, Fanning thought, bad as things had become, they were not yet unstoppable.

So the Bonneville sailed along the highway at cruising speed. Fanning watched it go. And what a temptation to begin viewing it from the outside now, the green sun-dulled finish growing fainter in the smoggy light, the car's bulk diminishing as it went and went.

But Fanning squired his attention back to the girl on the vinyl seat, who was compliant now, compliant in a rational and strategic way—no longer thinking of Miles Fanning, her assignation, her love, nor in so many words telling herself, *I'm being kidnapped, he's* . . . but just watching the road unfurl, feeling the tires tick against the seams of the bridge, and maybe she said, calmly, almost without inflection, "You didn't need to hit me," and perhaps Mr. Byrnne made one more attempt at normalizing things, perhaps he spoke that line Fanning had already heard him say, "Hey, Jeez, I'm sorry, I don't know what came over me. You're okay, aren't you? Let me see you." Or else not. Maybe he just drove, and Carly started to wonder what'd become of the big talk they were going to have. So maybe she said something about that, the talk, because not talking was eating at her, was making her bare arms shiver. Maybe *she* talked, not about Mitzi, or their situation there in the car, but about him, remembering a detail from his speech at meeting and asking about that, which was so obviously a ploy, and he wasn't letting himself get bamboozled by some high school girl, for Christ's sake, even if his thoughts were racing and jumbling the way they sometimes did, so maybe he cuffed her again, driving with one hand as the other went for her, the car actually veering between lanes now before he could right it.

Seeing the car behave erratically, Fanning thought: But what about the police, what about another driver witnessing . . . then found himself skipping ahead to the investigator Simon had engaged, Mr. Quinton, not some city cop on early retirement, but a fireplug of a man in his forties, a man the Travelers had employed in cases of insurance fraud.

Fanning's own interview with him had taken place at a worksite in Shirley, Fanning called down from the roof of a ranchhouse where he'd been nailing off plywood. Would he join Mr. Quinton in the front seat of his van, please? A hot day for early June, Fanning's skin setting up in the air-conditioning. The same basic questions the police had asked and asked, but put with a certain precision, an orderliness seemingly at odds with the man's physique. And there was his demeanor toward Fanning, his saying at one point, "Miles, look at me," and waiting until Fanning did, in fact, raise his eyes, before going on, "No one thinks you're the guilty party. I certainly don't. You can wipe that from your mind. But it's been my experience that people sometimes don't know what they know." So they'd gone over details for the better part of an hour, Fanning's new foreman periodically glaring in his direction. But in this case he really *did* know nothing, Fanning told Mr. Quinton, other than what he'd already repeated ad infinitum, and when Mr. Quinton broached the subject of sexual relations, Fanning said flatly no, Carly was a virgin. Mr. Quinton wrote quietly on his steno pad, not making Fanning defend the statement. That's what Fanning remembered. And one other thing about Quinton: Never once did he use the past tense in relation to Carly, it was, "But you'd say, generally speaking, she's a girl who goes out of her way to give people a hand if she thinks—"

In any case, Quinton was no burnt-out bulb.

Would he not have asked, in due course, if there were grudges held against this family, implausible as that seemed on its face?

Which meant that Mitzi had either spoken up, or not.

Perhaps, away from Simon's ears, she'd mentioned the Mr. Byrnne business, but had been so dismissive that Quinton had written it off as a dry well. But no, Quinton wasn't like that— if the police were ignorant of this morsel he'd have given it over, and Mr. Byrnne would've been questioned. Assuming he hadn't immediately bolted from the Clarion area, and Fanning guessed he hadn't, that he was too insecure on the basis of past infelicities about disappearing without stupidly leaving behind traces of himself. And why go missing at the very time the girl went missing, wasn't that just plain dumb? Better to let things proceed, to act as he'd been acting, going in for the occasional job interview, then to meeting on Sunday.

So he would've been in that bare white-walled room with Simon and Julia those first weeks, studying them from the periphery, listening with the others to Simon's stoic updates. One thing he *had* done was lose the Bonneville, turning up now in a mud-brown Chevy Vega, which people interpreted—insofar as they thought about it at all—as a token of his increased humility under the Messiah influence. The Bonneville was in the bottom of a water-filled granite quarry up in southern New Hampshire, near the town of Fitzwilliam. If anyone asked, anyone in authority, he had a story prepared, about falling off the wagon one night and forgetting where he'd parked, and then, sober, retracing his steps, and never finding it, but still believing it would turn up and so he'd yet to report it stolen—too embarrassed, a man trying to turn his life around, etc.

But wasn't it public record somewhere, whether a Mr. Byrnne had been detained for questioning? And of the several tasks that Fanning would perform this day, one of them was to see if such information yet existed.

And then he thought of Simon driving Julia to school in the dark that fall, saying gravely: "Mr. Quinton feels that all avenues have been exhausted." It occurred to Fanning that for whatever the reason—pride, utter distraction—Mitzi had not spoken up. It mortified her to think Simon might believe she'd encouraged the man. Perhaps, unknowingly, she had given Mr. Byrnne some hope that his interest might be reciprocated—or, Fanning thought, maybe Mitzi had been less than entirely forthcoming with Mrs. Schmidt, maybe she was more tempted than she'd let on, had seen Mr. Byrnne once or twice, brief meetings where she tested herself, where she remembered how it was to sit across a booth from a man and feel his impudent desire, a man her junior no less, a man she didn't trust, a man (as Fanning had imagined Julia saying) who couldn't hold a candle to Simon Lamoreaux when it came to intellect or sheer force of presence, but who reminded her of a self she'd abandoned years before, one accustomed to flattery, to cajoling, words she should let fly harmlessly by, but instead found herself not believing—she was too old for that—but enjoying, listening to like a discarded but still-familiar story. This Mr. Byrnne, whose first name Fanning didn't know. And even the *Byrnne*—who could say whether that was real? This Mr. Byrnne who'd slipped between the cracks.

The bathroom had fogged with steam, but it had long since cooled. Droplets ran down the wall, down the triptych of mirrors. Fanning finally stood dripping and reached for one of the white, absurdly luxurious towels the hotel supplied and stepped from the tepid water.

15

I need your street address, Fanning typed. *And I need to know if you're there or out in the hinterland. And whether there's any chance you could work at home tomorrow.*

He added his initials, logged off, and began the process of recaffeinating himself for the day.

It was light enough now to see that a listless snow was falling. He watched for a time but it grew no more menacing. *Nothing,* he thought, *flurries, won't last.* And there did seem to be, along the bottom of the eastern sky, a seam of lighter light, the color of fresh egg yolk. He shaved and rubbed lotion into his skin, dropped the cheapo razor in the wastebasket, and zipped his Dopp kit.

He rode the elevator to the lobby, asked directions for a travel agent. It was not yet eight-thirty. He returned to his room and lay down and at quarter past nine went and checked his in box. Nothing yet. Fanning pictured her flopped on her bed, dozing raggedly, bangs all askew. The thought pleased him unreasonably.

He left the hotel, ran his errand, and was back within the hour.

Nothing still.

Nonetheless, he sat at the desk in his room and took the folder of writing paper from the drawer, not knowing what he would say until he said it.

He wrote the day's date and beneath that:

Julia, the enclosed is for you. It's for tomorrow after-noon—that would be today as you're reading this. I hope to Christ you decide to take me up on it. An absurd request, I realize. If you don't, then you don't. But I want to talk to you about your sister . . . and other things. I think I understand the mechanics of that day. I could be dead wrong, but I don't believe I am. Of course you'll wonder how I can say this when we just got off the phone maybe six hours ago. All I can tell you is, it came to me—you'll have to trust me enough to hear me out. As you've made me aware, of all the grisly aspects of this it's the not-knowing that so corroded everyone's lives. What I have to say isn't the whole of it, but maybe it's enough, or I guess what I'm saying is it's a start. And I don't mean to use this as leverage—I'll tell you regardless, but I'd very much like to do it out here, face-to-face.

Then he wrote: *I want your face next to my face.*

He stared at this last line. After a minute he wadded the paper and batted it away. He stood and watched the flat February sky, then sat, took out a clean sheet of stationery and eventually began again, writing what he'd written before, not precisely word for word, but he kept going this time, filling three more sheets.

He had today to kill and most of tomorrow. He'd promised himself he'd look into what remained of the case. *Case*, he thought, driving. It had barely become a case—just an inquiry, questions with unyielding answers. Now Fanning remembered another detail he'd suppressed: there had been an abduction in the city two months before Carly's disappearance. The dregs of winter. Not a school girl but a young woman of similar build and coloring, a clerical worker at The Hartford, and no headway had been made on this case at the time of Fanning's questioning by the police—what he remembered was hearing speculation that Carly might be the second in what would prove to be serial crimes. That fear expressed within his earshot. But no others followed, apparently, or none to see as a pattern, so he imagined this hypothesis had fallen away.

To be replaced by what?

He knew the kind of day today would be, but didn't care. His limbs felt achy and unresponsive, yet his mood, though cut with unease, had a stubborn buoyancy. He parked and presented himself at the police headquarters on Jennings Road. He expected to be given the speedy brush-off, but instead received a hearing by a detective named Sepulveda, a man of an age and bearing and a look about the eyes that could have made him Fanning's older brother. Fanning apologized in advance, then explained why he'd come. Sepulveda said it was his job to listen to stories like Fanning's, however out of date. Besides, he had daughters of his own.

When Fanning reached a stopping point, Sepulveda said, "These days it's mostly runaways. You should see what's out on the streets now, how young. It would sicken you."

Fanning nodded, then reiterated that Carly hadn't run away.

Sepulveda said yes, of course.

Fanning asked if there might still be a file on the investigation. Sepulveda told him unsolved cases remained open, and that somewhere in the building would be stored the original case notes.

Sepulveda stretched his torso toward the phone and made a call.

"It isn't that I think there's anything you could do at this point," Fanning said. "It's just——"

Lieutenant Sepulveda said he understood perfectly.

Waiting, the two men talked, and the detective jotted on a flip-top pad. Fanning found himself rubbing the knees of his pants, caught himself and stopped—it was a gesture Kyra repeatedly warned him about, that it made people around him nervous. Now the phone sounded. Sepulveda excused himself and picked up. As it turned out, the Lamoreaux materials weren't where anyone could lay a finger on them. Misfiled, most likely.

Fanning said, "I wanted to verify whether he'd ever been talked to, I guess was the main thing."

"Byrnne."

Fanning nodded.

Sepulveda said he'd have them keep hunting.

Fanning repeated what he'd said earlier, "Something went wrong inside the car, I'm convinced. Something was said, I don't know what, something that made the outcome——" He pressed his palms together with his knees, immobilizing them.

Sepulveda wrote again, and looked up at Fanning with respect and said it was not impossible, what Fanning had speculated, not at all.

"And the file," Fanning said, "your opinion is it'll turn up—it wouldn't have been . . . disposed of, or——"

Sepulveda said there was every reason to think they'd find it. It might take a while, was all.

"I mean if even the file is gone——" Fanning said. "You know what I'm saying?"

Sepulveda nodded.

Fanning picked a card from his wallet and gave it over and Sepulveda tucked it in the upper corner of his blotter. Fan-

ning stood but was reluctant to have the interview end. Sepulveda seemed to sense this. He shook Fanning's hand and said
he would be in touch. Then Fanning was on the sidewalk
again, scanning the featureless sky.

Earlier, he'd paid and checked out of his hotel without having
heard from Julia. Then, on impulse, he'd left his bag with the
desk clerk and returned to the workstations upstairs, telling
himself he'd give her one half hour, no more, no less, and at
minute twenty-five it appeared nakedly on the screen: street
and apartment number, city, zip. Shortly thereafter, Fanning
located a FedEx box, inserted the cardboard mailer, heard it
slide and drop.

He drove northeast out of the city, taking the Wilbur Cross,
angling toward Massachusetts. It occurred to him that
Byrnne might have used the same route that spring day—
these fields, snow-blotched now, would've been the same the
two of them had watched from opposite ends of the Bonneville's bench seat as they thought their separate thoughts.
The same rows of hardwoods, the same rock walls. Yet as Fanning closed in on the border the more positive he grew that
Carly had remained in Connecticut. A small gust of intuition
that once he crossed the state line struck with an unevadable
force: he'd left her behind, she was gone without remedy.

He drove on, remembering again how they had stood in
the column of light below the barn's cupola, then the times
later in that short courtship when she'd reached behind her
with such simple dexterity, under her shirt, and unhooked the
clasp of her bra so he could touch her as they kissed, as they
told each other how they felt, eventually having to pull away,
to stop, agonizing as it was. He tried to let her face, her clear
gaze, the formation of her lips, materialize in his mind's eye,

but what came was more a picture of a picture, and nothing
he could do brought more life to it.

Carly, he thought.

He drove, passed through Sturbridge, intersected the Mass
Pike, and made for Boston.

Was it true, what he'd written, that he knew enough? Or
would it take bones? A squalid remnant of chambray cloth?

The salve of retribution?

How old a man would Byrnne be now? Early sixties at
best, not so old and doddering you'd be tempted to think why
bother with the son of a bitch. And how many more weeks
had he occupied his folding chair at meeting before turning
up absent one Sunday, then the next, until, over time, he
dropped from people's conscious memory? Most people's. And
which direction had he headed then? Not this way, Fanning
guessed. Not north into New England, but back out into the
greater country. Open space.

Though Fanning had felt robust enough leaving Hartford,
purposeful, he realized he'd grown too fatigued, too shaky to
keep driving. He spotted a restaurant and peeled off, gratefully, onto the exit. He thought he'd go in for coffee and a
sandwich, but didn't. Couldn't seem to extract himself from
the car, then he was reclining the seat and letting his eyes fall
shut. When he woke, the car was frigid and the daylight had
gone to a sooty dusk, and a crease ran down his cheek where it
had lain against his coat collar.

Another night in a rented bed, bludgeoned sleep, and one
more day to use up, hour by hour. Fanning walked, blowing
off the energy pooled in his extremities. Around the Common, up Beacon Hill, down past King's Chapel, pausing at the
gate of its burial ground to read its sign, to stare at the canted

slate markers, its pockets of ashen snow, before going on, as
far as the waterfront beyond the Quincy Markets. He stood
watching the herring gulls, their feathers hicked up by the
wind. The slow apparitionlike passage of freighters and
smaller craft across the water. He turned and walked back
toward Faneuil Hall and the tall gray buildings of downtown.
The city of his birth, though he saw it with the eyes of an
outsider. He thought: This Anna, whoever she was . . . hadn't
she come forward to say her part? Wouldn't Julia have learned
of it? This too would be in the case file, or not, should it reap-
pear. Anna, Christie, Lynn, Marcy, Fanning thought. Some
girl who believed she was in a world of hurt. Inside the market he bought a coffee, warmed his hands on the paper cup,
letting the steam fog his glasses. He walked again. Before
rush hour had abated he was in the car. Nothing to do but aim
himself toward the airport.

Halfway through the tunnel, a sudden flare of brake lights
and traffic halted—Fanning's eyes shot to the rearview and
he braced himself, but the car behind had stopped in time. It
was only then he thought of Mitzi's being plowed into in this
same dank-tiled hole in the ground. After the first minutes of
sitting, some of the men got out and walked a few car lengths
ahead and tried to see what the holdup was. Fanning stayed
put, checked his watch, resting his head on the seat back, hoping to inhale as little of the air as humanly possible. A sug-
gestion of movement and those afoot scurried back, doors
slammed, echoing. Everyone pulled forward thirty yards and
waited again. Ten minutes, fifteen. But Fanning was a man
with gobs of time. He tried the radio. Foolish. His foot beat
absently on the floor mat. He thought of what lay above
them, bedrock, yards of silt and unspeakable harbor bottom,
tons of turgid water. Suddenly, then, the tunnel's bottleneck
was dissolved without explanation, and everyone was cruising
at full speed, up the long incline and out into the evening.

At Logan, he parked in the short-term lot, needlessly

inspected his watch again, crossed to the terminal, passed through security, and checked the status of United 174 from San Francisco.

On Time.

His long legs carried him past the newsstands and gift shops and fast-food kiosks. He stopped at a cubbyhole of a bar and drank a few swallows of bitter microbrew, watching the Celtics-Pistons, then walked again, pausing beneath another set of flight-data screens. *On Time. On Time.* He went in and stood at the urinals among a long row of topcoated men. He washed and bent to the sink, kneaded water into his face, rinsed his mouth, spat and rinsed again before rejoining the concourse.

Opposite him, incoming passengers streamed from a gate. Men and women in suits striding briskly off, others shuffling aside, in search of a spouse, or a name inscribed on a grease-board held aloft. A Sikh boy of eighteen or twenty fell into the embrace of his mother and turbanned father. Behind him came more of the plane's occupants, variously loaded-down, glazed and stiff limbed, then a beaky old lady in a fold-up wheelchair, another few stragglers with garment bags, and the first installment of crew.

Fanning watched until there was no more to see and went on.

Julia's gate lay at the concourse's very end, one of four. No other flight would use it immediately, Fanning gathered—too many seats vacant in the waiting area. He stood at the window, studying the lights outside, the taxiing, the arcs of hand-held batons, the downdrafts of spent jet fuel. At length, he turned away. He lowered his body onto a black vinyl bench that gave a clear sight line toward the mouth of the jetway. He waited, pushing up his glasses and massaging his eyes— they were gritty and overworked, and he let them stay closed as he listened to the murmur of talk and the ambient noise of luggage wheels and footfalls and the distant overlap of amplified messages. Then, brightly, from a speaker overhead, the announcement of the San Francisco flight, and moments later he was watching the nose of the jet rock to a stop and the accordian folds of the jetway coupling with the fuselage, and soon thereafter a first-class passenger emerged, a woman in a fine beige suit, her traveling companion guiding her with a hand at the small of her back, then more came, followed by the common run of passengers, couples and students and mothers with babies and panoplies of baby gear. Fanning studied each face, and if his heart was hammering inside his chest, so be it, so be it, where was the harm in that, to let yourself go with wanting, with hope? He watched and he watched for the one face that sought out his. Oh, and then, finally, he was rising from the bench.